Along the

Dusty Road

A Novel by

JOEY JONES

ISBN: 978-1-948978-19-4 (PRINT)

ISBN: 978-1-948978-20-0 (EPUB)

ISBN: 978-1-948978-21-7 (MOBI)

For my amazing children:
Branden and Parker.
I am beyond proud to be your father.
You are the best adventure I've ever experienced.

Also by Joey Jones

WHERE THE RAINBOW FALLS
(The Rivers Series, Book 2)

"A riveting story with an ending sure to make your heart swell, WHERE THE RAINBOW FALLS is a novel that leaves you feeling satisfied and accomplished." —Brittany Curry, Librarian

WHEN THE RIVERS RISE
(The Rivers Series, Book 1)

"A threatening hurricane is on the horizon and love is on the line . . . this captivating story of love and loss will keep you turning the pages and wishing for more. This is Joey Jones delivering what his fans have come to expect!" —Riley Costello, Author of *Waiting at Hayden's,* a shopfiction™ novel

THE DATE NIGHT JAR

"A beautiful love story, capturing the poignancy of both new affection and the power of deep, lasting devotion. Readers of Nicholas Sparks, Debbie Macomber, and Nicholas Evans should add THE DATE NIGHT JAR to their reading list." —Jeff Gunhus, *USA TODAY* Bestselling Author

A FIELD OF FIREFLIES

"This is a tale of tragedy, romance, heartbreak, and, ultimately, redemption. With lyrical writing and strong character development, Joey Jones effortlessly pulls readers in." —Kristy Woodson Harvey, *NEW YORK TIMES* Bestselling Author

LOSING LONDON

"I read the entire book in one day... I could not put it down! WOW!! LOSING LONDON was incredible; I laughed, I cried, and I'm still in shock." —Erica Latrice, TV Host, Be Inspired

A BRIDGE APART

"Filled with romance, suspense, heartbreak, and a tense plot line, Joey Jones's first novel is a must-read. It is the kind of book you can lend to your mom and best friend." —Suzanne Lucey, Page 158 Books

Acknowledgments

It's hard to believe I have written seven novels. I am incredibly grateful to have one of the most amazing supporting casts an author could imagine. So many people have stood behind me, beside me, and led me through every step of this journey. First and foremost, I would like to thank God for giving me the ability to write and planting that passion within my soul. Branden, my oldest son, now has a child of his own, and it makes my heart happy to watch him as a parent. Parker, who just completed kindergarten, is full of energy, love, and laughter. I cherish our adventures together, making memories that will live forever.

I would also like to thank my wonderful family. My parents Joe and Patsy Jones taught me how to become a responsible adult, and I hope to leave a legacy that makes them proud. My dad now resides in Heaven, and I miss him dearly. My mom, my breakfast partner and one of my best friends, is the most humble person I know. My brothers and sisters DeAnn, Judy, Lee, Penny, and Richard are some of my closest friends. In many ways, their support is my foundation.

My editor Donna Matthews is incredibly talented at polishing my writing. My graphics designer Meredith Walsh did a fantastic job with each of my novel covers and supporting pieces. Polgarus Studio made the intricate process of formatting the interior of this novel a breeze. Once again, Deborah Dove worked her magic in creating the book blurb.

Lastly, I want to thank some people who have been influential throughout my life: some for a season but each for a reason. Thank you to Alan & Kathy Hammer, Andrew Haywood, BJ Horne, Billy Nobles, Bob Peele, Cathy Errick, Diane Tyndall, Erin Haywood, Jan Raynor, Jeanette Towne, Josh Haywood, Josh Towne, Kenny Ford, Kim Jones, Mitch Fortescue, Nicholas Sparks, Ray White, Rebekah Jones, Richard Banks, Steve Cobb, Steven Harrell, and Steve Haywood. It is a privilege to call each of you my friend.

Along the Dusty Road

Prologue

The view of the world outside my salt-stained bedroom window is absolutely breathtaking. I realize this for what seems like the millionth time as I watch the sea oats dance to a breeze that appears to be blowing the Atlantic Ocean towards me one wave at a time. The seagulls, pelicans, and sandpipers patrol the air and the ground, and the sounds of the beach whisper through the screens.

By the way, my name is Luke Bridges, but that doesn't really tell you *who* I am. To you, it's just another name. At this point, it means nothing at all. It's important to me, however, because it is *my* name . . . *my* heritage . . . and one day it will be the link to *my* legacy.

I have lived most of my twenty-eight years in this small town on the coast of North Carolina. Atlantic Beach is the place I call home and always will. Some would say living in one community nearly your entire life is a waste. They're entitled to their opinion. Just as I am entitled to the one I hold. I've learned that some people travel this world chasing dreams and others running from reality. Ultimately, it's every person's choice where he or she parks his or her boat. As for me, my boat is here amongst the sandy shores, the spidery live oaks, and a small-town ambiance that soaks into the soul and, like the oil stain on my driveway, never washes out.

My father taught me to introduce myself well. "You never get a second chance at a first impression," I vividly recall him saying.

So who am I?

I am my father's son. When my dad said to me, in the comfort of a burgundy reclining chair that became molded to his shape over the years, "When you meet someone for the first time, never start the conversation by talking about what you do for a living," I listened. The next part is the part that speaks volumes, and I've banked my life on it: "Tell me what you do," he said, his hands shaking slightly as he spoke, "during the hours when you're not at work, and that will tell us who you are."

When I tie my shoes, I tie them just like the next man, and when I walk beside him, I neither look down on nor up at him. That is how my parents taught me to treat people. The words "yes, sir" and "yes, ma'am" and "no, sir" and "no, ma'am" are as much a part of my vocabulary as sugar is a part of sweet tea in the South. If someone gives me something, I say "thank you," and if I make a request, I say "please." If I misbehaved when I was young, my rear felt as sore as a bumblebee sting which always faded away quickly, but the lessons seemed to stick.

In one hand I clutch the worn Bible my father gave me as I gaze at the beach beyond the window and then glance at the pictures surrounding me, constantly reminding me of what life is all about. This makes me wonder why some people's priorities are so out of balance these days. Do they not realize life isn't about who can drive the nicest car, answer all the questions on Jeopardy, or pay their way out of any dilemma they can get into? Not a good life, anyway.

Life is about love, about giving love and receiving love. If there is one thing I can say honestly with the book in my hand that our country's president swears on before taking office, it is that I have given love. More love than I knew my heart could pour out in an entire lifetime. More love than I thought existed in this world. On days like today I wonder if I gave so much because I received so much.

The photograph in my other hand is one of the few things I would take with me if the house beneath my body ever caught on fire and I could only carry out one load before watching the rest of my possessions burn to ashes. It was taken at my house on a whim and seemed awkward then. The people that I love most are all there. When I stare at the picture long enough, I can hear their voices, and sometimes I think I smell them too. I always find it interesting how we each have a unique scent. Looking back, that was one of the best days of my life.

I want you to meet all of the people in that picture. The one person I want to introduce to you right away is my wife. She came into my life, forever changing it.

This, the words that follow, is our story . . . .

1

Will you marry me?

Gazing into the twinkle in her deep blue eyes which reminded me of the vast Atlantic Ocean visible on the horizon, I wondered for a moment if Emily could read my thoughts. Maybe in another life on another night I would have the guts to whisper those four words—*Will you marry me?*—into her ear. Tonight, however, I knew they would only play in my mind as she returned the question in my eyes with an awkward glance before looking at the parking lot between our sand-stained toes.

On this brisk May evening in the town of Atlantic Beach not long after the final point of our coed beach volleyball match, a real nail-biter, Emily leaned against the hood of the Chevrolet Cavalier she drove for as long as I could remember. I settled in nearby but left a couple feet of space between our sweaty bodies. We heard the waves crashing one after another, maybe a hundred yards or so from our vantage point, a view about as good as it got whether at night or during daylight hours.

A boardwalk ran parallel to the ocean, and a blue concrete knee wall stood between the tattered wooden boards and the sandy beach. After the game we rinsed off at the outdoor shower stations where the foot wash was usually the main attraction. Still, it would take soap and a good scrub at home for my feet to look and smell like new. A wide path to the water opened up between eight volleyball courts—three on the left and five on the right—nestled between large rolling sand dunes that bordered the ocean for miles. I can't count the hours I spent playing here, but I enjoyed some of the best days of my life at this beach.

A row of dozens of erosion-preventing wooden slat fences positioned at angles to create little walkways sectioned off the volleyball area from the part of the beach where people packed in during the summer months. The permanent lifeguard station equipped with a viewing deck, American flag, and surf-status flags stood tall almost like a carefully placed centerpiece welcoming people to our slice of heaven.

The Circle was what we locals called this place. As I fiddled with the Atlanta Braves baseball cap I let fly into the illuminated sky after Emily blistered the winning serve which splattered sand on the other team's side of the court, I replayed that moment as well as others involving the woman sitting to my left.

Ten years passed since I kissed Emily Beckett. Still, in that instant when she leaped toward me in her lifeguard-red bikini, and I felt the weight of her body land in my arms, I considered our lips meeting for the first time since high school.

What would it feel like to keep her in my arms beyond the point of awkwardness? After a moment, I guided her feet to the ground and joined our teammates for high fives as if I never thought twice about the feeling of holding a beautiful woman against my body.

Emily and I weren't dating or seeing each other, and we didn't fall into any of the other categories adults used to describe a relationship of that type. We defined our relationship with two words—*only friends*. Over the years I learned that the *only* part of that phrase should raise a red flag anytime it described a friendship. We dated in high school or maybe a better choice of words might be *hung out*. We were sixteen then, and our biggest concern was whether to attend the football game or meet at the bowling alley. Now twenty-six, we worked full-time jobs, paid bills, and took on plenty of other adult responsibilities.

Emily's priority these days was the seven-year-old slouched over in the booster seat in the back of her car. When he called out, "Mommy," our conversation came to a halt. Before she could respond, his head nodded to a new position, and then he was once again out like a log. He had already adjusted himself a couple times since I carried him like a sack of potatoes across the sand and down the sidewalk to the parking lot. During the match he fell asleep with his blankie about twenty yards from the volleyball court.

"I think you wore him out," Emily acknowledged, a thankful expression circling her face.

Racing across the beach before every game from the first net to the fifth became a tradition for Ayden and me. To be honest, I enjoyed goofing off with him as much as being on the sandy court. I'd always been drawn to children, and my mother often told me I would make a great father one day. However, one of the main reasons I wanted Emily's and my relationship to stay at the *just friends* level was because I could barely imagine the difficulties of being a stepdad. When I imagined marrying someone, the traditional relationship came to mind. Spending a few years alone with my future wife, whomever that might be, before we even thought about trying to have children seemed ideal. For this reason, I doubted I could ever actually ask Emily the question lingering in my mind on nights like tonight.

However, not replaying our teenage years when Emily and I spent evenings together here at The Circle, where her brother and I used to play on opposite volleyball teams, was difficult. These thoughts made two words creep into my mind: *What if?*

I would be lying if I said I remembered which one of our teams won back then. I was a feared striker, and he was a phenomenal server; I remember that much. When my team wasn't playing, I would sit on the knee wall with Emily and other friends, and we would draw tic-tac-toe boards in the sand with our big toes. As the ball volleyed, we shared popcorn and gummy worms and drank Pepsi like water. Those were the days. If I could go back, I would make a lot of changes, but you know what they say about hindsight.

That thought made me think about my dad. I should have listened to him a little more back then, and I definitely should have heeded his advice over the phone this afternoon when he encouraged me to bring a jacket to slip on after the match. I folded my arms to block the steady stream of wind blowing off the ocean and causing Emily's shoulder-length, buttery blonde hair to dance in every direction possible. Moments ago, she let out a ponytail, and as I watched her attempt to capture the loose strands, I couldn't keep a straight face.

My dirty blond hair covered my forehead and almost touched my blue eyes, but it wasn't quite long enough to pull back. My driver's license listed the top of my head at two inches above six feet which came in handy when playing volleyball. The tanned legs sticking out of my yellow beach shorts, which I wore whether playing volleyball or swimming, provided most of my height.

Standing there, I continued to think about my dad. If I allowed anyone to believe I gained most of the knowledge I possessed from books or educators, I would be misleading them. Much of the wisdom I obtained in my years on this earth, I absorbed from a person who never spent a single hour in a college classroom. A man with the courage to tell me he barely graduated high school. Dad always encouraged me to further my education. Still, after six years in a well-known university and some firsthand experience in the real world, I realized that education doesn't define a man. A man is who he is, and who he is defines his life.

Life was about nights like tonight; playing on a familiar sand court beside my brother—my best friend in the entire world—and among other friends and acquaintances. Ben would rip off his right arm for me if I needed it. Life was about real hopes and goals, not artificial, man-made happiness; about finding the woman of my dreams and spending the rest of my life loving her best, giving up selfish desires, and starting a family. Something real. Something lasting. Something that satisfied the deep urges of the human soul. Something as close to Heaven as this universe offers.

As the parking lot cleared and the scent of salty air—one of my favorite smells—wafted into a wide-open area behind us that used to be a small amusement park, I realized the time to say goodnight to Emily had arrived. I hugged her a little tighter tonight and noticed that even after playing volleyball for over an hour, her neck smelled sweet like honey.

It's funny how when you are crazy about someone the human nose doesn't typically pick up on odors like sweat or bad breath. A scientist should study that if one hasn't yet. It wouldn't surprise me if that has already happened since I recently read an article about a study on ants passing gas. Do people not have anything better to do with their time and money?

I bent down to rub Ayden's little head. In my mind I whispered to him that I was sorry for not having the courage to give my heart to his mom all because I was terrified at the thought of becoming *his* stepdad. It was hard to make that decision mainly because I determined he was a great kid. Sure he lacked a little discipline, but that I heard had more to do with his biological father not being a solid role model than anything else. I hadn't been convinced of the polar opposite either—that the man deserved the worst father on the planet award. Truth be told, I didn't know. I hadn't met the guy, couldn't remember his name if my life depended on it, and never thought much about him. I tried not to judge him because I had never been a father, and I was the one who decided not to date Emily because if I ended up marrying her I would be a father—an instant father to *his* son. There would be very little 'just us' time for Emily and me to chase each other around the house naked or take off on a whim and head to the mountains for a weeklong getaway. Two little eyes would always be watching everything that went on between his mother and the man who married her. A man I sometimes wanted to be, but a man I didn't think I could be.

A casual relationship seemed to be the last thing I needed. My number one rule for dating was simple and safe: I either dated a woman because I could see myself possibly marrying her or I didn't date her at all. In my heavily researched opinion, having a romantic companion just for fun was a waste of time and energy. It seemed the short-term excitement was far outweighed by the risk of long-term consequences such as STDs, pregnancy, heartbreak, or even divorce if it went that far. Even though I wanted to doubt any of those things would happen if Emily and I became more than friends, I didn't want to chance it. I knew Emily well enough to know that neither of us wanted to have casual sex with anyone.

From that don't get the idea that either of us has lived innocent or sheltered lives. We haven't. We both made mistakes, wheel barrels full of them. Mistakes we wished we could take back but know we can't. Also, don't think for one minute that Emily ever considered Ayden a mistake. He was a gift from God, and in a way she could have never known at his birth, he saved her life.

A child once changed my life too, but I never told anyone about that. I made a huge mistake some years back and swore I would never mention it to another human being for as long as I lived. However, as the taillights from the last car to pull out of the parking lot faded into the distance, I suddenly and inexplicably felt the urge to tell Emily Beckett a secret I planned on taking to my grave.

2

The stars twinkled brightly above the Atlantic Ocean as the waves folded onto the shore. The scene seemed surreal. I felt like if I had ever seen more stars in the sky in my entire life, I couldn't remember the occasion. They became almost lifelike as the glow of the parking lot lights gave way to a clear night's sky in the distance above the horizon. It was as though the rest of the world disappeared, and this night was made especially for Emily and me.

When I was about to reveal my secret, Emily's phone rang. Based on the hesitant, somewhat guilty look she shot out of the corner of her eye, I assumed it must be Brad—another reason why I hadn't gotten involved with Emily. The two of them weren't officially a couple now although they had been for six months or so. However, they still hung out together as if dating. When they were a thing and he told her he didn't like her playing on my volleyball team, I decided not to like him. Of course, I can't say I didn't understand the guy's reasoning. Even though I had a girlfriend until a month ago, Emily and I had a history although relatively brief romantically. At the time it didn't seem to matter to him that she professed she wasn't interested in me. Him not being here and able to be a part of what went on before, during, and after the matches—like right now—made it worse, I'm sure. He came to a few games this season, but his work schedule made it difficult to attend often. I think she said he flew to Knoxville this week for a conference.

I wandered to my Range Rover, a few spaces away on the blacktop, and slowly lifted the back hatch just killing time. On the way I picked up my duffle bag off the ground where I left it between my vehicle and Emily's. Inside it I kept my personal ball, water bottle, a change of clothes, and a few other random items, some associated with the sport and others not. When not playing volleyball, I liked to ride waves on one of my surfboards, and the racks on top of my vehicle confirmed that for anyone who might not otherwise know.

Emily's back was turned to me now, and I saw her hand holding the phone against her ear. I spent the next few minutes reorganizing the storage space in the back of my SUV: jumper cables, lawn chair, loose volleyballs, board wax, and a weedeater I bought earlier in the week which still hadn't made it to the garage. After moving everything around half a dozen times, I couldn't think of anything else to do except stand there and wait for Emily to finish her conversation or crank my vehicle's ignition and head home.

She glanced my way several times, but I couldn't read the thoughts in her eyes. Did she want me to stick around, or was she wondering why I hadn't left?

Leaning through the passenger side of my vehicle, I wasted a little more time straightening a stack of papers from the office. Over my shoulder I could still hear Emily talking, but I couldn't make out any words. I didn't want to be nosy although I wanted to know if the conversation might end soon. I didn't have anything better to do, but I certainly didn't want to appear desperate.

When I made the decision that it was time to go, Emily sat on her hood staring out at the ocean with the phone still pressed against her ear. As I rounded my vehicle's frontend, I stopped momentarily to wave.

"I'll see you later," I relayed in a tone hoping it wouldn't travel through the phone at least for her sake. As for me, I didn't really mind what the guy thought about me.

Instead of lifting her arm to return my wave, Emily held up her index finger and slid off the hood. "One second," she mouthed as her hand temporarily covered the receiver.

I nodded then pushed my key into the ignition so I could listen to the radio while breathing in the new vehicle smell. As the first song played, I wondered again what Emily and Brad were discussing. I randomly considered whether I would rather be her some-of-the-time boyfriend on the phone from Knoxville or the guy who was *just* her friend waiting in an empty parking lot for her to get off the phone with him.

I knew it wasn't an ideal situation for either of us. My head rested against the seat as two more songs played before I watched Emily toss her phone into the front seat of her car and walk in my direction, flip-flops clacking all the way.

"Is everything okay?" I inquired.

She scuffed the sole of her shoe against the gravelly-looking pavement causing a slight grinding noise.

"I think he's irritated with me," she offered, standing tall with one hand resting on each hip. If I remember correctly, Emily once told me she was five foot six inches which also gave her an advantage in volleyball.

I wasn't sure if it was my business to ask why, but I did anyway. "What for?" I pried.

"He seemed upset that I was talking to you in the parking lot," she admitted.

My first thought was to defend our position by making up a few good reasons why being the last two people at The Circle was okay. However, they were no longer officially a couple, so it didn't make sense, and after all when they had been together, I was careful not to disrespect their relationship.

"I really don't blame him," I shared, mainly to stir the pot. "If I were Brad, I'd probably be a bit jealous too."

"Why? We're just friends," Emily replied combatively.

I debated whether she was talking about her and Brad or her and me. I also wondered if she had just finished the same argument with Brad. Some of her hand gestures earlier implied such. I also took note of those two words again—*just friends.* Instead of deliberating that issue or taking sides with Brad, who rubbed me the wrong way the first time I met him, I opted to make a joke.

"If I was Brad and I knew you were talking to a tall, dark, and handsome man underneath this sky while Jimmy Buffet sang in the background," I pointed out, glancing up with a mischievous grin on my face before reaching for the volume to crank the music a bit louder, "it would probably bother me."

I watched a smile ease onto her face. "You're so full of yourself."

What I said to her was the truth, at least the part where I said I wouldn't want a girl I was basically dating talking to another man in a situation like the one we allowed ourselves to get into after more than one match this season. As for the tall, dark, and handsome part, you would have to ask a woman's perspective. Sure, I looked in the mirror every day and came to the conclusion years ago that I probably wouldn't be defined by many as unattractive, but everybody's tastes were different. Most of the women I dated said I had sexy blue eyes and strong cheekbones, whatever that meant. They also seemed to like to run their fingers through my stringy hair. I worked out a few times a week, enough to keep myself toned but not so much I worried about my shirts stretching or my veins popping.

A steady breeze continued to blow, and all of a sudden Emily's face changed to serious. For a moment, I thought she might cry. "It's hard, Luke," she trailed off.

"What is hard?" I asked, a bit confused by the instantaneous surge of emotion.

"Having feelings for a man who spends more time out of town than in town; someone who is more concerned about landing his next big client than talking to the woman he has been dating or whatever we're doing now, for over half a year. He was supposed to call me before the game but didn't. He said a meeting ran late; he went out to dinner with a co-worker; and he just now returned to his hotel room." Emily paused momentarily as if considering whether she should continue expressing her concerns to me or bottle them up. "I just don't know if I want to be with someone like Brad," she admitted.

My feelings told me to offer advice by giving her a few different options on how to fix the dilemma. However, I'd read enough books on relationships to know all I needed to do was listen as her head shook in disgust.

Emily continued, "And it's not just his work schedule. He doesn't seem to want to spend time with Ayden either. The three of us drove to Kings Dominion last Saturday, and he didn't even ride a single kiddie ride with my son. Not one, Luke. He didn't ask if he wanted cotton candy, if he would like to feed the ducks in the pond, or if he wanted a piggyback ride. He was just there with me. He wanted to hold my hand and sit close when the three of us rode a ride together, but it was almost as though he didn't even realize Ayden was with us. I don't expect him to be his father, but Ayden needs attention too. He needs someone to make him feel special."

At this point I'm sure the look on my face spoke the thoughts in my mind. I wasn't sure if I should respond because this felt personal and took me out of my comfort zone. I had no experience dating a woman with a child, so I kept my mouth shut to see what else I could learn.

What Emily said next caught me off guard. "Why can't he be

like you are with Ayden?" She looked me dead in the eyes as she spoke but then turned and stared out toward the volleyball courts as though she had meant it but hadn't meant to say it out loud.

Like I was with Ayden. How was I supposed to respond to that? I couldn't. Her words surprised me, even frightened me a little. At the same time, though, I had to admit they made me feel tingly inside.

Emily's voice climbed to a new level as she continued with the hypothetical questions. "Why can't he chase him around and make him laugh? Why can't he wipe off his shirt when ketchup leaks out of the hotdog bun and has nowhere else to go? Why can't he just take him to the bathroom when I'm preoccupied? Instead of coming to find me and acting like Ayden is a contagious disease."

My mouth fell open by the time she finished, or at least it felt that way, but no words came out. All the things Emily rattled off I did with Ayden at the volleyball matches but never really thought twice about. The public restrooms at the other end of the boardwalk seemed to be in constant need of a good cleaning, so I didn't blame the guy for not wanting to help a child navigate that obstacle.

This would have been a perfect time to take advantage of Emily's emotional state and possibly end up with her in my arms and who knows where else. I thought about telling her that Brad sounded like a jerk and I was the guy of her dreams who could be just the man she needed. Once again, however, reality reminded me I didn't want to be a stepdad.

On my way home I slammed my hands against the steering wheel more than once. I watched Emily walk to her car, and then we drove in opposite directions. However, that hadn't made me mad or didn't explain why my palms turned red. What I couldn't believe was that I nearly told Emily my secret. She had her own issues, anyway, and the last thing I needed to do was open up a skeleton from my closet.

3

A week passed when I found myself standing in the same parking lot, but this time with the sun beating on the roof of my vehicle. Watching the nearby road to see if Emily's little green car might appear next around the corner, I knew she picked up Ayden from daycare before heading to The Circle, but she typically arrived early.

The last week of my life went well. I wore a smile on my face that said so, and I found myself eager to tell Emily the good news. After a weekend of fishing with my dad at the pier, I spent Monday morning in my mentor's office. Spending time with him was only part of the good news, but that's where I found the news I wanted to share.

"How's the practice coming along?" Larry asked in his usual stern and monotone voice when I entered his office through a narrow hallway tucked inside a small building he shared with a real estate agent and a photographer.

"I'm building a steady stream of clients," I responded with a smile, knowing Larry was partially to thank for referring his overflow my way.

"Before you know it, your calendar will be bursting at the seams and you'll be referring folks to another therapist, maybe eventually someone you mentor."

Larry constantly rattled off compliments which felt good coming from anyone, most especially someone as successful as he when it came to helping people improve their lives.

We spent the next fifteen minutes discussing the Atlanta Braves, analyzing the players' skills, and critiquing the manager's decisions. Like most other fans, we assumed we could manage the game more effectively, but we both knew better. There was a reason at the beginning and end of every season we would likely be here, in Larry's office, *talking* about the people making the decisions for the team. Somehow the conversation transitioned from baseball to my personal life. He had a way of shifting subjects without me even realizing it which made me confident about learning from the best.

"Are you dating anyone?" Larry asked, and somehow I instantly interpreted the exact direction of the conversation. Although he posed that question in some form or fashion nearly every time we met, the look in his eyes was different today. I quickly deduced that he was about to try to fix me up with someone he knew personally.

A moment later, I found out I was on target. When Larry told me her name, I didn't recognize it. As far as I remembered, I hadn't gone to school with this person or heard anyone mention her which could be good.

"She is my cousin," he clarified. "She moved here recently, and I'm trying to introduce her to a decent guy."

"Decent?" I protested needing to buy some time and wanting to give him a hard time.

Larry laughed because he knew what I was doing. However, I doubted he knew Emily Beckett popped into my mind the moment this conversation started.

"If you're interested, I'll let her be the judge," he snickered.

"That's nice of you, *Cousin* Larry," I teased.

"What do you think?" he probed.

I needed to know more. "Tell me about her."

Before he could respond, the phone rang causing both of us to lose our train of thought momentarily. Letting the call go to voicemail, Larry shifted his focus back to describing his cousin. "She's related to me; we're just alike actually. What more do you need to know?" he offered, smiling.

"So she's a bodybuilder with a deep voice?" I surmised then paused, allowing myself a moment to enjoy my own amusement. "I think I'll pass."

"Seriously," he replied. "She's a nice woman. Blonde hair. Pretty green eyes. She's not unattractive I promise. Just take her out, you don't have to marry her."

I processed the opportunity. Larry was right. What did I have to lose?

Blonde hair. Pretty green eyes.

As I watched a volleyball match from the hood of my vehicle, those two attributes began to rummage through my mind—as they had all week—and then Emily's tires rolled into the parking spot next to the one I'd pulled into a bit crookedly. We said our hellos, and as we often did, Emily, Ayden, and I headed toward the sand court—together. As usual, I wondered what people thought, but then I let it go as the sound of Emily's voice interrupted.

"I have something to tell you," she commented as Ayden ran ahead.

"Really?" I responded wondering what had her excited. I figured she might tell me she and Brad were a couple again or something along those lines. "I have something to tell you too," I admitted.

"Okay," she responded, sounding excited about my news.

For a while now Emily had been asking when I was going to go on a date with someone, and every time I made up some excuse to avoid sounding pitiful. Honestly, until today there hadn't been any opportunities recently, not ones worth exploring anyway. A few women in the volleyball league showed interest, but none of them seemed like my type. Some were nice, even attractive, but I couldn't see myself with any of them long term.

"Brad and I are no longer together in any capacity," she announced suddenly, seeming relieved to get the news off her shoulders. "You are the first person I've told," she added, smiling widely.

I was surprised to say the least. She talked about completely breaking things off with him a few times and even made mention of it after our last match, but I didn't really think things had reached the point where she would actually follow through. I found myself excited; however, not as enthusiastic as I probably would have been if I hadn't just agreed to go on a date. For some reason, my news didn't sound as much like good news as it had a minute ago.

"It makes me feel special that you chose to tell me first," I acknowledged while pausing to let everything happening around us—kids running, moms pushing strollers, dads carrying volleyball equipment, balls flying through the air—distract me for a moment. "What happened?" I queried.

I could tell by the tone of her voice that she initiated the split.

"I told him what I was talking to you about after our last match. That I didn't think he was the man I needed to be with. He's a good guy, but I don't think he's ready to be a father. A husband? Maybe. But he's not what Ayden and I need right now, and there is no sense in dragging out something that I know isn't going to last. I've done that before, and it's not fair to Ayden. He gets used to a man, and then the man disappears. I don't want to expose him to that lifestyle."

When she finished, I realized I couldn't give better advice if she walked through my office door and asked. "It sounds like you really thought it through and made the best decision for you and Ayden.

I'm proud of you," I admitted, excited and sad simultaneously.

"That's my news. What's yours?" she asked expectantly.

It didn't seem right to tell her about the date, not after what she had just shared. *Hey Emily, sorry you and the guy you've been spending time with for more than six months parted ways today. But guess what? I have a date with a hot chick tomorrow night.*

What else could I come up with on the fly? I asked myself.

"If we win tonight, we'll be in first place," I announced.

She chimed right in as though our standing in the volleyball league had been the news I planned to share all along. "You know the team we play tonight has only lost one game, right?"

I looked toward the beach to figure out who *that team* was; Emily always told me who we were playing, their record, and what strategies we should employ for each game. It had been that way for the two seasons she played on the team.

When we reached the sand, we went in separate directions. I started a conversation with my brother Ben, who coached our team and played, and he and I jogged around to loosen our legs. People often tell us we look a lot alike, but the resemblance isn't close enough that others confuse us for each other. Ben's hair is a little lighter and shorter than mine and a bit wavy. At the volleyball matches, the sports goggles that shield his green eyes are the most significant contrast between us; in everyday life he wears glasses. Another difference is the inch or so I have on him in height but who is counting except for me.

Emily joined another teammate and began stretching utilizing the barrier wall between the boardwalk and the sand to steady her balance.

After Ben and I finished a few sets of wind sprints, we headed toward the wall to meet with the rest of our teammates. While I sat there halfway watching the current set and talking to Ben as he filled out our team's paperwork, I felt Ayden's dump truck crash into my leg at least three times. The little fellow looked up and smiled after each collision, and I told him he needed to be careful to avoid hurting somebody. I decided he wasn't trying to bruise my ankle before the match started but that he just wanted somebody to acknowledge his presence. When Ben finished the paperwork, I asked if Ayden could run it to the scorekeeper, a lady with big hair sitting in a lawn chair beside the net. When Ben said yes, Ayden's square-shaped little face lit up like a Christmas tree on the day after Thanksgiving—at least that's when my family decorated ours to kick off the holiday season.

When the first serve flew over the net, I lost track of everything outside the rectangular court. Focusing on the match and nothing else came naturally to me, but I'd be lying if I said I didn't notice Emily's athletic frame nearly every time a brief pause in play occurred. Like me, Emily had been gifted with long legs. I enjoyed watching her move around the court; she never shied away from a ball no matter how hard the opponent spiked it, and diving across the sand seemed to be in her blood. Even today with the sun blaring in our eyes, she just threw on a pair of sunglasses and sacrificed her body for the team's sake.

If the first volley of the set indicated how the match would go, we knew we were in for a challenge. We recovered two spikes from our opponents, dove several times, and were nearly out of breath when they scored the point. I felt like I already needed water. Ben recorded our team's first point when smashing a serve that landed in the middle of two of their players who immediately began to argue about who should have returned the ball.

From there, the set went back and forth. The first time the ball zoomed toward the knee wall near the boardwalk, I watched Ayden's little legs scurry behind. I think his favorite part of volleyball was retrieving the out-of-bounds balls.

When he made it to me with the ball and a dirty face from playing in the sand and mud he apparently found somewhere, he asked me a question he liked to ask every time we saw each other.

"How old are you?"

"The same age I told you last week," I reminded him.

He smiled, and I knew he remembered. "The same age as my mommy—"

His little boy voice was so cute. "Yep," I answered, reaching for the ball.

Along with being the same age, Emily and I graduated high school the same year, only wearing different colors. Rival colors. She graduated top of her class from East Carteret High. My rank at West Carteret High wasn't all that important, or at least that's what I convinced myself of, after discovering my name near the bottom of the list. Anyway, I made up for all the tests I failed in high school when I graduated college with a 3.9 GPA. After walking the big stage, I made it a point to return to West Carteret where I handed my transcript to my former teachers. I caught most of them in my arms as they fainted. Sports seemed to cause conflict between Emily's high school and mine, but I had friends at both. My best friend in high school actually went to East Carteret, and it was okay to tell people that, so it wasn't like we were Bloods and Crypts. He moved to Florida after college to take a job in the hotel industry, and we grew apart over the years. We still message occasionally, and when he's in town to visit his parents for the holidays, we grab a bite to eat and talk about the good old days.

After talking to Ayden, the next play scared me half to death. One of our teammates set the ball for Ben who spiked it and scored a point, but when we all went to share high fives, Emily collapsed onto the ground and lay there motionless like the ball in the sand after being rolled back to us beneath the net. Our team converged on her, and eventually she sat up holding her hand on her forehead.

"What happened?" I asked, my hands shaking noticeably.

Others asked similar questions, but Emily didn't respond. I bent down close to her wanting to do something—anything—to help. A man on the other team called for his wife, a nurse.

4

"It looked like there were three balls in the air," Emily finally uttered, noticeably dazed.

Return the one in the middle would have been the cliché response and would likely be said later jokingly, but at that moment no one knew exactly what happened or if it was serious.

"My vision started getting a little blurry a few volleys ago," she informed the rest of us.

The nurse made her way through the circle of concerned players and nearly pushed me to the ground before digging her knees into the sand next to Emily. She went through the "How many fingers am I holding up?" routine and asked Emily if she felt dizzy. Then, we all realized the nurse hadn't been watching the match very closely. "Where exactly did the ball hit you?" she asked.

"It didn't," Emily clarified. "I think I am getting a migraine. Can someone get my Ibuprofen out of my bag?"

This wasn't the first time Emily felt a migraine coming on at the court, and as stubborn as she was, I knew she would try to play through it. I'd only seen her pull herself out once due to a migraine, and she had to be driven home that night.

A cup of water and two pills later, Emily was back on her feet taking practice shots to ensure her vision would hold up. I tried to convince her to sit out for a little while, if not the rest of the game, as did others, but she wouldn't listen.

Throughout the remainder of the match, I think the other team purposely tried not to hit the ball near her which I found very gracious of them. When the game ended, Emily, Ayden, and I walked out the same way we walked in—together.

"What are you doing Friday night?" Emily asked out of the blue as we headed for the parking lot with a steady ocean breeze at our backs giving us a little extra push.

Why was she asking? was the first thought that popped into my head. The second was: *Should I tell her?* "Friday night—" I trailed off, unsure which direction to take. Buying time near the knee wall as we took turns letting the spray from the spigot rinse the grains of sand from our bare feet, I pretended to get caught up in a play on one of the other courts. "Let me think," I finally responded, absentmindedly holding my finger to my chin. "It seems like I have something going on . . ."

Emily interrupted, and for some reason I feared she might say: *You can't remember that you have a date?* I figured there was a possibility Ben had told Colleen, his wife and my sister-in-law, and Colleen mentioned it to Emily. But I wasn't sure why talking about it or not talking about it seemed to matter so much to me. So what if Emily knew I had a date? I was a single man. That is what single people do; they go on dates, I thought to myself. After all, Emily and I were *just friends.*

"Saturday night," she corrected, "I meant Saturday night."

Just in the nick of time, she saved me. I probably needed to wipe a few sweat beads off my forehead. This time, I instantly shook my head as I twisted the knob on the spigot. "Nothing important," I replied. "Why? What is going on Saturday night?" I asked, hoping she hadn't noticed me clam up about Friday night.

If she did notice, she didn't say anything. "Colleen and I are getting together at her house to cook. Ben will be there, and I am bringing Ayden. We thought you might like to join us."

I think I furrowed my brow because it seemed odd being invited to my own brother's house by Emily. I'd been there a hundred times and seldom needed an invitation. In addition to being brothers, Ben and I were best friends. "How ironic" was what everyone always said when I mentioned he was exactly one year, one month, and one day older than I am. Colleen wasn't much of a volleyball player but had come around quite a bit in the five years since the team originated. She started playing only to spend time with Ben doing something he loved. Colleen would have earned my vote for the Most Improved Player if we handed out awards. She hadn't missed a single ball tonight although she hadn't made any noticeable plays either.

I began to analyze Emily's question, wondering if she was asking me on a date. I felt my heart pumping which must have pushed air upward because my head swelled just a little. Okay, a lot. Not in a conceited way, I thought, but in a *is this really happening* sort of way. Would two dates in one weekend make me a womanizer?

With a smile on my face, I was about to say, "Yes, I would love to eat dinner with you all," when Emily added to the invitation, or maybe I should say she took away from it.

"I thought maybe you and Ben could take Ayden bowling or something like that while Colleen and I go to the grocery store and make dinner," she mentioned.

I fought the muscles in my face trying not to let the smile fade. All I thought was that she was asking me to babysit so she and Colleen could spend time together which would have been fine if I hadn't already formed a different assumption.

"I know he would really enjoy it," she shared as she stood in the doorframe of her car.

In his booster seat, Ayden's eyes began to bubble when Emily uttered the word bowling. The smile on his face reminded me of a kid walking into Chuck E. Cheese for the first time.

"He doesn't really have any positive male role models in his life right now," Emily whispered so her son's tender ears wouldn't hear.

My mind began to ramble. Babysitter? Role model? Date? Did the title I put with it matter? No, it didn't, I concluded. Like I said, I liked the kid a lot, even though losing races to him destroyed my image at the volleyball courts. I ran track in high school and could probably still outrun anybody in the league but not the seven-year-old waiting for me to make his day.

"Emily," I answered, still holding at least part of a smile, "I would love to."

I bent down to see Ayden, and he seemed to fixate his eyes on mine. "Is that okay with you?" I asked, leaning into the car to catch a glimpse of a face so dirty it looked like he camouflaged himself for a game of hide-and-seek in the woods.

He tilted his head just a bit. "Can we go to the park instead?" he asked in his cute, convincing little boy voice.

At that moment he could have asked if I would take him on a rocket ship to the moon and I would have said *yes*. "If it's okay with your mother," I answered instead, looking to her for approval, attempting to mimic the puppy dog eyes tactic he so eloquently used on me.

I figured the park must be pretty seven-year-old friendly. Still I didn't want to make a decision without consulting Emily first. The last thing I wanted to do was tell the boy he could do something only to be shut down by his mother and then listen to him cry for the next five minutes while she explained why he couldn't go even though I said he could.

"Mommy, I want Luke to take me to the park," he pleaded. He said it more than once but less than ten times. I lost count at four.

"That's fine, Ayden. That will save Mommy some money which has been tight lately." She shot me a look that made me think she hadn't meant to say anything out loud about her financial situation, but I wasn't sure why it mattered. She knew all about mine. Since I moved back to the beach, she'd been my banker. As a loan officer, she handled my mortgage and vehicle loan and set up all my other accounts. Emily quickly moved to another comment. "Good idea, Ayden," she added, winking at me.

Soon after that we plopped into our vehicles. I followed her around the circular drive to the main traffic light on the island where if we were heading to our respective houses, I turned left and Emily went straight which led across the high-rise bridge connecting the island to Morehead City. I purposely followed her taillights this time so I could drive behind her long enough to ensure the migraine wasn't affecting her driving. In the parking lot I tried to convince her to let me drive them home, but she repeatedly assured me she would be fine. "Anyway," she pointed out, "it would be a hassle trying to work out the vehicle situation tomorrow. You have work. I have work. Ayden has school. I'll be fine." None of that mattered to me; the inconvenience on my part would have been none at all.

I kept a few car lengths distance as we stayed around the thirty-five mile per hour speed limit for the half a mile or so stretch that led to the foot of the bridge. As our vehicles began the rather steep climb, an image of her car ramming through the guardrail suddenly popped into my mind. It took me until we reached the top of the high rise to shake it. The thought didn't completely evaporate until we reached the mainland, where a red light awaited us at the Highway 70 intersection, the busiest road in Morehead City.

At this juncture, Emily headed straight across where the street led into residential areas. I decided I better turn so she wouldn't think I was following her. Downtown was to the right and so was Beaufort; to the left was where most of the restaurants and shopping centers could be found, at least the ones still open this late in the evening.

I decided to turn left and grab a bite to eat. As I drove, I couldn't help but wonder if Emily had noticed the odor escaping from my body. The t-shirt I threw over my head in the parking lot was already soaked to the point that it was sticking to my back, and I could feel tiny grains of sand poking my skin. I always hated that feeling which is why I preferred not to wear a shirt when leaving the beach. As that thought circled my mind, I couldn't remember why I put the shirt on in the first place. At the next stoplight, I yanked it over my head and tossed it into the floorboard.

We beat the second-place team, and I did my share of chasing down balls and diving in the sand, so it made sense that I wouldn't smell like fabric softener. It was a good night. I served well, landed a handful of spikes, and could only think of a few plays I would like to have back. Plus now I had a date not only for Friday night but also on Saturday night although the latter was unofficial. I wasn't sure I wanted it to become official. For now I was satisfied with it being something less. Not only did that terminology keep me from going down a path I wasn't sure I wanted, but, hopefully, it would keep me from being tagged with the *player* title.

By the time I pulled into my driveway, I'd devoured the chicken sandwich and fries I grabbed at a drive-thru. Rather than going inside the house right away, I decided to sit on the front porch steps and soak in a little more of what had turned out to be a pristine evening. There, my conscience began to eat at me for not letting Emily know I had a date Friday night. I wasn't sure why it bothered me. It wasn't like I was in a serious relationship. Heck I didn't even have a girlfriend was what I kept telling myself—just a date.

Once indoors, I opened nearly every window so that the sounds, smells, and breezes of the ocean air filtered through the house. I grabbed a washcloth and a fresh towel from the linen closet. When I stared at the mirror in the bathroom, I couldn't force myself to erase the smile that seemed to be stapled to the ears on either side of my thin face.

After tossing my sandy, sweaty clothes into the bin, I stepped over the side of the tub and pulled the shower curtain shut. Beneath a steady stream of water, I went back and forth between being happy and feeling guilty, the emotions I'd been battling since leaving the volleyball match. Choosing happiness, I sang every song on Lady A's most recent album, some more than once and most awfully. I often tell others that many people sing when they are happy. Some sing beautifully, and some sing poorly, but life is probably going well if they're singing, at least at that particular moment. I myself have never been much of a vocalist which is why I elect to do most of my serenading beneath a flow of water in the privacy of my home.

I lived alone since graduating college and preferred it that way. I didn't want to worry about a roommate cluttering my coffee table with unwanted magazines, leaving piles of dirty dishes in the sink, or bringing gobs of friends over for get-togethers at *our* refrigerator's expense. Living by myself was a bit expensive since I chose to invest in a home on Ocean Ridge Drive, a family-friendly neighborhood, but I decided the pros outweighed the cons. Although I didn't have a family yet, I hoped to well before my hair began to gray or fall out, and I wanted it to be in a place suitable for a wife and eventually children. This place would be where kids with helmets rode their bikes and couples walked beneath street lamps without fear of what might happen if they wandered the neighborhood after daylight faded.

In fact, my next-door neighbors, who both drove trucks for FedEx, had been on the way out for a walk when I arrived home. Russ, whose parents left the house to them a few years ago, threw up a hand, and by the time I settled on the porch, I watched him pass Dr. Nesbitt's house and slowly fade into the distance. Dr. Nesbitt lived on the other side of me, and his house was one of the largest in the neighborhood. I guess I should mention that mine is probably the smallest. If I didn't point it out, he would. He did, actually, to everybody. Sarcastically, the man let everyone in the community know my house brought down the value of his which probably cost three times as much. "I thought psychiatrists made a lot of money," he once declared to me. "Why don't you add another story to that house? It can't be more than twelve hundred square feet," he laughed as if the square footage of a man's house made the man.

In reality my brown cedar shake sided house with dark blue shutters measured seventeen hundred square feet, but who was counting? And the title on the door at my office read "Counselor" not "Psychiatrist," but he wouldn't know because he never took more than two minutes of his time to have a real conversation with me. For some reason the ones we shared had always been negative.

When I moved back to the area after finishing my master's in professional counseling, I practiced under my mentor until obtaining my own license, then I opened an office in downtown Morehead City. I fortunately attracted enough clients to pay the bills, but I hadn't been able to bring in adequate revenue to justify hiring an assistant. Maybe one day.

Before heading inside to get ready for bed, I spotted some neighbors strolling in front of my house. I couldn't help but wonder when was the last time they realized what they had: Someone to walk with beneath the stars, talk to about the moon, and pray with about eternity. Whether he admits it or not, almost every man yearns for a woman to share his life. For twenty-six years, I longed for someone to fall deeply in love with, marry, and spend the rest of my life getting to know her like the back of my hand. It just hadn't happened yet. I loved two women or at least thought I had. Still, I hadn't found the sort of love I was searching for—the kind the human heart can't beat quite right without, the type of woman that slows your engine without even trying.

In the past ten years I'd been through a three-year relationship, a four-year relationship ending in a broken engagement, and a one-year relationship that was more of a fixer-upper than a real relationship.

As my eyes grew too tired to keep open, I shifted my head on the pillow and wondered what would happen this weekend. Would it be the beginning of what I searched for my whole life, or would it be a disaster?

5

They didn't realize what they had, I thought while listening intently to the couple sitting across from me in my office.

"We haven't had sex in two months," she announced.

"Whose fault is that?" he retaliated with an elevated voice.

"Well, it's certainly not mine," she shot back.

"So then you're saying that it is my fault?" he questioned while searching for clarification.

"I've been walking around that house," she started pointing as though it were just outside the office walls ". . . half naked." With tears beating their way out the corners of her eyelids, she continued, "Not once have you touched me or even looked at me."

I watched him squeeze the armrest on either side of the chair, and I was thankful that his physical anger was being channeled into an object. Not once had his wife shown up in my office with bruises, scrapes, or cuts to accompany a story about how she fell down the stairs. Others had but not her.

"When?" he asked, as though the two of them had been living in different houses.

"Why do you think I walk around in my towel for ten minutes after I get out of the shower?" she asked. "To dry off my already dried body?"

I watched his eyelids shut, and his lips curled at the exact moment. "How am I supposed to know that means you want to make love?"

When I hear the term *make love* used in the place where many would say *sex* or another similar noun, it causes me to smile inside. I believe there is always hope for a couple dealing with a conflict in my office, and in this case that particular terminology reminds me how close we are to turning a corner. Some counselors won't let couples argue in their presence, which is a shame. If I can learn firsthand how they fight, I can manage my way into intricate details of their marriage that are not often accessible through mere probing. I think this method works better than if I talk to each of them alone or if I demand that they speak only when it's their turn. Of course there are times when such is necessary, but there are also times when this is best.

"You don't say that you want to have sex, and you don't touch me or look at me?" he stated, still dumbfounded by her accusation.

"I shouldn't have to—"

She made a valid point.

Many men would jump at the opportunity to meander slyly into the bathroom where their toweled wife stood halfheartedly toiling with her hair. Her soft skin peeking out of places that only he is allowed to explore and even though he knows what lies beneath, his eyes light up when the towel slides off her soft skin. The smell of sweet bath oils erupts from her body, and one thing leads to another. But, there are always two sides to every story.

I learned to be neutral—not to jump to conclusions. I also learned not to let certain images seep into my mind. It always surprised me how open both men and women became in front of a therapist. It forced me to become like a pitcher on the mound in the ninth inning of the world series with his team leading by one run and bases loaded. He has to drown out the crowd, release all emotions, and let his ability do what he does best—take control, or else get sidetracked and lose the game. This couple's marriage, however, wasn't a game; it was real life.

"I shouldn't get turned down every time I try to have sex with you," he clarified. "At least I ask," he noted. "I don't just beat around the bush and hope you know what I want. How do you think that makes me feel? You're upset with me for not knowing that you in a towel equals you wanting to have sex with me, and all I'm asking is for you to say *yes* every now and then when I *actually* ask."

I learned that many men find it okay simply to ask for sex while women prefer to drop hints. This may come as common sense to some, but it doesn't to most couples who visit my office. They are as lost as sheep without a shepherd.

"I shouldn't have to ask," she blurted out. "You should know."

"Know?" He shook his head repeatedly. I could tell he wanted to throw up his hands. "How am I supposed to know?"

Case and point.

"You just are."

"Like I knew that night that you were sitting on the couch listening to music instead of watching TV? When our son was at his friend's house and the mood seemed right?" He waited for a response, but she said nothing. She only hid her face in a hand that hadn't touched her husband in a sexual connotation in far too long.

"Because—" Her tears kept her from saying anything more.

My cue to step in. "Do you find your wife attractive?" I asked.

With the door shut, blinds pulled, and no one else in the room, questions often become very personal in my line of work. Therefore, I always assure my clients they have complete confidentiality. I would only expose a client if I feel a person's life is in danger. I let each client know that up front. We sign a contract, and we shake hands.

He glanced at the clock ticking on the wall before speaking. I knew he wasn't concerned about the hourly rate or getting anywhere. It was just a nervous habit. "Yes."

My focus was directly on him. I leaned forward just a bit, relaxing my elbows on the knees of my light-colored khaki pants. The shirt tucked into them was almost as dark as his mood seemed moments ago. Business casual was how I preferred to dress because I believed it less intimidating for my clients than if I wore a suit and tie.

An adequate distance separated us to make him comfortable. Still we were close enough to make the conversation personable.

"What thoughts go through your mind when you see your wife walking around the house wearing nothing but a towel?"

I could tell he was thinking. He put his finger to his chin, and I watched his eyes dart upward. "I think that she is busy getting ready. She is fixing her hair or picking out which outfit she wants to wear that day."

I knew I needed to step in again. "Beyond that," I probed, "when you see your wife," I glanced at her to see if he would. "What do you think about her? Not about what she is doing or thinking; how does seeing her in a towel make you feel?"

He studied his wife for the second time in the past ten seconds. The mood in the room shifted from bitterness to thoughtfulness in a matter of minutes. Outside my office windows, people went about their daily routines walking to and fro just living at their own pace. Some had problems similar to the couple sitting in front of me; others had more significant issues; and some had lesser ones. I learned no matter where folks were in life—single, married, divorced, widowed—we all deal with conflict and confusion. Sometimes this can be fixed, and sometimes it can't. Some people want their problems resolved, and others are so comfortable complaining about them that they wouldn't know what to do if their issues disappeared. They would probably rush into new ones.

He began to answer my question precisely as I thought he would. "I see a beautiful woman," he responded honestly, a single tear winding through the stubble on his worn face. "I admire the way she takes care of herself—how she eats salads and works out so that the towel is flat when wrapped around her not because I ask her to but because she wants to look good for herself and me. I want to rip that towel off her and make love to her just like the first time we stumbled into that dingy motel and fell onto a bed that made more noise than a rusted trampoline." He said more, all in a similar context, and I watched his wife's eyes light up the room. Her mind, I could tell, flashed back to the honeymoon years when neither of them could do any wrong and arguments led to sex instead of slamming doors and walking out. I wish the two would go home today, make love, and live happily ever after, but that's not the reality. That's a fairy tale that romance movies depict; this is real life, and I know they have more steps to take. There are a lot of unanswered questions.

When I saw Russ and Mary heading up their driveway last night, they hadn't been holding hands and walking slowly. They were four rose bushes apart, and he stormed in one direction and she in the opposite. My window hadn't been rolled down, so I was not sure if the banter between them consisted primarily of profanities, but the expression on their faces caused me to think that it just might. I worried about them often. Having this couple as neighbors made counseling them different, but knowing the two personally made me want to help them as friends. We weren't close, but every now and then we met at the spot between our yards where his turf-farm-grown-grass and my hand-thrown-seed-grass collided. We talked briefly about the wacky North Carolina weather, the dog that bit the mailman last winter, and the Atlanta Braves for whom Russ is a huge fan. I never actually saw his memorabilia, but he once told me he had a bat given to him and signed by Dale Murphy.

The session was nearing an end. "Here's what I want you to work on this week. Mary, when you want to be intimate with Russ, make sure he knows it. This doesn't mean you have to do the whole male roll over in bed 'Wanna have sex?' routine." Russ and Mary both chuckled. "When you're in that towel, sit beside him and put your hand on his thigh, or when he walks past you in the mirror, wink at him, and if you have to, use that towel to pull him a little closer."

I left it at that. Homework is usually no fun, yet homework that includes making love to your spouse should be.

6

After the session with Russ and Mary first thing this morning, I filed a stack of documents plaguing my desk, met with two more clients, made a couple dozen phone calls, and talked briefly to Larry about tonight's plans.

When the clock in front of me reminded me that it was time for lunch, I shut off my computer and walked outside where the fresh air felt fantastic. The downtown streets buzzed with traffic, and tourists filled the sidewalks armed with backpacks and cameras pointing at the old buildings and landmark signs. To them, they were beautiful, magnificent, and alluring. Even though I appreciated their value to the town, overlooking them simply became part of my routine.

I hopped in my vehicle and drove across the bridge to meet Ben at Bella Pizza & Subs, a tiny restaurant on the island. I soon learned that my brother intended to provoke me.

"Two dates in one weekend," Ben applauded and then attempted to high five me over the pepperoni pizza sitting on the table in between us, "that's what I'm talking about."

"It's not like that," I scoffed, leaving him hanging.

He worked up a false look of disappointment and let his hand hang in the air until the point of embarrassment. "Why not?

You're single. Live life a little. Have fun," he encouraged, finally dropping his hand.

"It just doesn't feel right," I admitted.

"It's like you said when we talked earlier, Saturday night isn't a real date. It's just spending time with a friend and her son. It's not like you and Emily are planning a romantic candlelit dinner at your place. You're having pasta at our house. And even if you were, who cares? Go out tonight with Mindy and see what happens. Then spend time with Emily tomorrow evening and see what transpires with her. Decide which one you like best and tell the other you're not interested." Ben paused as the waitress made her way to our table to top off our glasses after checking in with the folks in the booth behind us. "This is a great opportunity, man. It's like you are one of those guys on that dating show . . .," he trailed off, a puzzled look on his face. "What's it called?" he asked, wanting my help. "You know, the one where the man picks between all the beautiful women."

I knew the show; watching television is one thing the average single man often does. I seldom tuned in to *The Bachelor* although if asked while hooked up to a polygraph I would admit I saw it a handful of times. I understood the premise well enough to realize that one so-called *lucky* man spends time with fifty different women. Over the course of the season, he narrows them down and chooses the one he wants to be with by the final show. It's like real-life dating on steroids and in fast-forward. Typically, during the season finale, *The Bachelor* asks the woman of his choosing to marry him. I have no idea how many women have said "yes" or "no" since the show began airing, but I presume that if someone were to research the number of these couples who end up happily married, the percentage would be low. For that reason, the show always troubled me a bit. As I watched the wheels in Ben's brain churn, I let him wallow in pain. *Fifty women*, I considered, and I thought *I* had troubles.

By the time we cleaned the pizza pan, Ben still hadn't remembered the name of the television show. Between bites, he continued to encourage me to make the best out of this weekend, and the more he talked, the more I realized he had a valid point. Maybe I had been a little too uptight about the situation. There have been times when I would have eaten a worm to have *one* date on a lonely weekend.

After lunch, I spent the rest of the afternoon in sessions with clients, and in the moments in between, I caught myself watching the clock. I worked my regular eight-hour day, but it felt longer than usual.

Friday evening rolled around, and I found myself breathing heavily as I paced through the house getting ready for my first ever blind date. Larry offered for him and his wife Janet to join us for dinner, so they could introduce Mindy and me. I agreed because I was comfortable with the two of them and figured it would make things less awkward if Mindy and I didn't connect or have anything in common.

I kept on the same pants I wore to work but changed into a green collared shirt. I wasn't sure if the idea of a blind date was what had my stomach in knots all day or if it was the fact that I had plans with two different women on consecutive nights—maybe a little of each.

When the time came, I drove to El Zarape, a local Mexican restaurant everyone in town, except for me, seemed to be nuts about. In the parking lot, I took a deep breath. What if Mindy wasn't my type? Or what if I liked her but she didn't like me? These questions and dozens of others danced around my mind like lottery balls as I stepped out of my vehicle and prepared myself for *THE* introduction.

I found Larry and Janet waiting for me on a bench just outside the front door. I glanced around at the dozen or so folks crowding the sidewalk on a busy Friday night, waiting for a table to become available. I couldn't help but wonder if any of these people were Mindy. It didn't take me long to pick out a couple I hoped weren't. A woman standing in front of a row of holly bushes lining the restaurant somewhat resembled Larry's description, but she was smoking a cigarette, a habit I refused to deal with in a relationship. I knew too many people who died from lung cancer. In addition to the fact that smoking is unhealthy, I just can't stand the smell of a burning cigarette. It makes me cringe.

Another woman, leaning on the bench to Larry's and Janet's right, had more earrings than I could count without staring, tattoos for sleeves, and skintight black leather pants. Honestly, she wore it all well but wasn't my type. Out of nowhere, an image of a bedroom bombarded my mind: black walls, handcuffs hanging on the headboard, a whip on the nightstand, and a large mirror on the ceiling. Interesting I thought but no thanks.

By the time I made it through the crowd to Larry and Janet, I concluded that Mindy hadn't arrived yet. I figured she probably spent a little longer than needed on her hair and makeup and was running late. Or maybe she was inside freshening up, I considered, on second thought. *Oh, crud.* That reminded me that I probably should have looked at myself in the mirror before hopping out of the car. I began to consider all the things a nervous person thinks of during the moments before a date. What if I had toothpaste on the edge of my lip or a piece of fuzz in my hair? Or even worse? Before taking another step, I covered my mouth pretending to clear my throat and then inconspicuously brushed the tip of my nose as Larry stepped in my direction.

All clear.

"Hey, Luke," he greeted, shaking my hand. Janet and the people on the bench to their left stood up. A moment earlier, Enrique Iglesias's voice, coming from speakers not hidden very well in potted plants on either side of the entrance, was interrupted as the next name on the list was called. I assumed the three people I didn't recognize must be "The Claytons" since that is what the nasally sounding person called out, twice, following the announcement with: "Your table is now ready" emphasizing the "now."

They weren't The Claytons I soon found out, and in a matter of moments all three of these folks were staring at me. My next thought was that they might be friends of Larry's and Janet's whom they'd run into here and been chatting with while waiting. It was a small town after all. If so, Larry would probably introduce us; we'd shake hands maybe; and that would be that.

"This is my cousin, Mindy," Larry announced, motioning to a woman with the promised pretty green eyes and bleached blonde hair that blended quite nicely with her yellow dress. On my walk up, she'd been hidden behind the middle-aged couple sitting beside her on the bench. I approached my blind date, and she took my hand as I reached for hers. Our eyes met momentarily, and we exchanged a friendly "hello." I immediately noticed her soft skin, and by the smell her hands left on mine, I could tell she moistened them with a sweet-smelling lotion. Vanilla, I presumed.

Larry was right after all, I concluded. Mindy was pretty, and I made sure to thank God she looked nothing like her cousin. I shuttered a few times throughout the week imagining what thoughts might swim through my mind if I had to spend the evening sitting across from a woman who resembled my mentor. Yuck.

"And these are her parents," Larry added.

Huh?

What?

Who?

Those were just a few words that nearly escaped my mouth as Mindy's hand fell from mine. For a moment I knew I must look like a deer caught in a spotlight. I almost blurted out my next thought: *I'm sorry, I thought I heard you say that these people standing next to my blind date are her parents.*

Had I heard him right? Mindy's parents? Seriously?

I waited for someone to speak.

Not only would I have to deal with the pressures of a blind date, but I also had to meet Mindy's parents for the first time on the same night? Is this the way all blind dates work, I wondered? In order to have a chance at approval for a real date you have to meet the parents? No wonder I steered clear of this form of dating. Suddenly, the situation seemed more awkward than I ever imagined possible. I knew that all five people shining their headlights at me could tell I was having difficulty hiding the emotions unconsciously brought to the surface, courtesy of the thoughts rattling my addled brain.

After an awkward silence, I gathered my composure and shook Mindy's parents' hands. "It's nice to meet you both," I said, bending the truth. I even added a joke, "I'm just sorry it has to be under these circumstances." Thankfully, they got it, or at least they pretended to. On second thought, they probably didn't get it. However, I did appreciate the courtesy laughter.

On the way to the table, Mindy walked beside me as the hostess, followed by her parents, then Larry and Janet, led us to our seats. Mindy stepped close and whispered, "I'm so sorry."

"For what?" I asked.

"About two minutes before you arrived, Larry told me he forgot to tell you my parents were having dinner with us tonight."

"Oh, that's okay," I fibbed, and without skipping a beat I added, "I asked my parents to come, too, but they already had plans to play bingo."

Thankfully, Mindy took it as the joke it was intended to be, and when she laughed out loud, I felt the tension dwindle for the first time. "Tonight is their thirtieth anniversary," she informed me. "Larry and Janet are treating them to dinner."

The three of us men sat on one side of the table and the women settled in across from us. Since Mindy and I were the last two to sit, I had no other option than to pull out the chair next to her father, a hairy man with broad shoulders and a reddish face. The waiter took our drink order, and then we all began conversing. For the next ten minutes I felt like I was on the hot seat, answering questions like: Where do you work? Where do you live? How long have you lived in Atlantic Beach? Then came the usual questions that inevitably come up when you meet someone new in any small community: Who are your parents? Who are you related to? Do you know so and so?

Although Mindy recently moved to this area, her parents had been living here since she graduated high school and attended college in Virginia. The interrogation continued until the waiter brought out a second round of beers for everyone except Mindy and me. No one warned me that tonight, along with the surprise already encountered, there would be a beer drinking contest.

Mindy's dad tried to tempt me early on with the ole peer pressure routine. "Have just one with us," he encouraged. At least he didn't add, "It'll put hair on your chest, young man." Although by looking at his collar, it seemed to have worked for him.

It didn't take long to decide that Mindy seemed like a sweet person, and I couldn't help but be impressed by how she stood up for me when her dad tried to convince me to drink alcohol with the rest of them. However, there had been a time when I could have drunk him under the table. In a conversation between Mindy and me while the others were preoccupied with their swigging contest, she told me she didn't care for alcoholic beverages either. We kept our reasons to ourselves for the time being, and then when her dad butted in, she told him that we were hoping to remember tonight. I almost fell out of my seat when he said, "I'm just hoping to wake up naked with that woman right there," he announced, pointing at his wife. A little to her left actually, but I think that had something to do with his aim after emptying six glasses.

Other than feeling awkward for all the obvious reasons, I was never a big fan of Mexican cuisine; I typically stuck with American food. A meat and potatoes kind of guy was what I'd always been. The last time I visited a Mexican restaurant, I made the mistake of ordering one of the only two options on the "American" section of the menu: a hamburger and fries. A few bites into the burger, I realized there was a reason the restaurant was called a "Mexican" restaurant. However, before that day, I assumed a burger and fries would be a safe choice on any menu.

I didn't let Mindy's dad talk me into getting drunk with him, but I did let her mom talk me into ordering a chicken fajita instead of another "American" option—chicken nuggets and fries—which I knew would have been the joke of the night. I could hear Larry now, "I wonder what toy you'll get with your kid's meal?" He knew me well enough to give me a hard time but also knew me well enough to know that I would have had a comeback cocked and loaded for such a comment.

As the night wore on and I enjoyed my fajita, I prayed the waiter would bring the check instead of another round of beers. Mindy's mother spent half the evening talking about her daughter's ex-boyfriend Joe, a hard-core New Yorker. She described him as a six foot four inch, 250 pound man with tattoos who had stalked her daughter since the day she ended the relationship. I wasn't sure what to think about that or how to respond, so for the most part, I just listened, nodding my head occasionally, saying things like "Wow" or "Interesting."

When the check came, I couldn't talk Larry into letting me pay for Mindy and myself. By the time we made it back out to the fresh air, she and I decided to spend a couple more hours together. I was pleased to learn I would have to take her home since her parents had picked her up on the way to the restaurant.

"That was your way out if you didn't want to spend more time with me, huh?" I teased as I opened the passenger door and waited for Mindy to get in, already enjoying the one-on-one time and being away from the hot seat.

After a brief conversation, we decided to head to downtown Morehead City and walk along the waterfront. We parked in the large lot next to Dee Gee's Gifts & Books, and when we stepped out of my Range Rover, Mindy slipped on the cute lightweight cropped jacket she'd been carrying with her throughout the evening. Most of the shops were closed for the night, so we opted to peruse the storefront windows and found ourselves in random conversations about outfits, antiques, and mermaids. I soon began to think about how nice it was to spend time being silly with a woman as beautiful as Mindy.

The highlight of our evening came when we wandered into a gift shop. I had to use the bathroom so badly I thought my bladder would erupt at any minute. I guess I drank too much Pepsi at dinner. Of course, I didn't tell Mindy, not at first anyway.

"Is it okay if we head into this store so I can use the restroom?" I said nonchalantly.

When I pulled on the door handle to the bathroom, it wouldn't open which made me wonder why there aren't *occupied* signs on all single-unit bathrooms? Suddenly I felt like a kid standing barefoot in a mud puddle. I had to go, and I had to go now. As hard as I tried to hide my desperation, Mindy, who had followed me inside the quaint store, must have seen it because she caught herself on the potato chip rack. That's how hard she was laughing.

She pointed to the other door, her aim about as good as her dad's. "Why don't you just go into the women's?"

Believe me the thought crossed my mind, but I wanted to be respectful especially on a first date. "That seems weird to me."

"You mean," she paused continuing to find humor in my pain, "weirder than how you're acting right now?"

I guess I set myself up for that one. I never needed to use the bathroom so badly in my entire life, and here on the night we met, my bladder felt like it was going to explode—literally. When I couldn't take the pressure anymore, I opened the door with a woman's silhouette on the front.

Two minutes later, I came out to find Mindy's face precisely as I left it—bright red. Only this time, she held a tin bucket and a pack of diapers. I still don't know how she found those timely items so quickly.

"I gathered some things that might help next time you find yourself in a predicament like this," she teased.

I never felt so embarrassed yet so at ease at the same time. Mindy was witty and down to earth, and I liked that.

We spent time relaxing on one of the wooden deck swings overlooking the Intracoastal Waterway. Afterward, she took a photo of King Neptune, a giant statue that stands guard over the waterfront docks as well as the restaurants and shops. I showed her Big Rock Landing, where the Big Rock Blue Marlin Tournament weigh-ins occur yearly during the area's largest fishing tournament. It was also a major tourist attraction.

We made it to Mindy's house a few minutes after midnight. When I guided the gear shift into park, I felt her eyes inviting me to stretch across the center console for a kiss goodnight. My heart pounded. My fingers trembled just a bit. Slowly, gently, the distance between my lips and hers—glowing with sparkling lip gloss—closed. This was it; the moment I'd been waiting for. A connection. A spark. An explanation that everything happened for a reason tonight, and all my worries about this weekend were over. But then, something else happened. Something I didn't expect.

Mindy brushed her thumb across my lower lip pushing it slowly, passionately, as her fingers slid across my freshly shaven face.

"Would you like to come in?" she asked.

7

The following morning, nature's alarm clock—thin rays of golden sunshine glaring through the spaces between the blinds—warmed my body and eventually brought my feet to the floor. The first thing I noticed was my pants tossed loosely into the corner sometime late last night. The next thing I realized was that the smile I fell asleep with seemed to have hung around for approximately seven hours. The luxury of waking up to anything besides a ringing in my ear always seemed to help my day start off better than when the last thing I did before hitting the pillow was to punch in a set of numbers, causing me to sigh like a young boy being made to lie down for bed on a school night.

I remembered begging my mom to let me stay up after dark when I was a kid, thinking it was a sin to go to bed before the sun fell below the tree line. Of course I couldn't comprehend that just as the seasons of the year changed, so did the sun's ascent and descent, not to mention the time changed, which always threw me off when I was young. "All the other kids," I grumbled, "get to stay up later than me." I had no clue if that was true, but I couldn't imagine why any loving parents would send their kid to bed at such a time.

As I got older, I wanted to stay up later and later which called for me to get smarter and smarter. When I reached my teens, I became interested in sports. I watched them on television and played them at school and in the recreational leagues. On nights when I knew there would be a game on television, I reminded my dad of the big event—every game was big in my mind—and I learned to do so when my mom wasn't around. Dad was a sports nut too, and I could tell he enjoyed my company even when I was learning the intricacies of each sport. We spent countless hours in front of the television watching various sporting events, including football, baseball, basketball, NASCAR, and even the occasional golf tournament or tennis match. I sat as close to his recliner as possible, and the two of us got so caught up in the game that in those moments it seemed there were no worries in the entire world. The concerns on our minds—for him, politics and his job as a heavy equipment operator at the local port, and for me, teenage girls . . . and more teenage girls—vanished.

During football season, I always prayed for close games; those were the nights when my dad became my personal attorney. "Cathy," he said to my mom in the same voice he used with me when I knew he meant business, "I can't make the boy go to bed when the Dolphins are tied with the Broncos in the third quarter." Now that I'm older and wiser about the friction between men and women in such circumstances, I imagine Dad had a word or two waiting for him when Mom finally tucked me in after an overtime game on a school night. Our favorite, though, had always been watching baseball. Again, I prayed for close games, and when there were, Mom rarely bothered trying to pull me away from the television. She would find a book and glare in our direction on her way to her bedroom. I wouldn't see her for the rest of the night.

That reminded me the Atlanta Braves were playing the Chicago Cubs this Monday night, and I promised Dad I would watch the game with him. The Braves had always been our favorite team. I even owned a jersey autographed by Chipper Jones, a hat signed by Bobby Cox, and all kinds of other Braves memorabilia collected over the years. Some of it I bought with my own money, and other items came as Christmas and birthday gifts.

Some say sports occupy a man's mind more than anything else. I say *They're wrong*. Feeling the fibers of the carpet wiggle their way in between my toes as I headed for the bathroom and thinking of Mindy in a way I probably shouldn't, my mind quickly shifted from the upcoming game to the time the two of us spent together last night—the reason for my prolonged smile. *Women* is my answer to what occupies a man's mind more than anything, especially a single man. This raised the question that tormented me since Mindy asked me to come in last night: Had I made the right decision?

Initially, I convinced myself that the invitation was harmless—we'd share a cup of coffee or a glass of iced tea and get to know each other a little better. That's all. But then, somehow, in the heat of the moment, with Mindy's thumb pressed against my lips, my body began to desire things my heart didn't need right now. I remembered I made a promise to God. As quickly as that thought popped into my mind, another took its place. I suddenly recalled that asking for forgiveness had always been easier than asking for permission. I made mistakes in the past. I slipped up and said, "Yes, I'll come in," thus tricking myself into thinking we'd only have a glass of wine and a nice time. The next thing I knew I was floating in paradise beneath the covers of a woman's bed who didn't even know my middle name. Temporary satisfaction overrode my desire to keep my pants buttoned. Even then when things were said and done, God in all His grace somehow picked me back up and let me try again. Why He gave me so many chances, I wasn't sure.

I couldn't help but notice that the bed was a mess this morning as cool air blew through the windows I left open last night. I remembered this during the middle of the night when I woke up, heard the ocean's familiar voice, and pulled the covers to my neck shielding my bare chest from the brisk temperature. I slept without a shirt on for as long as I can remember, so my boxers were the only item of clothing keeping me warm at the present moment.

After a few minutes in the bathroom to freshen up, I gathered my pants, belt, shirt, and socks. Instead of putting my clothes on and kissing Mindy on the cheek, I did something else.

It wasn't the initial question—"Would you like to come in?"—that caused me to stumble last night, but it was what happened after I said, "I would love to, but I'm going to have to take a rain check." I hadn't fully prepared myself for what the woman in my passenger seat was about to whisper ever so sensuously into my ear. Those words would cause most any man to jump across the center console and end up where I found myself.

Even now, eight hours later, her words still tingled my spine. "Then I guess I'll have to pray for rain," she uttered. A moment later our lips met, and one thing led to another. I remember looking into a dark, cloudy sky, wondering if water drops might fall between our bodies or if that was even possible since we were nearly connected at the hip, tiptoeing toward her front door, trying not to trip over each other's feet.

I threw my dirty clothes into the laundry basket in the bathroom and thanked God for giving me the courage to say goodnight to Mindy at that door, realizing my vulnerability would only lead to one place. At first, I thought I hurt her feelings, and I still wasn't sure I hadn't. When I said, "No thanks," for the second time, she didn't attempt to talk me into it again. All she said was, "I wouldn't typically invite a man into my house on the first date." I began to shake my head and was about to tell her I hadn't gotten that impression, but she wouldn't let me get a word in. She continued, "It's just that you seem like such a nice guy, and . . .," she paused as though she was afraid to say the words that tickled her tongue. Her eyes glanced toward the clouds that I glimpsed earlier, now moving more rapidly, as if in a race against one another. Crickets chirped in the bushes, and I heard a frog croak just as we reached the door. "It's been a while since I've met anybody like you," she finally uttered. "All those stories my mom embarrassed me with at dinner are true. I somehow always end up with the bad guys. I think I can change them, but I never do. You seem different. I'm used to my dates trying to put their hands in places they shouldn't and rush me through *their* front door. Now, I'm doing that to you, and I'm sorry. I just wanted you to know that I really like you, that's all."

Overhead, a row of pole lights illuminated the apartment building's parking lot and highlighted the tears forming in the corners of Mindy's eyes causing her eyeliner to run just a smidge. If I had any inkling that she was the kind of woman who found pleasure in one-night stands, her current state convinced me otherwise. "I had a nice night too," I admitted honestly. "I think we both did. Why don't we just leave it at that for now and see what happens," I suggested, wanting to let my guard down and plunge through that closed door.

"Good idea," she replied simply, smiling and realizing she needed to wipe her eyes in hopes that I hadn't noticed.

Still content with my decision after a night of sleep, I made my bed. I slept well last night, and now I could open my Bible without feeling guilty. God always had a way of reminding me when I ignored my moral compass, at least until I asked for His forgiveness and actually meant it. I remember this most evidently from my teenage years. No one I know labeled me as a wild teen, but I attended my share of parties. I was known to throw down a few too many brown bottles and silver cans as my friends and I made memories we soon forgot and others we wished we could forget. Following late Saturday nights out on the town, I attended church the next morning with my parents who didn't know the details. I often found my tired body sinking into the pew, wondering how many people had a hunch about what I and some of the other teenagers within earshot of the preacher's voice had been up to the night before. Eventually, I realized it didn't matter if they knew. God knew, and He, not the others, was the one working on me. They were there to worship Him and hear the message. Back then I thought all adults had it figured out, especially Christians. Boy, was I wrong. When sitting in church now, I don't wonder what the people sitting near me did to embarrass themselves in front of God this week. I focus on my personal relationship with Him. I haven't been drunk in years, but there are also other things I know better than to do now like judging others or feeling guilty for mistakes God forgave me for years ago.

An image of Emily's face suddenly popped into my mind, and I thought about her and Ayden as I read a passage in Psalms. When I reached the last word, I placed my Bible on the nightstand where I like to keep it. Emily was one of the main reasons I chose to become a counselor. During the four short years we spent in high school, she lost her father to an overdose, her mother to a stroke, and her brother followed the same path as their dad. Back then I tried my best to help her through the grieving process, but I felt helpless as I listened to her cry on walks down the beach. She asked why she'd lost everyone more times than I could count. As I worked my way through my core classes in college, I realized I gave Emily some of the best natural medicine available—I listened. I shared my time with her and showed her compassion. Looking back, I know I have God and my parents to thank for teaching me how to love others.

In the morning, before my day begins to fill with the hustle and bustle of life, I usually spend time reading. I wish I could say I read my Bible daily, but I don't. Sometimes I spend part of my morning in another book or an article from a magazine I ordered through a school fundraiser from the boy next door. I never set a time or chapter limit or anything like that; I just read until I decide to do something else or when it is time to head to the office.

That's what I love about Saturday mornings, I thought as I cracked an egg and dropped it into a frying pan. No schedule. No counseling sessions. No research. No phone calls to return, other than my mother's.

When I dialed her number, she answered on the second ring. We chatted while I scrambled three eggs.

"How did your date go last night?" she asked.

Mom always kept up with me. She knew my schedule as well as anyone these days, and just as I'd told Ben about my back-to-back dates, I filled her in on my plans.

"It wasn't what I expected," I started then paused, unsure exactly how to describe the night. It had been a roller coaster of sorts I guess. "But it was nice," I concluded.

"You sure about that? I heard a little hesitation in your voice."

I explained the situation about Mindy's parents—the shock of them being there, the drinking, the stories about the ex-boyfriend. Then I told her everything else, leaving out the part where I nearly lost my virginity. As far as my mother knew, I was still a virgin.

"So you'll see her again?"

For a moment there was a lull in the conversation. Mindy and I hadn't made plans for a second date although we exchanged phone numbers, and I didn't have any reason not to give her a call sometime soon. Maybe I should ask her out to a movie or to have lunch one day this coming week. "I think so," I finally answered. "I don't see why not. Mindy seems sweet; I'd like to get to know her better."

"Is she pretty?"

My description always seemed to focus on her bleached blonde hair and green eyes.

Without notice Mom changed the subject. "What about Emily? Are you looking forward to spending time with her this evening?"

I sprinkled a dash of salt and pepper over my eggs and stirred butter into a bowl of grits I cooked in a small pot on one of the back burners. The smell of breakfast was taking over my house, and I loved it. There may not be a more pleasant aroma in the world. In fact, someone should create an air freshener that smells like a country breakfast along with one for coffee too.

"I think tonight is more of a just friends thing." As soon as the words trickled off my lips, I furrowed my brow.

Had I seriously used those two words? *Just friends.*

"She sure does have a sweet little boy."

I furrowed my brow again and stopped stirring for a moment. "Sweet?" I questioned drawing out the word. I never heard anyone use that word to describe Ayden. He'd always been a bit of a terror at the volleyball court.

"He just needs a lot of love." Mom paused. "And a good father-figure in his life."

"What does that mean?" I asked, jumping to conclusions.

"Exactly what I said. Ayden seems to have a great mother, but being a single mother is rough. I lived that life with my mother and witnessed the struggles firsthand you know," she stated matter-of-factly. "You have to work at least a full-time job to support you and your child then come home to an empty house and pretend everything is okay. Cook dinner, help with homework, force your child to bathe, brush teeth, and get into bed without pulling out what little hair you have left after a miserable divorce. Your child becomes your life. Your best friend. Your everything which is not healthy despite what society suggests in this day and age."

I guess it's evident that my mother was another reason I chose to become a therapist. "I think Emily is doing a good job," I pointed out. "She's okay."

"Come on, Luke. You're a counselor; you deal with these types of family environments every day. Sure, Emily is doing a good job, but you know she isn't doing okay. She's keeping afloat; there's a difference."

Balancing the phone between my shoulder and ear, I raked my eggs and grits onto a plate with a spatula. Eventually, I poured a glass of milk to wash down all the great smelling food.

"Of course she has struggles, Mom, but like you said every single parent does. That doesn't mean she needs a man to help her with Ayden."

Mom cut me off, and I picked up my milk and took a sip as I listened. "Every woman needs a man in her life, and every child needs a father. You just said what you said because you think I'm saying *you* should be that man, but I'm not. I think you would make a great husband to any woman and a great dad to any child whether he was your own blood or not. You know exactly what Emily needs and what Ayden needs too for that matter. That doesn't mean you have to be the one to give it to them, but that little boy looks up to you. I see how he follows you around at the volleyball games when I come to watch."

"You just said you weren't saying I need to be that man. Aren't you contradicting yourself?" I argued like a defense attorney in a crowded courtroom.

"You don't have to marry her, Luke, to be a positive male role model for her son. You know that as well as anyone. Emily is reaching out to you. Why do you think she asked you to have dinner with them?"

"Because she thinks I'm sexy," I teased, knowing my mom didn't like that word.

"You're handsome," she corrected. "You have a good head on your shoulders, most of the time. Just don't hurt her, okay? And more importantly, don't hurt that little fellow."

When I finally hung up the phone, I didn't feel as chipper as earlier. My head had been straight when I woke up. I had a good time last night with Mindy, and I looked forward to spending time with Emily and Ayden this evening. Somehow it became that simple after an entire week of allowing myself to stress over the details. Now my mother made my head spin again, and I didn't know what to think. Why had she done that?

I carried my plate—that I'd merely picked at while on the phone—to the deck at the back of the house and ate as I watched the seagulls and pelicans soar above the rolling waves. A steady wind, strong enough to force me to keep one hand on my napkin so it wouldn't become a kite without a string, blew the flimsy sea oats on the low-lying dunes separating my small backyard from the beach. There was almost always a constant breeze out here; this morning it felt good on my skin. Before coming out, I pulled a pair of shorts up my legs but opted to remain shirtless.

Mom had been right about everything she said. No matter how much I wanted to deny it, I knew that. Ayden did look up to me, and Emily needed me in her life maybe not as a boyfriend or potential husband but as a friend who adored her son and thought an awful lot of her too.

As aggravated as I was with my mom at this very moment, I appreciated what she did in such a subtle yet unsubtle method. I'd have done the exact thing if I had been in her shoes. She reminded me there was more at stake here than a fun weekend which helped me recall that I needed to be careful with Emily and Ayden tonight. I needed to set boundaries.

Mom had always been the mediator in our family. She kept us grounded and made us face our struggles head-on. "We're going to settle this right now," she said. "No matter how long it takes, we're going to get to the root of the problem so that we don't bury it in our hearts and have to deal with family conflict for years to come." I imagined she learned a lot from her mother. My grandmother's ex-husband was a drunkard and spent half their marriage in bars and the other half behind bars. She put up with him as long as possible, and then when my mom was five, she finally packed as many of their belongings as would fit into the trunk and empty seats of a Chevrolet Chevette and left him for good. It was the hardest thing she ever did, she once told me when she was still alive. She grew up in a home where divorce wasn't an option. It was a last resort and only considered when infidelity or physical abuse was present. When her husband crossed that line, she drew hers.

I despise divorce and work with clients daily to help them grow in their marriages. There are rare occasions, like my grandmother's, where I believe walking away is necessary, but the divorce rate should not be anywhere near fifty percent in this country. In my opinion—call it expert or just another average Joe's perspective—it's that way due to lack of commitment. People these days place too much emphasis on feelings. One day they decide they feel like they have fallen out of love, so they give up on a marriage of five, ten, or even fifteen or more years without a fight.

Last year I counseled a couple who had been married for twenty years. The kids left home, and this couple decided out of the blue that they were no longer compatible. The love they shared before the kids were in the picture somehow faded into something else. If I remember correctly, they said their relationship had become more of a businesslike partnership over the years. The sad news is that many people fail to understand that love isn't *just* a feeling. I spent weeks trying to encourage this particular couple that true love is a compilation of acts. It begins with a single action, and as it grows, it turns into hundreds and thousands of continuous, simple acts that make up the complexity of the meaning of love. I realize that love cannot be lost but only relinquished. Every marriage will inevitably face days, maybe weeks, months, or years when at least one partner feels like he or she doesn't love the other; I often tell my clients this. Love is like a flower. It will grow back as long as you choose to water it. So, in the end, it comes down to a choice. That choice is called commitment. I tell my counselees their marriage will last if they are committed to loving one another, but if they choose to make rash decisions based on what society calls the *feeling* of love, their marriage is most likely doomed.

I was about to leave the wind, the waves, and the fragrance of salt air, which had overtaken the smell of my breakfast, to go back inside when Russ walked over with his son.

"Hey, Colton," I greeted, offering the little guy my hand to complete a high-five technique we patented over time. "How did school go this week?"

"Good," he answered shyly, hiding behind his daddy's leg. He'd started first grade this year.

I turned my attention to Russ. "Hey, neighbor," I said. "I see you've been cleaning out your dunes this morning." The entire time I'd been outside with a plate on my lap, he'd been wearing a pair of gloves while picking up trash. I waved at him moments after I ventured out the back door.

"This wind has blown all sorts of objects into the dunes, and I've meant to clean the area out for a while."

It always amazed me how much trash ended up on the beach. Along with keeping the dunes behind my house clean, I walked the shore frequently and picked up empty cans, broken toys, and other random items.

"I haven't looked at the weather forecast, but I expect this wind is bringing some rain with it," I stated, glancing up at the clouds I noticed in the distance upon stepping outside.

"Yeah, the weather is supposed to get a little rough later tonight. The meteorologists are calling for winds up to forty miles an hour." That was a bit high even for the beach.

"Really," I responded with surprise. I was so busy this week that I hadn't heard anything about it. Come to think of it, I'm not sure if I turned on the television at all. "I'll have to make sure to take everything inside so none of it ends up in your immaculate dunes."

Russ laughed. "You better, especially if it means anything to you. It might be months before I clean that area out again. Mary's been nagging me for a while about this project."

I smiled. "How is Mary?"

"She's having a good day. It's been a long time since I saw her smile as wide as she did this morning when I told her I would finally work in the dunes."

"That's great to hear," I announced, happy to see improvement. "I know keeping a tidy yard is a priority of Mary's, and I've noticed you've been full steam ahead lately. I saw you mowing the grass Thursday after work and weedeating yesterday evening."

"She appreciates a freshly trimmed yard. I can't believe that I never realized that was part of why our marriage was failing."

"Well, it's like we discovered a few weeks ago in one of our sessions that it's not really about the end product of a beautiful yard, it's showing her you care about taking care of things especially when they're important to her. I remember both of you agreeing that she spends countless hours tidying the house's interior. When women see us men sitting around watching television all day Saturday while they clean and the grass grows, it doesn't settle too well."

"I know. I'm learning," Russ admitted.

"We all are. Remember, though, there is a healthy compromise. Make sure you don't spend all day outdoors. You need to take time for her too and Colton," I reminded my neighbor, reaching down to mess up Colton's hair so he could laugh in the midst of all this adult talk.

"I'm taking the family out for dinner tonight. We're going to—"

Before Russ could spit out the restaurant's name, the three of us turned our heads at the sound of Mary's voice. "Russ," we heard her call out. We watched her look toward the dunes then to the left and right. "Russ," she said again, not noticing him standing on my deck.

"Over here, Mary." He waved as he spoke.

Standing on the back porch with a glass of iced water in her grip, she waved back, holding it up with a smile on her face.

"That's what marriage is all about, Russ," I acknowledged. "Taking care of your spouse."

A moment later, he and Colton stepped back across the property line, and Mary handed him the glass.

I started to open my sliding glass door. "Russ," I called out first, "Make sure you catch a few innings of the East Carolina versus N.C. State baseball game today."

He held up his thumb and smiled. Mary put a hand on her hip but also smiled knowing that her husband deserved to watch his alma mater in a big game against an in-state rival. The three of us had also talked about "Russ time" and what it meant to their relationship.

Inside at the sink, I couldn't help but grin realizing that we were in the process of redefining my neighbors' marriage and, just as importantly, helping sculpt a positive lifestyle for Colton.

So far in my short career, I helped keep more than a dozen marriages together, and I only lost two. Russ and Mary filed the papers at one point but decided to rescind them after a month of counseling. Those were the ones that made my job so special, the reason I woke up every morning and gave every ounce of energy God provided me each day. I still wanted more purpose I realized. I wanted someone to wake up with, not necessarily tomorrow or next week, but forever.

8

spent the rest of the morning and early afternoon working through a to-do list I drafted earlier in the week. I tackled one of these every Saturday since moving into the house. By two o'clock, I had taken out the garbage, given the new weedeater a test drive, cleaned my vehicle inside and out, worked out at the gym, and showered and shaved.

I dabbed a hint of Old Spice aftershave on my face and double-checked the areas on my neck that my razor often missed in my rush to get to the office on weekday mornings. I sang into the showerhead until my voice became crackly. This time, instead of Lady A, I did injustice to the lyrics of every Kenny Chesney song I knew. My dad often said, "If you can't carry a tune in the shower, you might as well pack up the instruments and take them to the nearest pawn shop." I never fully understood that comment because it seemed to make sense and not make sense at the same time. Who would have instruments in the shower?

After my karaoke session, I called Ben and Colleen to find out if I could bring anything to help with or complement dinner, and then I headed to the closet to select my clothes for the evening. An assortment of khaki-colored pants and collared shirts—my usual work attire—filled the racks. My shoes were arranged by color on the floor and placed side by side neatly. By many, my wardrobe would be labeled casual, but casual is the norm when you live at the beach. In fact, the majority of locals prefer to wear flip-flops and shorts most of the year. There aren't many establishments where you'll find a "No Shoes, No Shirt, No Service" sign. Such notices have always made me wonder: Are underwear and shorts or pants optional at these places? Around here having lunch next to a group of people wearing bathing suits is no big deal.

The Crystal Coast, the name given to the coastline extending from the Cape Lookout National Seashore to the New River, had long been a tourist attraction. Still it seemed more out-of-towners were finding out about the place each year. The primary towns that made up the area included Atlantic Beach, Emerald Isle, Pine Knoll Shores, Indian Beach, and Salter Path along with soundside communities such as Beaufort, Morehead City, and Swansboro. Visitors often first came for vacation and then ended up retiring here. The Crystal Coast was one of those love at first sight places.

I tugged at a few pairs of pants and pulled out a couple different shirts before finally deciding to wear a pair of blue jeans and a blue and black pinstripe polo. The new pair of shoes I bought last weekend at Belk would go well with my outfit, so I slid them over my socks. I'd worn them a couple times this week to break them in, and for the first time they felt like they belonged on my feet.

Checking myself in the mirror, I wondered what Emily would wear tonight. Would she dress casually like me? Or would she slip into something fancier, such as dress slacks and a button-up blouse? It didn't really matter, I decided. We didn't need to match. She might even wear her volleyball shorts and a cotton t-shirt. What would be wrong with that? That was how we became accustomed to seeing each other over the past couple of years.

I imagined Emily was probably getting ready right now too, and she was likely helping Ayden with his clothes. I wondered what being a single parent was like. Could I have done it? Do it? Would I have done as good of a job as Emily? One thing I knew about Emily Beckett was that she had a heart of gold. If anything bothered her, she felt like she had to come clean. There had been more than a few volleyball matches when after the game was over and we were headed in opposite directions, she called me to apologize for how she played that night. In my eyes, it usually wasn't what I labeled a bad game, but if she felt she had not performed her best, she wanted to let me know. It was as if she knew she couldn't sleep that night if she didn't confess to someone. I also thought that sometimes she used that as an excuse to call. We often ended up talking for fifteen or twenty minutes.

I remember one night in particular when she called. She said she had played terribly because all she could think about was Ayden who had spent the evening playing happily in the sand with a teammate's child. We played the late game that night, and she worried about her son not getting in bed at his regular bedtime. She feared he would be sleepy at school the next day and wouldn't perform at the level needed. He had started second grade in September, and all she wanted, I remember her saying, was for him to do well in school. She wanted him to have more opportunities than she did growing up. Emily already started saving for his college education probably because no one ever did that for her.

Nonetheless after getting pregnant, married, and divorced since graduating high school, she paid her own way through college. Along with playing volleyball, working full-time, and raising a son, Emily earned a degree that helped score her a promotion at the bank. I felt bad for her and envied her at the same time.

As I was thinking about Emily and putting on my clothes just outside the closet door, my cell phone rang. I pulled my jeans up to my waist and hobbled toward the blinking screen hoping to find Emily's voice on the other end.

When I reached for the phone, I recognized the name.

"Hey, Ben. What's up?" I answered, a little disappointed.

"Can you pick up some basil on your way over?"

In the background, I heard Colleen call out the aisle number for the spices section at Food Lion, the only grocery store on the island.

"Sure," I answered. "I think I know where it is," I added.

A good thing about being single was that you were forced to learn how to cook; otherwise, you gained weight eating pizza and fast food every night of the week. I did that in college—back when my metabolism could handle it—but now with more responsibilities and less gym time, I created meals that would treat my body well, not just my taste buds. There weren't many spices on aisle four that I didn't know by name, and most I could pick out by the aroma spiraling throughout the house as soon as the top was twisted open.

"So what are we doing with Ayden?" Ben asked. "I hear we are supposed to babysit him tonight."

"He wants us to take him to the park."

I sensed a bit of hesitation on the other end of the line. "Are you sure about that?" Ben questioned.

"Yeah, unless he's changed his mind since Thursday night when he begged me to spin him in circles on the merry-go-round."

"No, not about him *wanting* to go to the park. About us *taking* him to the park?"

"What do you mean?"

"Couldn't you talk him into sticking with bowling?"

"I didn't see the need to try," I said, shrugging my shoulders as if he could see me.

"I guess we'll figure it out when everyone gets here," were Ben's last words before we said bye.

Battling the increasing wind, I made it in and out of the grocery store in less than ten minutes. By six o'clock, I was pulling into my brother's driveway. Emily's car was parked on the street. When I walked through the front door, I couldn't help but hope Heaven would smell like the aroma working its way into my nostrils. Ayden flung himself onto my leg and hung there as I halfheartedly tried to wiggle him off and keep from dropping the bag in my hand. He laughed louder every time I swung my leg playfully.

"Are you excited about going to the park?" I asked.

Ben barked at me from the other side of the room with his eyes. *Oops*, I thought.

Ayden fell to the floor and quickly found his feet. "Yes, whet's go now!" His *L's* always sounded like *W's*.

From the kitchen, Emily's motherly voice floated into the living room. "Ayden, you are not going to the park. You wanted to bring your scooter instead. Remember? That is why Mrs. Colleen and I started cooking early. We'll eat, and then Ben and Luke will take you outside to ride your scooter in the neighborhood."

I had no idea what Emily and Colleen were cooking, but I knew I wanted some of it because it had to taste way better than American food at a Mexican restaurant.

"But, Mom . . .," Ayden started.

She cut him off like a pro and told him that if he kept whining he wouldn't get to play at all. I thought about taking his side because, for a moment, I kind of felt like I was being punished too, but I didn't need to because he seemed to have it covered.

"I don't want to ride my scooter anymore. I'm going to the park with Luke."

Ben shot me another look, and I laughed through a grin. I had been looking forward to spending time with Ayden, whether at the park, in the bowling alley, or whizzing around on the Spiderman scooter I nearly tripped over on the front steps.

"Ayden," Emily said, raising her voice in an effort to prove her sincerity.

Immediately he began to whine.

"That's enough, Ayden," she added.

"Park," he exclaimed. "Park . . ."

I only caught a glimpse of Emily so far when she scurried through an opening as I walked into the house. I could tell she and Colleen were busy in the kitchen, so I decided to see if I could influence Ayden who appeared intent on getting his way.

I picked him up and twirled him around, and in moments he seemed to forget about the disagreement with his mother. I knew it wasn't the best way to solve the problem, but I didn't want Emily to have to battle with him in front of all of us.

We ended up on the floor playing with toy cars, and when I realized that his attention was focused on the sound of the siren he was making, I stuck my head around the corner.

"Hey, Emily."

When she turned, I couldn't help but stare for a moment. Her outfit was much different from volleyball shorts and a cotton tee which always served her well. This evening she was another wave of beautiful. My eyes gently worked their way down her outfit, and the way she looked at me in return made me feel that it was okay to notice how magnificent she looked. A simple, button down white blouse covered by a red and white checkered apron added a certain appeal to her overall appearance. A pair of brown linen pants that she wore so well fell perfectly on her long legs.

She smiled as if thanking me for the unspoken compliment. "Hello, Luke," she greeted.

I saw steam rising from a large pot on the stovetop behind her. A smaller pot covered one of the other eyes, and I assumed it was for macaroni and cheese—something Ayden loved. I couldn't help but take another whiff of what I smelled the instant the front door opened.

"If whatever you are cooking tastes as good as it smells, then we are in for a real treat."

I caught Emily's eyes moving up and down my body quickly before she said, "Actually, this is vegetable soup, but I doubt you'll like it."

She knew me well enough to know that I was a picky eater.

"I might like it," I contested, "especially if you put this in it," I added, reaching into the bag with the basil.

She laughed. "Too bad that doesn't go in the soup. It's for the chicken."

My eyes must have lit up.

"You were afraid you were going to have to eat this soup, weren't you?" she queried, her hands resting on the hip of her apron.

"Hey, I like vegetables," I replied.

"But not vegetable soup, huh?"

"I don't know. I've never tried *your* vegetable soup."

"What vegetables do you like?"

As soon as I mentioned liking vegetables, I knew I would have been better off keeping my mouth shut. "I like corn."

She waited a moment for the list to continue. "Is there another vegetable you would like to add to that list, or is corn as far as it goes?"

I smiled. "It's just corn," I admitted.

"Is corn even a vegetable?" Ben questioned from the other room.

"It's debatable," Colleen announced.

"Either way you need to expand your horizons," Emily encouraged.

Ben entered the kitchen to share his humor. "He doesn't just like corn, Emily. He likes canned corn, frozen corn, corn on the cob, cream-style corn . . . my brother is a real healthy eater."

I threw the bag in my hand at Ben. "Mind your own business," I declared.

"Any conversation in my house is my business," he countered.

My eyes darted from Ben back to Emily. "Next time we want to have a conversation, we'll have to go outside," I suggested.

"I'd rather watch the two of you bicker about vegetables than get blown away," she laughed.

I smiled. "It appeared rain clouds were moving in too," I informed Emily.

"Oh, Ayden might be unable to ride his scooter or go to the park."

Where Emily couldn't see him, Ben smirked in my direction and immediately suggested another idea to keep Ayden entertained which I suddenly realized had been his intention all along.

In Ben's video game room, we let Ayden turn on the console and pick out the first game which lasted a total of three minutes. Then the little fellow proceeded to choose a second, third, fourth, fifth, and sixth game. I guess we would have let him select a seventh, but six was all Ben had in the cabinet that were appropriate for kids his age. Most of the games were a little too difficult for Ayden, and he kept asking Ben or myself to help him push the buttons on his controller. Anytime his player got knocked out of the game, he wanted to quit. It didn't matter if Ben or I were still playing. At first we gave in, but after it happened repeatedly, we made him wait until we all finished a level or match or some other defined stopping point.

Eventually, Colleen peeked her head into the room. "Are y'all ready for dinner?"

As Ayden and I continued trying to knock one another off a pedestal on the screen, Ben answered for us. Shortly afterward we all sat around the kitchen table with loaded plates and smiling faces. While Colleen came to get us, Emily dished out food for everyone, and I had to admit it was kind of nice to have my plate prepared for me. When I was growing up, Mom always made Dad a plate because he'd usually just arrived home after a long day of physical labor, but Ben and I dished out our own food. These days at my own house I rarely even use real plates. Keeping a stock of paper plates prevented me from washing dishes any more frequently than necessary.

Everyone was eager to dig in, so I didn't wait to find out who would bless our food. The way it smelled, I figured it had already been blessed, but I offered to do so again just to make sure. When I finished, everyone rattled, "Amen." For the next few minutes, all I heard was the sound of forks scraping against plates and raindrops pounding the shingles while the wind blew hard against the house's exterior.

It didn't take long for Ayden to speak up, though. "Mommy, I don't like vegetables," he announced, pronouncing it "begi-tubbles."

"You have to eat some," she insisted.

"Ayden, I don't usually like vegetables either, but these are yummy." I took a small bite of the soup, which tasted relatively good for a mixture of vegetables I hadn't tasted since I was ten. When I mentioned that I learned to eat healthily, I should have also mentioned my downfall.

Ayden glared at me with his fork sticking in the corner of his mouth and shook his head from side to side.

Ben finished his meal first, and Colleen and Emily ate the last bites off their plates just after he set down his fork and wiped his mouth with a napkin. Emily scooted out of her chair and began to take up everyone else's plate except mine and Ayden's.

"So you're not just a picky eater," Emily stated, "you're also a slow eater."

I grinned as I pulled my fork from my mouth. I chewed for a moment and then swallowed as Emily stood there waiting for a smart aleck comment that she knew must be coming.

I didn't want to disappoint. "I like to enjoy my food instead of scarfing it down like you three little piggies."

"What are you insinuating?" she asked.

I pointed at each of the three empty chairs at the table individually.

I knew her well enough to know I could make such a comment without worrying that she might get offended. It was a joke, and she knew it, but she pretended to be upset and turned her attention to her son.

"Ayden, you didn't eat your veggies."

He snapped back. "I did."

"What, two green beans and a spoon full of corn?"

"I ate most of them."

He might have eaten a tenth of what was in his bowl, but when he begged her to let him play games with Ben again, she let him after making him eat two more spoonfuls resulting in a disgusted look on his face.

When Ayden disappeared into the other room, Emily rinsed his plate at the sink. Out of the corner of my eye, I watched her off and on as I finished my piece of chicken and the small cup of vegetable soup I poured just to prove her wrong. The decision was also an attempt to be a positive influence on Ayden.

"Let me get that," she offered as I pushed my chair away from the table and stood.

I wasn't used to anyone picking up after me, and I wasn't sure if I liked her taking my plate out of my hand and rinsing it off for me. It made me feel a bit helpless. I watched my mom pick up after my dad and brother for as long as I could remember. They left their plates wherever they took the last bite—the living room coffee table, the bedroom nightstand, the front porch, or elsewhere. It was as though they didn't have two arms to pick up their own plates and two legs to walk it to the kitchen sink.

I didn't reference it though, and I let Emily know again how much I appreciated all she did for us this evening.

"Thanks for dinner," I acknowledged, knowing it was the best meal I had eaten in quite some time.

After enjoying the results of Emily's time invested in the kitchen, it was evident she had been blessed with the gift we southerners call *good ole fashioned country style cooking*. There seemed to be fewer and fewer people worthy of this title in any part of the country, or at least that was what my mom often said, and I agree with her since I had yet to find one. A good cook was not necessary when it came to the attributes I was looking for in a wife, but I sure did like Emily's cooking.

"Mom," Ayden shouted, running out of the game room toward the front door. "We're going to get more controllers so everyone can play."

Emily furrowed her brow, and when Colleen followed him into the kitchen, she added to his comment. "If it's okay with you?" she asked. "We are going to run into town to buy two more controllers. Ayden wants all of us to be able to play."

"You guys shouldn't buy new controllers just to appease him."

"But, Mom—"

"It's alright," Colleen assured Emily. "Believe me, they're for Ben; he has been talking about getting extra controllers for a while now. This is just a good excuse to go get them."

"If you are sure," Emily agreed. When Ben walked into the living room with a cheesy smile covering his face while shaking his head up and down, we all knew Colleen's comment was valid. "Ayden, let me finish up here real quick, and we can all go," Emily confirmed as she wiped a plate dry.

It suddenly became apparent that Ayden didn't care much for that idea. His face turned red and began to take the form of one of the rain clouds outside whose bottom was about to fall out. For the moment, the precipitation seemed to have let up.

"Mom, I want it to be just them and me," he proclaimed. Apparently, he had formed a new bond with Ben and Colleen.

Emily playfully threw up her hands. "Okay. I'll stay here and finish cleaning up Mrs. Colleen's kitchen. Then when you get back, we can all play, okay?"

Ayden grinned from ear to ear.

"You are welcome to stay here but certainly don't have to do more work," Colleen insisted.

I wasn't sure whether to offer to stay or go, so I waited to see if Ayden or Emily preferred either option. However, as everyone put on their shoes and grabbed rain jackets, no one mentioned anything specifically.

In a light drizzle, Emily went to her car and moved her son's booster seat into Colleen's vehicle. I went into the game room to turn off the racing game left on pause, but I ended up sitting down to finish the race. Hopefully, Ben and Ayden wouldn't be upset with me.

When Emily came in, she sat beside me on the couch—a little closer than expected, but I didn't mind.

"I want to play," she affirmed.

I'm not sure why I furrowed my brow. I should have known that Emily, such a fierce competitor on the volleyball court, would like most any competition.

"What, you don't think I can beat you?" she questioned acknowledging my facial expression.

"I didn't say that."

"You didn't have to. It's written all over your face."

"There's something written on yours too." I squinted and inched my face toward hers, close enough to breathe in the scent of the watermelon-flavored bubblegum she was chewing.

For a moment I considered reaching six more inches and surprising her with a kiss, but I couldn't. I'd made rules for tonight. No kissing. No holding hands. No prolonged hugs. It sounds elementary, but I started something with Mindy last night. Even though I didn't know where that was going, I felt it was headed somewhere. Kissing Emily would only cause a big mess. It would force me to have to make a decision—a decision, I reminded myself, that I made over and over since Emily started playing volleyball with my team.

I wasn't ready to be a father.

"It says L-O-S-E-R," I said instead, spelling it out slowly.

It sounded corny, I'm sure, but it seemed to fit the moment perfectly.

I imagined Emily could sense that I was flirting. I think she could also tell I purposely broke up a certain chemistry that seemed to be present between us.

Emily picked up the controller, and we began to race. The room darkened quite a bit as we circled the track repeatedly. I would like nothing more than to take credit for beating Emily at our first race, but that would be a bald-faced lie. In my defense I hated to admit that she cheated. On the final stretch I was about to catch up with her car and, in my expert opinion, pass her and take home the checkered flag. However, when my Ferrari's front bumper became even with her Porsche's rear bumper, she reached across my lap and knocked my controller onto the floor.

Instead of picking it up, I tackled her onto the other half of the sofa, and somehow in the midst of us rolling onto the floor, her car still crossed the finish line. Unfortunately, my car stopped two inches from it, and every other driver in the race passed me.

I gently held her down by her arms and felt my control over my body slip away. I felt her breath as my lips moved toward hers, and I knew our hearts were beating faster than they ever had at the volleyball court. This was the moment we both anticipated, the moment we longed for even though I didn't want it to happen for many reasons. A moment that I couldn't help but wonder if we would spend the rest of our lives talking about.

9

Our ears quickly perked up at the twisting of a doorknob as the front door creaked open.

"Mom," Ayden called out.

Emily and I both jumped up and barely made it back to the upright position before Ayden ran into the room nearly finding us tangled on the floor. I was thankful we were able to collect ourselves, at least for the most part, by the time he bounced into his mother's lap and gave her a great big *I missed you* hug. From my perspective, it seemed like they'd just driven away. Ayden studied us for a moment after the embrace, and I couldn't help but wonder if he noticed that something didn't quite add up. I knew from counseling kids his age that seven-year-olds can be a lot smarter than most adults give them credit. The way he looked at me next before saying, "What are y'all doing?"—like a mother stumbling in on the same situation with teenagers—made me wonder even more.

"We're racing," I answered quickly as if I were the kid in the room.

Still breathing heavily, I playfully snatched him from his mother's lap and tackled him into the couch cushions, knowing he would love the excitement of being jolted through the air.

As if working as a well-seasoned team, Emily used the moments while I kept her son occupied to fix her hair and straighten her shirt. Colleen would definitely notice that once she walked in although Ben might not.

After unwrapping two brand new controllers, the five of us played video games for the next few hours.

We took turns using the four controllers letting Ayden keep one in his hand almost the entire time. Some games were team-oriented, and others were for individual players only. Emily and I played on a team against Ayden and Ben in an Army tank game at which they beat us pretty badly. Ayden believed he did all the work, but I think Ben stayed up past his bedtime a few too many nights practicing for such opportunities. Colleen wasn't as interested as the rest of us, who could have played all night, but even she enjoyed Mario Kart.

When it was time for Emily and Ayden to head home, I escorted them to the car and ensured they left safely. Beneath the hazy glow of the neighborhood street lamps, I thanked Emily again for cooking such a delicious meal. When I strapped Ayden into his car seat, he reminded me that I forgot to take him outside to ride his scooter now packed in the trunk on top of the jack. Emily explained that he had made that decision earlier after the rain stopped. We asked Ayden twice if he wanted to quit playing video games and ride for a little while. It would have been a nice night to ride, I thought, as the wind kissed our faces gently and the stars twinkled to a pattern that made me wonder if Heaven had an orchestra and tonight was the symphony.

The huge smile on my face as I walked up the driveway heading to my own vehicle described the night's outcome from my perspective. It was so much fun. Dinner. Racing. Rolling around on the couch with Emily. Racing some more. Eating a bowl of cookies-and-cream ice cream to top it all off.

When I cranked my vehicle, I thought back to last night. There was no kiss to compare with Mindy's; even if there was, I wouldn't have been so shallow as to make a big deal of it. When Emily and I had been wrestling, I thought one of us might make a move—most likely me—but when we heard the door creak, all the emotions pouring out of us ran and hid just as we concealed our new connection from Ayden. The night went well, very well, in fact. And I couldn't say I wouldn't like to do it again next weekend.

❦

The pastor at my church is a lanky fellow in his mid-forties; he wears glasses and doesn't have a single hair on his head. When I shook his hand on Sunday morning, I was surprised that I got out of bed in time to make it to the service. Last night I attempted to fall asleep soon after getting home, but for hours I felt like a little kid on Christmas Eve, wondering what might happen next.

I yawned a few times as the musicians played, but for some reason, I constantly yawn when I sing in church, no matter how much rest I get the night before. I'm not sure if my vocal cords haven't woken up yet or if it is something else altogether. Who knows? I think I sometimes yawn when singing in the shower as well.

Today I could blame Emily because before silencing my phone and crawling into bed last night, I called her to make sure she and Ayden made it home safely. She complained about how she hated driving at night. Each day she wore either contact lenses or glasses, depending on how she felt when she woke up. If her eyes were tired, the contact lenses dried out quickly, and she was more prone to experience a migraine, especially if she didn't use the rewetting drops frequently. She mentioned to me before that it was harder to see when driving at night. Everything became more blurry, and the lights from oncoming traffic, especially the super bright LED lights, caused her to see splotches which often triggered migraines. I found out that Ayden fell asleep before they made it to the first stop sign less than a block down the road. That didn't surprise me. He had a long night and a lot of fun playing with Ben and me although we hadn't made it to the park, the bowling alley, or even outside for him to ride his scooter.

After church, Ben and I met at my house to watch the Braves game. Later that night, Mom and Colleen joined us, and we sat at the kitchen table for our weekly Scrabble match. This particular board game had always been my mother's favorite, and we played as a family every Sunday night for as long as I can remember. None of us had yet to enter a Scrabble tournament, but we were all solid players.

Midway through the game, I heard the doorbell ring just as I used all but one of my seven tiles. Glancing around the room, my brow furrowed. Everyone was here; Dad was in the recliner watching a baseball game between the St. Louis Cardinals and New York Mets. I knew he wouldn't leave a tied ball game to find out who was at *my* front door. He wouldn't have gone to the door if we were at his house; he would have said, "Cathy," even if she were in the back of the house with her book, "someone is at the door."

"Are you expecting company?" Ben asked quizzically.

In the meantime Colleen jumped up from her chair and headed toward the front of the house. "Oh," she shared, her words trailing behind her as she walked away from the rest of us, "I bet it is Emily."

What? The expression on my face probably explained the puzzle in my mind. Colleen hadn't mentioned anything about Emily coming over, and I didn't remember it being brought up at any point last night. Not that it was a problem. If I had known, though, I probably would have worn something other than a ragged t-shirt and a pair of gym shorts I literally owned since high school.

"Her groceries are in your refrigerator," Colleen announced.

Huh? As if her showing up at my house on a Sunday evening

wasn't already confusing. Ben and I exchanged glances, seemingly asking how Emily's groceries got into my refrigerator. I shrugged my shoulders.

"Is there something you're not telling us?" he asked.

It was evident that my mom was lost. On the other hand, my dad was lost in the game, and I don't believe he even realized someone rang the doorbell. Selective hearing is what Mom always calls the condition.

When I tugged at the refrigerator door, I spotted two bags that didn't belong on the bottom shelf. Neither had been there when I pulled out ingredients to make egg and cheese sandwiches for dinner less than an hour ago.

"Emily and I went grocery shopping yesterday afternoon, and she accidentally left a couple of bags at our house last night that she meant to take home. I brought them over for her to pick up here," Collen informed us just before inviting Emily inside.

In the years I'd known Emily Beckett, she had never stepped foot in any house where I lived. When we dated in high school, we always met at a neutral location like the beach or movie theater. The only time I went to her house, or I should say her parents' house, was the first time we kissed; the memory stuck out in my mind like it was last night. The two of us stood on the front porch. A cold rain just swept through on a November evening, and a thick fog covered the open field across the street. It reminded me of a scene from a horror movie the entire time we were out there, talking and carrying on like teenagers do. I remember that I kept checking our surroundings, looking over my shoulder, waiting for something or someone to jump out of nowhere. It made it worse that Emily decided to tell me a story about the mother bear and cubs she and her mom saw in the field across the street the previous week. The story was one of those cutesy, cuddly stories about bear cubs frolicking around with their mother watching over them. However, I only pictured a giant black bear with enormous paws slapping me around like a rag doll when it came time to walk through the darkness between the porch and my car— a bright red Ford Mustang.

Emily and Ayden were on their way home from a Sunday night church gathering, I heard her tell Colleen before they made their way into sight. Emily wore a black dress dotted with white flowers, and Ayden looked like a little man dressed in a button-up shirt and khaki pants. The smell of perfume danced across the room, not strong enough to elicit a sneeze, but just the right amount. I couldn't help but glance down at my clothes, and I felt like that guy who showed up at a costume party without a costume. Out of place. Why hadn't I run to my bedroom to put on something more appropriate when I had the opportunity? It didn't matter, I decided; I didn't need to impress anyone, right?

"Long time, no see," was my opening line, and I caught Emily checking out the holes in my shirt, showcasing my tanned skin.

"I have a few pairs of jeans that would go perfectly with that shirt," Emily teased.

Everyone laughed. I always thought it was interesting how people bought brand new jeans with rips, but maybe Emily's were from high school and had worn out over the years, like my shirt. However, the ones she had at that time probably started with holes in the material. I could still recall some of the jeans the girls wore back then with opened windows to places that aroused teenage boys. Many guys spent entire class periods trying to find just the right angle to catch a glimpse of one of the girls' backsides.

I smiled mischievously. "I think you've been wearing jeans with holes since high school," I replied, batting my eyebrows.

Ben chimed in with a holey jeans comment. "It's always been a mystery to me how clothing with less fabric seems to cost more."

"How do you know?" Colleen quizzed. "I can't get you to stay in a clothing store for more than two minutes when I'm trying on outfits."

After everyone finished making fun of my holey clothes, which I happened to be wearing on a Sunday nonetheless, we paused our Scrabble match. Emily, Colleen, and Mom talked in the kitchen while Ben and I took Ayden into the living room where the TV and my dad were. We attempted to explain the concept of strikes and balls to Ayden as we watched the game, but he enjoyed listening to my dad argue the calls with the umpire more than absorbing what we had to say. It didn't take long for Ayden to ask if I had any toys. Thankfully, I came across a box of my old toys from childhood when I was cleaning the garage yesterday, and I let him play with them while the adults talked. We tried to talk, anyway. Ayden demanded our attention almost constantly, making sure we knew that he couldn't play with Tonka trucks all by himself.

Mom wandered into the living room and started taking pictures of us with her cell phone while we played on the floor.

"What are you doing?" Ben asked.

"Do you know how many years it's been since I've seen my little boys playing cars?"

Laughing at Mom's comment, Colleen and Emily nestled on the couch behind us.

"Everybody stay right there for one minute," Mom instructed as she walked to a nearby shelf and propped up her phone.

"What are you doing now?" I asked.

"I'm going to set my camera timer and then sit by your dad and take a picture of all of us."

I glanced down at my shirt and shook my head. "Emily and Ayden may not want to be in our family portrait," I teased.

"Of course we do," Emily disagreed, not helping my cause.

Mom pressed the camera timer button, and ten seconds later, a moment was captured on camera that I wasn't sure I ever wanted anyone to see. She snapped a few more photos, and then we all chatted while playing cars and watching baseball.

Ayden wasn't a happy camper when Emily stood up and announced, "Hey, buddy, it's time to go home."

"Whet's stay here," he pleaded, continuing to roll the trucks across the floor.

"Awe," everyone sighed.

"Mommy has work tomorrow, and you need to get to bed." She glanced at the old clock in my living room that had once hung on my grandparent's wall. "It's already past your bedtime."

I hated it for him.

The only way Ayden walked to the car was by the force of his mother's hand pulling him in that direction as he kicked and screamed. With a grocery bag in each hand, I followed them, trying not to analyze the situation. I had enough of that to deal with Monday through Friday.

"You can come back and play again," I promised Ayden.

He managed to calm down momentarily, and I handed him the truck he seemed to favor when scurrying around on the carpet making fire engine noises.

"What do you say, Ayden?"

Ayden said nothing. However, he sounded the siren loud enough for my neighbors to realize there was an emergency but not one requiring real first responders. Over the row of bushes separating my lawn from Dr. Nesbitt's, I spotted the man standing at the foot of his garage. I made a mental note that I would probably receive a formal complaint letter later this week claiming we violated the neighborhood noise ordinance. He always kept the homeowners association on its toes. I waved at him anyway and then watched him turn the other way, pretending not to see the gesture.

The lights at Russ's and Mary's were all turned off, and through the short trees that dotted the front side of our yards where our property connected, I could only make out the shape of their house, thanks to the street lights.

"This is a nice neighborhood," Emily noted. "Seems peaceful."

Even though the ocean was on the other side of my house beyond the backyard, we could hear its dull roar in the driveway.

"It is, for the most part. A couple of grumpy old people have retired here for no reason other than to join the community patrol, but I guess it could be much worse."

"It's better than drunks and druggies living all around you."

I figured that comment was literal, but I wasn't sure whether it applied only to where Emily grew up or also where she lived now.

"Even though I handled your home loan, I never knew exactly where you lived," Emily admitted, leaning against her car with her legs crossed at the ankles.

As far as I remembered, she never told me where she lived either. Of course I knew the direction she headed when she left the beach volleyball courts, but other than that, I had no idea where to find her if I ever needed her. If I was being honest, I was beginning to think that it would be kind of nice to know where she lived.

We talked about my neighborhood for a few more minutes; she went on and on about how relaxing it seemed. "Sitting out on your back porch and listening to these sounds every night must be nice."

"I try to take full advantage of it," I admitted. "However, spending time on a dark porch alone gets kind of lonely even though the beach is right there." As soon as I made the comment, I wished I could take it back, wondering if it sounded like I wanted her to think of me as a poor, pitiful man with no friends and no happiness in my life. My life wasn't like that; I had plenty of friends. My best friend was at my house as we spoke. I guess I said what I said because sitting on my back porch with my buddies only satisfies certain needs. Sure, it's fun to talk, joke around, and catch up with one another, but male bonding doesn't make up for the urges of the human heart—a place where only a woman can meet a man.

"Maybe you should—" I paused momentarily, realizing I needed to think the idea through in my head before making any plans.

"Should what?" Emily pushed when I didn't finish the statement.

Arms crossed, I dug my hands into my armpits. "I was going to say that . . . maybe you should come over sometime, and we could put the porch and those rocking chairs to good use." I picked up on a comment she made earlier about the rocking chairs when the three ladies were gazing out the sliding glass door at the ocean.

"I think I would like that," she replied easily.

"Can I come, too?" Ayden inquired, jumping into the conversation as though he'd been a part of it all along.

"We'll see, baby."

I knew Emily needed to get Ayden home, so I did what felt right. I took two steps toward her and wrapped my arms around her neck, squeezing tight. Her arms slid around my shoulders, but her squeeze was quick and gentle. I let her go when I felt a slight tug and noticed her foot had slid backward on the driveway. Instinctively, it seemed, she turned to Ayden. He smiled, and for a moment, I wondered why she looked at him instead of me. Had my hugging her without any warning or apparent reason bothered her? Then, about the same time she explained her hesitation, I realized precisely what had happened. It wasn't Emily's approval that I needed; it was Ayden's.

"He hasn't let a man hug me in front of him without complaining since me and his daddy split up," she confessed in a whisper, ensuring he didn't hear her. She seemed relieved, though. I watched her turn to glance at him through the open window again before finishing. "Usually he throws a temper tantrum and even hit my ex once when he hugged me."

Siren going at full blast in the back seat, Ayden continued to smile at us periodically. It seemed as though the weight of the world fell off Emily's shoulders, and I couldn't think of anything to say that would cause the night to end any better than it would right now. I shut the car door gently after Emily slid in, and then I watched them back down the driveway slowly, making it obvious Emily noticed the enormous palm tree at the foot of my driveway. A few people chose to play chicken with it, and the tree—still standing proudly—always won.

Walking back into the house, I continued to think about the plans Emily and I made. An hour ago, I hadn't even known she would show up at my house tonight, and now we would soon be spending an evening together at my place. Doing what, I had no idea. Maybe we would grill steaks. Listen to music. Talk about the past. It didn't matter what we ended up doing; the important thing, I began to realize, was that I would get to spend time with someone who was growing on me more each time I saw her.

We finished our Scrabble game a little after ten o'clock then I stood at the front door and watched my parents drive away. Ben and Colleen lingered a little longer, mainly to ask questions about Emily and me, I derived.

"Did you have a good time last night?" Colleen started. "Do you think you two will start dating?"

"Did you kiss her?" Ben probed.

I answered the questions the best I could.

"What about Mindy?" Ben asked at one point. They gave me their thoughts and opinions, and I listened with appreciation but knew I had to make the final decision. I stopped trying to please others years ago; it is a tiring activity. Ultimately, it seems everyone gets hurt, especially the one doing the pleasing.

My Scrabble skills tanked since Emily arrived; if that is a sign for the future, we might be in trouble. However, I am not impressed by superstitions based on lucky numbers, horoscopes, tarot cards, and all that jazz. Most predictions are vague thoughts anyone can run with if gullible. Making a person believe they should leave a relationship, start a new career, move to a different state, or make any important decision based on a random source is dangerous guidance. This rings especially true when nothing is known about the individual other than the basics like birth information or general data. The significant choices deserve careful thought and wise counsel. Little ones often do as well because our everyday actions build our character. Doing small things with a good conscience helps develop us for the meaningful challenges that affect the outcome of our lives and those around us. I've met people who disagree, and they have their reasons, but I am not convinced. I believe God gives us the ability and free will to forge our own paths in life. We are not robots. Some humans make wise selections based on solid understanding while others toss a coin into the air and drift in the direction the wind blows.

These thoughts occupied my mind as I knelt beside my bed after everyone left. Prayer is a power I do trust, based on truth and faith. When those two align, the potential is unlimited.

"God, what should I do?" I asked, my eyes closed and my heart open. I doubted he would flash a name in my mind in bright lights or whisper a definitive answer into my ear. Still, I hoped for gentle guidance in realizing something that would help me decide which woman could possibly be part of my future, if either. The latter, I recognized, had to be an option as well.

Through the opened windows, I still heard the waves talk to me as the occasional moth flew into the screen on the other side. The noise that a large bug bashing into a screen made on a quiet night always scared the bejeebers out of me, and I nearly jumped out of my socks the first time it happened tonight.

What were the pros and cons, I asked myself? Between Emily and Mindy, who was a better match for me? Emily and Mindy were each attractive in their own unique way. Emily's athletic frame had always been appealing. Mindy, oh my goodness, was one of those women who caused men to do a double take. Blonde hair, green eyes, nice curves. Smiling as I thought of both women's physical attributes, I knew there was so much more to these amazing human beings. Looks are an integral part of the package, but what about the inside? Mindy seemed sweet, but I didn't really know her yet. I knew Emily much better, and though she wasn't gentle in the way Mindy seemed to be, she had a kind way about her. She cared for others and would do anything for anyone, even a stranger when she could. Emily was also funny. I remembered Mindy showed wit too. The bathroom scene kept me cracking up for a long time, and even now when it popped into my mind, I couldn't help but chuckle.

Then there was Ayden. I loved the little guy. I enjoyed spending time with him and playing together, but I knew from past experiences and even this weekend that he was spoiled. He would make dating Emily challenging in a way I wouldn't have to consider if dating Mindy.

That was what it came down to, right? My mind had been set for so long; why should I alter my thought process now? Why should I date a woman, even if it was Emily, who had a child? Another moth tried to bust through the screen, and my thoughts drifted briefly. I still couldn't believe I blew a forty point lead in Scrabble. I should have seen it coming; I set my mom up for a triple word score, and she beat me by three points. "Idiot," I called myself out loud. *Focus, Luke. Focus.*

"Do Emily and Ayden deserve a second chance?" I found myself asking God, knowing His answer, but trying instead to answer how I wanted. Of course they did, but there were many extraordinary single men who would make an excellent stepdad for Ayden. "God, give me something, anything to go on," I begged.

At that moment, two things happened, and I wasn't sure which, if either, came from God.

My mind suddenly flashed back to a time when I made a huge

mistake—the secret I wanted to tell Emily after the volleyball match. What would my life be like now if I'd chosen the other option? There had only been two choices, and I made the one I felt I had to at the time. But looking back on it now that I was older and wiser, maybe I could have done something to change it. Perhaps I should have put my foot down for what I believed. Then I wouldn't have thought I had to fall on my knees repeatedly as I did throughout the years and ask God to forgive me for letting this happen. But He, I knew, hadn't been the one who *let* it happen. It was my fault, and although He forgave me the first time I asked, for some reason I had not fully let it go.

If I could stop the tears from streaming down my face, I would. I didn't want to cry. I didn't want to think about this. Not now. Not again. I tried to gather myself, knowing I could do nothing about it now.

But was there?

In the midst of what seemed to be a revelation, the second thing happened. My phone rang.

It startled me initially, but then I crawled toward the nightstand and smiled when I saw the name on the screen. She wrote her number on the backside of one of my business cards Friday night. I added her to my contacts Saturday morning, but this was the first time either of us called the other.

"Hey, Luke, it's Mindy," her sweet voice chimed.

10

*I*t was kind of late to receive a phone call on a Sunday night, but I didn't mind. I let the sound of Mindy's voice take me back to her smile, which became a permanent fixture in my mind's eye every time I thought of her since our blind date.

"Hey, it's nice to hear from you," I replied, meaning it.

For a moment there was a lull in the conversation. Not good, I thought, since we'd been on the phone for less than fifteen seconds. Usually I said something else to keep the flow moving, but I was still trying to collect my tears and my breath, and I took a moment to clear my throat.

"Is this a bad time?" she asked hesitantly.

"Not at all, I was just—" I wasn't sure why, but I didn't want to say what I was doing possibly because we had yet to have a conversation about her beliefs, although that shouldn't have kept me from telling her I was praying. "Relaxing, thinking about some things," I ended up saying. Perhaps the hesitancy had more to do about whom I was praying than with the spiritual part.

After lifting my knees off the floor, I rolled onto my bed to get more comfortable. I was still wearing the same clothes I wore during Scrabble night. The lightweight material provided plenty of breathing room. Still, I decided to pull the shirt over my head and throw it into the corner. Then I tucked myself in so I could fall asleep without having to do anything else when I got off the phone. Thankfully, I already brushed my teeth and flossed.

"You're not in bed, are you?" Mindy checked. I pushed the covers aside, rolled back off the mattress, and walked toward the window. "I know it is a little late," she added.

Beyond the pane of glass worn from salty air beating against it over the years, the moonlight glistened atop the surface of the ocean. "I don't usually go to bed before eleven unless I'm sick or I've had a long day at work," I replied, completely honest about my current whereabouts.

"I've always been a night owl, myself. My friends sometimes get irritated at me for calling them too late. I usually don't think about the time until I hear a raspy voice on the other end of the line."

I cleared my throat again. "Was my voice raspy?" I inquired wondering if it prompted her to ask.

"A little," she admitted. "But in a cute sort of way."

I somehow felt Mindy's smile through the phone. As I relished the breeze blowing in through the lower half of the window causing a few chill bumps to bubble up on my bare chest, I asked myself if I just blushed. I noticed the sea oats dancing in the dunes, and the twinkling stars were even more visible now than when I walked Emily and Ayden to their car a few hours ago. Suddenly a thought popped into my mind about the awkwardness of talking to my Friday night date after having my Saturday night date at my house tonight.

"Do you have a girlfriend?" Mindy asked out of the blue as if she just read my mind.

Oh, crap. Did she know I'd been with Emily Saturday night? When I thought it through, I realized she couldn't unless she was a stalker. Emily and I hadn't been out in public together at any point last night. We stayed at my brother's house the entire evening. Suddenly, I felt a twinge of guilt though.

"No," I answered honestly. There didn't seem to be a reason to tell her about Emily, not yet, anyway. There was no commitment from either side.

"I'm still afraid you are too good to be true. My friends would be all over a guy like you if they knew you were single. In a small town like Atlantic Beach, I figured everyone knows everybody's news and that a handsome, charming, and successful man such as yourself wouldn't stay available long."

"Well, I guess that is true in some respects, but you have to understand there's a flip side to it," I informed Mindy.

"What's that?"

"In a small town, there aren't many kind and attractive ladies like yourself available." I hoped she would appreciate the compliment, just as I allowed my head to swell an inkling more each time she flung one my way. I meant what I said. Of course there was Emily, but there really weren't many unmarried women in this town who I was dying to date.

"You sure know how to make a woman feel good about herself."

I pictured Mindy sitting on a sofa, twirling the ends of her hair with what sounded like the soft sounds of Kenny G floating across the room. I wondered how the inside of her apartment looked. Was it decorated with antiques? I doubted it, probably something modern, stylish. With a smile, I paced around my bedroom, stopping to sit on the dresser's edge once but finding myself moving again soon. I'd been fidgety since answering the phone.

"I'm sure you hear compliments all the time," I stated.

"You'd be surprised. More often I get whistles from the construction workers and frightening stares from fast food cooks."

"I know some good guys who work in construction," I acknowledged, thinking about friends from high school who chose that path. "They say there's nothing like a man in a hard hat," I teased.

"You must not have seen the shady characters making repairs to the library's exterior this week," she declared.

I laughed. "So what do the guys you typically date do for a living?"

As soon as I asked the question, I sensed that it seemed odd. I also realized that even though I spent more than four hours with Mindy Friday night, I hadn't asked what she did for work. My dad would be proud, I thought. Maybe even more surprising, she hadn't asked me. However, I assumed Larry probably told her when he talked to her about setting us up.

"I'm not sure." She paused. "What do you do?"

Was that a suggestive hint? Did she want to categorize us as *dating*?

"Larry didn't tell you?" I inquired.

"Nope. He only said that you are a friend. I actually inquired about your career, but he said I'd have to ask you. Larry's real secretive when it comes to disclosing information about other people." She paused for a moment. "I think that is because client confidentiality is so important in his line of work."

"Yeah, that makes sense," I remarked with a grin.

"He wouldn't even tell me if you make a lot of money," she said with a chuckle. I could tell she added the following comment to ensure I hadn't taken the previous one the wrong way. "I'm just kidding; that doesn't matter to me. My last boyfriend *actually* worked in construction. He earned a decent wage because he worked in roofing since turning fifteen, but he wasn't smart enough to buy health insurance. What he lacked in brains, he always thought he made up for in brawn."

At this point, I didn't really want to ask questions about her ex-boyfriend. Of course if she offered information, I would listen. On that note, I continued on the same subject, leaving out anything involving exes. "If you had to guess what I do for work, what would you go with?"

"Hmm—" Mindy hesitated, apparently thinking long and hard about what type of career seemed to fit my personality. "You seem to do well with words, I've noticed," she mentioned first. If we were playing the hot/cold game, she'd at least be lukewarm and headed in the right direction. "It's funny; we were actually wondering about this yesterday."

"We?"

"Mom and I took turns guessing what you do for work."

Interesting. "And what did y'all come up with?"

"We had a few ideas. Mom thought you might be an attorney. However, you don't seem to have the arrogance about you that many attorneys carry, at least the ones I've been around in other places. You do seem confident." Many of the lawyers in this area were just as cocky as anywhere else. Around here, it was all about who you knew. A few attorneys could just about get anyone out of anything. "My mom's next guess was a salesman, but I told her that seemed wrong too. Even though you are confident and well-spoken, you don't come across as sly, which many salesmen tend to be." Next, she added the fine print: "You'll have to forgive me if it turns out that I'm wrong."

This was fun. For only one date, Mindy picked up on my personality and character traits pretty closely. Maybe she was a therapist as well—Larry had in fact said they were just alike.

I had been a salesman once, during college, for a company that sold fine cutlery. That didn't last long; my manager wanted me to twist customers' arms to convince them to buy the most expensive knives in our selection. When I wouldn't use the sneaky sales techniques he taught, we both concluded he'd be better off hiring a different salesman.

"So what did *you* guess that I do?" I found myself wanting to know.

"I'm scared I'll be wrong," she admitted, and I could sense the hesitancy in her voice.

"Hey, what more damage can you do?" I challenged. "If I'm an attorney or salesman, you've already drug me through the mud," I teased.

"I know. I really hope you're not," Mindy pleaded.

"I'm not," I admitted, letting her off the hook easily this time.

She loosened up as the game went on, and I continued gazing out the window, where I could make out the faint lights of several large cargo ships and fishing boats in the distance.

"I have a few ideas. You seem like you would be a good teacher, but I don't know any teachers who drive Land Rovers," she concluded with a chuckle.

Good thinking, I thought. "It could have been a gift, or maybe I'm in debt up to my eyeballs." The latter wasn't the whole truth, but with the house on the beach and a luxury vehicle, I had bitten off more financial obligations than I needed to chew.

"Maybe, but I still don't think you're a teacher. My other two guesses are an accountant or a medical professional."

"Like a doctor?" I asked.

"Maybe some type, but not a traditional medical doctor."

"Like a chiropractor?"

"I hope you are a chiropractor; maybe then you can help me with this kink in my neck," she laughed.

"In that case, I wish I was too," I admitted aloud, surprising myself as I imagined working my hands around the back of her thin neck before moving to other places. I wondered if the same thoughts floated through her mind upon making the suggestion.

"My final guess is an accountant or a physical therapist."

At this point, I decided Mindy had probably stopped twirling her hair. Now I pictured her with the tip of her fingernail between her teeth, hoping she had my career pinned down. It seemed she was holding her breath for the big reveal, but I had to make her wait. "That's not a final answer," I debated. "That's *two* answers."

"Okay, okay," she paused to think. "You make it hard on a girl.

If I had to choose only one . . ." Another pause. "I would go with a physical therapist. You seem to have the patience to work with people going through a tough time."

With half of my job title correct, she was now burning hot.

"Not bad," I admitted. "Due to all the retirees who move to the Crystal Coast, there are certainly a lot of physical therapists in Carteret County," I pointed out. "I actually know one who plays his guitar and sings to his patients as part of their therapy."

"That's pretty cool," she responded. "So, that guy is your coworker, right?" she remarked confidently.

"For the sake of this game, unfortunately not."

Mindy exhaled, sending the sound of defeat across the line. At least that's what I figured the expression meant. Or maybe she was bummed that I couldn't help her with her neck, and I kind of was as well although previous girlfriends touted me as the best amateur massage therapist they'd ever met.

"You must be an accountant," she stated.

"Nope. You were much closer with the physical therapist guess," I acknowledged. "Just take off the first word, and you have my career figured out."

"Are you serious?" She sounded stunned. "You are a therapist like Larry?"

"Yep."

"Do you work together?"

"I have my own practice, but Larry was and still is my mentor," I explained. "I actually worked under him until I earned my license."

Mindy and I spent almost an hour on the phone. I went through the same process with her, attempting to figure out what she did for work. I contemplated a few occupations that might fit her personality: veterinarian, social worker, and nurse. I imagined she must be in a rewarding career with a position where she could help people. She came across as too friendly to do anything else with her life. After trying to probe her like the attorney her mother thought I could be, my final guess was a schoolteacher.

"Larry told you, didn't he," she complained.

"He didn't say a word, I promise. The only thing he revealed about you is that you are pretty. Oh and he did say you are just like him. Of course the second part frightened me to death. I had never been on a blind date, and I told him more than once that if you ended up being anywhere near as ugly as him, I'd find a new mentor."

We both laughed at the comment and many more as we got to know each other better over the phone while the moon moved across the dark sky outside my bedroom window. I found out she taught first grade at one of the local elementary schools and that she started this semester. She loved it so far, the kids more than the parents. The latter was the challenging part of teaching, she confessed.

When I finally closed the blinds and tucked myself in a little past my bedtime, I felt like I knew Mindy a lot better. I liked talking to her. She was witty and interesting at the same time.

As I drifted off for the night like the vessels I watched move across the water ever so slowly while on the phone, I'm not sure which person crossed my mind the most or who I thought of last, but Mindy and Emily both consumed my conscious thoughts.

11

As the morning sun rose above the horizon, I talked myself into rolling out of bed. I was never a huge fan of Mondays, not because the workweek lay ahead—I mostly enjoyed my job—but because the weekends always seemed to fly by so fast, especially the fun ones like I just woke up from. Others weren't quite as interesting, such as when I spent more time on the couch alone watching movies, surfing channels, and eating pretzels. Those weekends typically moved in slow motion.

One of my favorite weekend activities was playing in men's volleyball tournaments. They usually started on Saturday mornings and sometimes flowed into Sunday depending on how many teams entered a particular tournament and how well our team played. After those weekends, I spent half the following week recuperating from minor injuries and sore muscles from playing too many sets. My team traveled up and down the east coast from Virginia to Florida. One year in the state tournament in Wilmington, we played exceptionally well and ended up playing twelve matches to make it to the championship. Unfortunately, we lost to a team of former professional volleyball players, but we gave them their money's worth.

There were times when we played through heavy rain and high

winds. Nearly every summer weekend in the southeast felt as hot as blue blazes whether involved in an outdoor sport or walking your dog down the sidewalk. At least when playing volleyball at the beach, we occasionally jumped in the ocean to cool off. The early spring and late fall tournaments were often the opposite, and during those we all geared up in our long sleeves, especially when the temperature fell right along with the sun. Unfortunately, no coeds played on this team, which made keeping warm consist of smelling the sweaty armpits of another man instead of girlfriends and wives although they often came along to watch.

Being single allowed me to play more frequently, and I looked forward to playing in a tournament in Myrtle Beach a couple of weekends from now. Our team usually consisted of the same group of men. Many of us grew up playing beach volleyball together all the way through high school. We knew each other's tendencies on and off the sand, which usually helped in tournaments. Traveling often got expensive, although our team picked up a corporate sponsor a few years back after getting some notoriety in the local newspapers. They paid for our tournament fees, new volleyballs, and other gear. The players still covered hotel expenses, meals, and coolers filled with water bottles and iced-cold sports drinks.

The drive to my office on a weekday morning takes ten minutes when the traffic and stoplights cooperate. On Mondays, I flip on the lights and head straight for the thermostat. Today, I have just enough time to prepare myself and the office for the first session of the day. It takes about fifteen minutes for the air to reach a comfortable temperature, after being adjusted for the weekend to save on the utility bill, which would happen about five minutes before Jackie Jones enters the office at nine o'clock with a knitted sweater draped over her left arm and a cup of decaf coffee in her right hand.

When Jackie first started coming for counseling, I wondered if the garment had something to do with her being cold. I didn't ask, and after a handful of sessions, I realized she never put on the sweater. Instead, I observed how she treated the piece of clothing the way a young child treats a security blanket.

In the moments before Jackie arrived, I checked my email and voicemail—nothing important: one cancellation, two counseling inquiries, and one lady looking for a job. As usual, I peeked through Jackie's file to reacquaint myself with the topics we discussed last week and my running notes on her case.

Knowing exactly when the door would open, I welcomed my client with a smile and a casual greeting. I knew she would follow me through the reception area—where there had never been a receptionist to fill it—and down a short hallway to my office.

The décor in my therapy space intentionally creates a flow of positive energy. The area is free of clutter, distractions, and obstacles. Lights and lamps are dim, and a soft dose of classical music serenades the session through the surround sound. Based on my mood today, I selected Bach and Beethoven. I am always observant of the body language of the individual meeting with me, and I check in with them to ensure their comfort.

I watched Jackie nestle into the same spot she sat in every time when visiting my office. A sitting area occupied the space in front of my desk where I always chose to meet with clients. I learned when the counselor stayed behind the desk, it gave the client a feeling of inferiority, and it often took longer to connect on a personal level with that individual. Sometimes it was even the factor that kept the two from connecting.

In my years as a therapist, I've always taken every step possible to reach my clients on a subconscious level, and I discover new techniques daily. Interestingly, my clients often teach me as much as I teach them. I believe that life, in general, is a classroom, and we are all teachers and students simultaneously.

Suffering from depression most of her life, Jackie found

comfort in a single-person chair instead of sitting on the couch opposite the one where I sat or the love seat across from her chair. A rectangular, cherry oak coffee table was the centerpiece in the middle of the family style sitting area.

Jackie waited for me to slide a coaster in her direction. When I did, she immediately placed her Santa Claus coffee cup perfectly in the center. Rarely did she take a sip, and usually, she spent most of the session picking at the sweater her grandmother knitted in the early nineteen hundreds. Her eyes flickered between the tattered garment and me, and her hands shook ever so slightly when she talked.

We conversed easily and even laughed together, something Jackie didn't enjoy with many people besides her mother and me. Her father died when she was eight years old, and because of troubles with Jackie's birth, her mother couldn't bear a second child. Jackie wasn't one for making new friends.

I asked her how her weekend went, and predictably, she answered, "It was okay." I didn't need to ask to discover how she would answer; I asked simply because I cared, and I needed her to know that.

Depression is what Jackie struggled with the most, and she isn't alone, even in the small communities that make up the area I serve. The three types of clients I see most commonly are those dealing with depression, marital conflict, or addiction. Many are dealing with two of the three, and too often, my clients deal with all three simultaneously. Any of these issues can cause the second and, in due time, the third. On a positive note, if I can help a client conquer one of them, it is much easier for her to overcome the next.

A case of depression often led to other issues that invited deeper depression. In Jackie's case, depression caused her to become overweight to the point where she no longer felt concerned about her outward appearance, at least not openly.

Often her body odor lacked the freshly showered appeal. On Monday mornings after I walked her to the door at the end of the session, I sprayed disinfectant in *her* beige chair because her odorous condition nearly brought me to tears.

If any counselor, psychologist, or psychiatrist ever suggests that his client's problems don't touch him on an emotional level, find a new one. The only way I'm ever able to benefit these people, aside from the intervention of God Himself, is because I care deeply about them and value their lives and the lives of those around them. Humans, in my book, are not a commodity. They are a rarity, and every individual I can help save is a miracle.

Today I pleasantly realized that Jackie showered recently, if not this morning, at least last night. This was a good day. We talked about shame and guilt, two topics that often plunged their way into our conversations. It wasn't her fault her father died, and even though I wanted to think we conquered that mountain, I knew we had a steep climb ahead.

It often bothers me that I at least appear to have more fun on the weekends than many of my clients, but some have more fun than me. Especially temporarily. Those people sometimes spend the mornings hung over or in the county jail. Others arrive and claim they might be pregnant or have impregnated someone or believe they have an STD. Many clients have asked: "Do you think I have a disease?" Of course I can't answer this question for them. The plate on my door reads *Luke Bridges, LCMHC*; no title precedes it. The master's in Professional Counseling degree hangs on my wall in a simple frame, and I don't like to draw attention to my education unless asked about it.

If I determine a client needs medication, I refer them to a psychiatrist, where they become a patient. That's the difference between what they do and what I do; I have clients, and they have patients. There are cases when I feel medical treatment is necessary. However, way too many medical professionals overprescribe, which is one of the reasons our society has so many troubled people.

At my desk, I jotted notes from today's session with Jackie. Then I lowered my pen and turned to my file cabinet next to a large bookshelf that nearly covers the entire back wall of my office. The shelves contain hundreds of books from professionals in my area of expertise, as well as literature from related fields covering various topics.

Although some colleagues disagree, I approach many depression cases, like Jackie's, as well as addiction, as an opportunity to make choices that can bring a person out of the condition. The factors that lead a human being into depression are often not a choice, although sometimes it results from a careless decision or a string of poor choices. In fact, most everything in life is a choice. We choose to get out of bed in the morning. We choose to eat breakfast. We choose to go to work. We choose to put in an honest day's work. We choose to stay loyal to a spouse. We choose to be a parent. We choose not to pick up a drink. We choose not to isolate ourselves from others. Or— we don't. Some choices are right. Some choices are wrong. Some are neither. Some choices are easy. Some are difficult. Others are merely choices.

Often, right and wrong are left up to moral interpretation, which opens a new discussion on choices. Either way, each decision we make in life, no matter how small or large, will result in a consequence or consequences. Some good and some bad. Some lead a person into depression, and some lead them out. Even life itself has been made into a choice, although I disagree with the option to alter what God ordains.

At that moment, I chose to answer my phone when it began to ring, and on the other end, I heard a voice that made me smile.

"You're still planning on coming over to watch the game tonight, right?"

Monday Night Baseball featured the Atlanta Braves versus the Chicago Cubs. Where else would I be than on my parents' couch in a pair of comfortable sweatpants hanging out with my father and brother. Ben reached over me to dip his hand into an open bag of roasted peanuts in the shell and, in haste, turned them over into my lap and onto the floor. Klutz.

"Dude," I clamored, pretending to make a bigger deal of it than necessary.

When it came to making messes, Ben was the king. If there was a drink to be spilled, leave it to him. If there was dirt on the carpet, blame it on him. Dad didn't seem to notice; he just kept eating from the handful of peanuts he grabbed a few minutes ago. Mom, on the other hand, watched us like a hawk as if we were still kids, with her hands on her hips, waiting to see which of us would pick up the peanuts.

"Now you don't even have to reach in the bag," Ben pointed out enthusiastically. "You have peanuts readily available in your lap."

I picked up one and cracked open the shell like a pro. With my shoe, I swept the others into a neat pile on the floor and pushed them toward my brother.

"Those are for you," I announced.

There was already an array of empty shells scattered about on the hardwood floor in the area surrounding his feet, and the only reason Mom didn't have a conniption was that she knew I would throw them away later if Ben didn't.

"Thanks," Ben laughed.

"I'm still not sure how Colleen puts up with you," I questioned.

It was dark outside now and raining. A steady flow of droplets beat on the sliding glass door, and if I wasn't watching a baseball game, it would have been a perfect night to spread out on the sofa and fade into a deep sleep.

"What did you do today, Dad?" I asked during a commercial break.

There was an unwritten house rule that no one talked about anything other than the game while in progress.

"Worked in the yard most of the day."

What was new?

"I thought you did that this weekend," Ben said.

"I did, but there's always more to do."

"What are you doing tomorrow?" I asked Dad.

"If it's up to your mom, I'm going to take it easy," he mentioned, grinning in her direction.

"You need to. I know it's only May, but you can still get overheated out there," Ben reminded him.

"And you're not a spring chicken, Dad," I added.

"I know, but somebody has to do the work around here."

Ben and I basically made the same comment at the exact time, "We'll help; just let us know what you need."

Dad was one of the old-timers who wanted to do everything himself, his way, and in his time. No one else could do it better. There had been times when I came over and hopped on the riding lawn mower. However, before I made it around the front yard a few times, he stood on the porch while holding a glass of water insisting I needed a break. I hadn't even broken a sweat yet, but as soon as I stopped he commandeered the mower and didn't get off until the yard looked like the grass at the Braves' stadium. I then spent the rest of my time inside the house talking to Mom about how he needed to slow down.

Mom cooked spaghetti for dinner earlier, and I enjoyed every bite even filling a Tupperware dish for tomorrow's lunch. Continuing to wash dishes in the kitchen, she chimed in. "Your father won't tell you he was getting short of breath today," she announced.

"I'm fine," he interjected. "I just needed a glass of water."

Ben and I didn't like the sound of this, and we both waited for the other to say something to him first.

Finally, I said, "Have you been to the doctor lately?"

Dad replied, "The doctor tells me the same thing every time I see him: 'Here's another prescription, now please pay me a wheelbarrow full of money before you walk out the door.'" He paused, and I could tell he was getting agitated already. "They spend five minutes talking to you and think they know what's wrong. I'd be better off doing what my grandmother always told us to do if we didn't feel right."

"What's that?" Ben inquired.

"Sleep. Eat. Breathe. Drink plenty of water. And let God take care of the rest."

"Those might have been the best options in the early 1900s, Dad, but we've graduated from home remedies. You can't expect God to take care of you if you aren't going to take care of yourself."

Dad knew I supported home remedies and natural medicines in cases where proof existed but not in his specific case.

"Home remedies still work," he demanded as the commercial break ended, and we all knew it would be best to grow quiet when the announcers began to talk.

As the Cubs piled one hit after another, I didn't even care when they scored two runs and took the lead. My concern was more about my dad's health and his reluctance to have his condition checked out. It was like pulling teeth just to get him to have an annual physical. Mom told us he never went to the doctor until Ben and I got older and started giving him a hard time about needing to be around for his family, especially his future grandchildren. Those would have to come from Ben and Colleen if they came in the near future, I thought, as one of the Braves' outfielders caught the final out of the inning.

When the commercial break began, we started on Dad again. "Why don't you get it checked out, Dad," Ben suggested. "It won't take thirty minutes."

"I'm busy," he muttered.

Mom spoke up again, this time stopping and glaring at him with a bit of passion in her green eyes. "You are not. The only thing you have to do tomorrow is grocery shop with me," she reminded him while holding a dirty fork in her hand and pointing it at him. "We can run to Dr. Nesbitt's office before or after."

Dr. Nesbitt? "Since when is *he* your doctor? What happened to Dr. Thigpen?"

I looked at Mom because I knew she would be the one with that information. "Dr. Thigpen and his wife moved to Arizona. Their son lives there and apparently has a lot of land and is giving some to his parents, so he decided to retire."

"What do you know about Dr. Nesbitt?" Dad growled.

"He's just as stubborn as you are," I replied, shaking my head.

Ben chuckled. "Is that your neighbor?"

"Yes," I exclaimed. "The man drives me crazy."

Dad laughed for the first time since this discussion started. "Well, the three of y'all are driving me crazy, so we're even."

The game went on, and the subject came up during one more commercial break. Then Dad put a stop to it. We all knew well enough to let it go at that point. Once he put up a wall, we might as well walk out the front door and try talking to him through the actual brick wall. Plus, we didn't want to see his face turn any redder than it already had. He was mad, and I knew Mom would catch the brunt of it once Ben and I left. Of course, he wouldn't say or do anything out of line, but he probably wouldn't talk to her much until tomorrow.

The next few days went well. I talked to Mindy on my way home from Mom's and Dad's house Monday night. Later, after I settled in at home, I called Emily. We chatted until she got sleepy. During our conversation, we decided I would grill steaks for the two of us

Friday night. Ayden spent every other weekend at his dad's, and as much as Emily hated having to deal with him going over there, she revealed her excitement about spending time with just me this weekend.

"It will be nice to have someone my own age to talk to," she mentioned. She explained Ayden mainly liked going to his dad's house because his father let him drink unlimited Mountain Dew, watch inappropriate movies, and go to bed at midnight. "How can I compete with that?" she asked rhetorically when we talked on Tuesday.

On Tuesday evening, I found out that Dad boycotted Mom for almost the entire day, but she said he finally came back around. That night, I fell asleep talking to Mindy, who shared funny stories about her students each time we spoke. The best one today was discovering that a kid she often caught picking his nose kept a collection in a plastic pencil container in the back corner of his desk. Gross. The next day she told me about a little girl named Kate who liked to chase the booger collector around the playground. When she finally ran him down, usually in the corner, she kissed him until he cried.

Those images in my mind made me ponder the responsibility of having kids. On Wednesday night, when Emily said she had to get off the phone because Ayden wet his bed again, I realized how simple life was for someone like me, who wasn't a parent or a teacher.

This week the worst thing that happened to me was when a client's husband cussed at me on the phone. The Braves lost two games in a row, which was also a downer, but it didn't change my life.

Russ and Mary came in for a session on Thursday morning, and it pleased me to find out they'd been intimate twice in the past week. This was twice as much as any other week since they started counseling. All of the news wasn't positive, however. Colton acted strange ever since overhearing an argument about how his behavior at school had become "Too much to deal with," as one of them put it. Unfortunately, parents often don't understand how their problems affect their children. We talked about how the turmoil of their marriage contributed to Colton acting out at school. The boy wanted and needed attention, and his parents were so busy fighting that they had not been parenting him the way they should. Throughout the week, I watched them come and go from the house. I paid particular attention to mannerisms—the speed at which they walked, if they held their heads high or low, and other signals that hinted at what was happening inside a home. I noticed if they held hands as they walked out in the mornings and if they kissed goodbye. Even though they both drove for FedEx, their route completion times conflicted by about an hour, so they chose to drive separate vehicles. I observed Colton too and could tell he was happy to be leaving the house some days while on others not so much.

Children are much like adults. One day their disposition is sunny, but the next it might be the opposite. Typically there is a reason behind each.

Tonight at the coed volleyball match, I knew it was going to be time for me to tell Emily exactly what was on my heart and mind. I talked to her and Mindy a handful of times this week, and even though I enjoyed the conversations with each of them, it wasn't right. I knew that. Becoming emotionally attached to two different women simultaneously couldn't drift into anything good, which meant it was time for me to make a decision. I needed to quit running from my own fears.

12

Three strikes are all you get in baseball. Once you watch the third strike, or if you swing and miss, you're out. You walk back to the bench, and you let the next batter take a turn. That's where I felt like Emily was in her life. Her ex-husband had been strike one, and Brad strike two. Now she was ready for another pitch, but this time she wouldn't swing and miss or let a good pitch get by. I sensed that she was looking to hit a homerun. She was ready to find the man who would spend the rest of his life making her and Ayden happy. A man who could complete her family, which started before him, yet would be incomplete without him.

Was I that man?

That is the question I pondered for some time now, but even more so when Emily said what she said about Brad not being the man she and Ayden needed in their lives. I always convinced myself that I didn't want to be a stepdad, but after spending time with Emily lately, I began to wonder if I needed to adjust my thinking.

I couldn't wait until after the volleyball match tonight to talk to Emily. So I picked up the phone, dialed her work number, and asked if she could meet for lunch. I was pleased when she agreed to join me at noon at the picnic area behind the Crystal Coast Visitor's Center. The view of the Bogue Sound engulfed the horizon as I drove around the u-shaped drive that outlined a grassy lawn dotted with outdoor tables beneath a canopy of live oak trees.

Even though my nerves wore on me, a smile grew on my face when I spotted Emily's car parked on the far side of the lot. I hadn't quite figured out how to break the news to her, but I thought she sure looked great in dress slacks as we walked toward one another. I couldn't help but notice the gleam in her eyes when I told her where the bag in my hand was from.

"I love Venice Italian Kitchen," she exclaimed.

Great start.

On the phone, I asked what her favorite Italian dish was, and she told me it was a tossup between lasagna and chicken parmesan. Inside the bag, I carried both. Thankfully, I picked out a red polo shirt this morning, so if I spilled sauce on myself it would blend in and probably wouldn't show up very noticeably on my dark khaki pants either.

We wandered over to an empty picnic table beneath a tree that appeared as old as the town itself.

"We have options," I explained when we settled in across from one another.

"Oh yeah," she replied, tilting her head slightly and smirking.

"I like both of your favorite Italian dishes," I shared, "so I figured we can split them, or you can pick the one that sounds the best to you right now, and I'll eat the other."

"Splitting them sounds fun," she responded with childlike jubilee.

When I ventured over the Atlantic Beach Bridge to the restaurant, somewhat of a hole-in-the-wall type of establishment, I made sure to grab knives, forks, and plenty of napkins. It was one of those places where I preferred takeout because the seating area was small, but the food was authentic.

"Do you mind if I say grace over our meal?" I asked after

securing the napkins so the wind wouldn't blow them like leaves.

Emily blushed. "I would love that."

While we ate, small talk crowded the conversation. My plan coming into this outing was to eat fast so that I would finish in plenty of time to say what I had to say without worrying that Emily would be rushed to get back to work. Like Jackie Jones, my hands trembled when I ate the last bite of lasagna, and with a full stomach I prepared to pour out my heart to Emily Beckett.

"What are your thoughts on us?" I asked right off the bat.

Emily's facial reaction told me she hadn't expected such a question, and her body language showed a bit of tension. She instantly went from resting her elbows on the picnic table to sitting up straight with her arms folded.

"Us?" she asked, obviously buying time.

I immediately began to second guess asking the question.

"Yes, us. Do you see us as *just friends* or . . ." I paused and rephrased, wanting her to know where I stood so she wouldn't be the only one on the spot. "This past week has been great. I had so much fun with you and with Ayden. But before we get too close, I need to know if you want something more than what we've been?"

The question was blunt but exactly how I intended, and releasing it made me feel good inside. I felt my shoulders relax when the words evaporated from my mouth. It reminded me of slipping into a steaming hot tub after swimming laps in a chilly pool. I waited impatiently for Emily to respond, knowing what I wanted to hear.

"Luke," she started, tucking a stray hair behind her ear before crossing her arms again. "Don't take this the wrong way." That didn't sound good, I thought. "But as much as I would like for me and you to be together, for us to be an *us*, something, in particular, has always kept me from pursuing a relationship with you. Other than that, we seem to be in relationships at opposite times."

In the past, when Emily was single, I was dating someone, and vice versa. Of course there were times when we had both been in a relationship, but this, as far as I could remember, was the first time we'd actually been single at the same time since high school.

Wondering where this was headed, my brow furrowed. I took a sip of tea, hoping to cover my emotions. I wanted to ask why, but I thought she might tell me exactly why if I waited a few more seconds.

And she did. "There is something I overheard you tell Ben a while back at one of our matches." There was a lull in the conversation for a moment, and I instantly began to rummage through every conversation I could remember having with my brother at The Circle. "You'd been playing with Ayden, and Ben asked if you thought you could be a stepdad."

My face must have turned fire engine red; I instantly remembered exactly what I said and how I said it. I had no idea anyone, especially Emily, had overheard the conversation. Where had she been? How had I missed her? All this time, I had these thoughts about being a stepdad, even expressed them to people close to me like Ben, but I never thought Emily, or anyone with a child overheard me speak them out loud. I wanted to kick myself. Literally. I imagined standing up, reaching my leg as high as possible and kicking myself right between the eyes. I probably couldn't physically achieve that, but I felt like I needed to.

That day, Ben and I stood near the boardwalk, and I plucked Ayden off the knee wall at his request. When his feet hit the sand, he ran toward the volleyball net, and I kept my eye on him because Emily asked me to while she went to the restroom. That's when Ben asked the question.

"You said you had enough problems of your own and didn't need to inherit a child," Emily reminded me.

Those were pretty much my exact words, and the gesture on her face looked exactly as it should—disappointed. She must have walked up behind us as we stared out toward the ocean. The constant roar of the sea lends itself to people sneaking up on you, and the wind is its partner.

What could I say? Should I even try to explain? Would it make a difference? I'd dug a hole as deep as the Atlantic Ocean, and I didn't know if I could find my way out.

I decided I needed to give it a shot, a genuine one. "Emily, I've always cared for you and wondered what life would be like if we were together. And you're right; I've never *wanted* to be a stepdad. The thought of being a dad seems stringent enough, let alone adding an extra step to that enormous responsibility. However, I've been doing a lot of thinking lately. Praying, too. The truth is I once had a chance at being a dad." My mind shot back to six years ago when I had more muscle and less sense. I dated a girl at college for about a year. We were young and carefree, and one night after arguing for about a week straight, we got careless and let the emotions of making up take control of our bodies. One thing led to another, and by the time we realized what we let happen, it was too late. Creating a baby doesn't take much, especially when you leave the condom in the car and are so focused on ripping off your girlfriend's clothes that you neglect to take sixty seconds to run out the door and grab it. Right there on her bed in her parents' house during a holiday break on a night I'll never forget, I got her pregnant. Well, for the most part I'll never forget it. Whether the sex was good or if it mended all the broken pieces the harsh comments and phone call hang-ups brought on, I don't recall. Those things were pointless now, I remembered once again, as tears began to form behind my eyelids. Fighting hard, I held them in as I spoke. "But I screwed it up. I made a big mistake and hate myself for it," I admitted. This was the secret I'd never told another human being. Not Ben. Not my father. Not Mom. No one. One tear fell. Then another. My face dropped so that Emily couldn't look me in the eyes, and I continued talking through the hands that covered them. "I agreed to an abortion even though I didn't want to." I paused. I hadn't come here intending to tell Emily any of this, but now more than ever it seemed relevant. "*My son would be about Ayden's age.*"

I needed a moment to collect myself, and Emily was gentle enough to give me all the time in the world. She stood up, walked around the table, reached her arm across my shoulder, and rubbed my back like my mother used to when I was upset about making a bad grade at school or getting laughed at by a kid I looked up to. This moment was therapeutic. I always knew I needed to talk to someone about the abortion but never had, not even Larry. Every time I counseled teenagers, young adults, and even mature adults contemplating an abortion or riding the roller coaster of emotions with their decision one way or another, I knew I needed exactly what they did. I needed someone to listen, accept that I made a mistake, and remind me that it didn't make me a bad person. It didn't mean I was bound for hell or that God would punish me for the rest of my life.

"I was young and stupid," I admitted, "but that isn't an excuse. Neither is why I gave in to her request six years ago. She told me I had no choice in the matter. That if her parents found out she was pregnant, they would make her have the abortion anyway and that I wouldn't get any say in the matter. So, we made it all go away. We took the easy road." I paused to collect myself and my thoughts. "Or at least what we thought was the easy road. But now, there isn't a day that goes by that I don't think about that choice. I hate myself for it. But I can't take it back, Emily. Just like I can't take back what I said about not wanting to be a stepdad. Just like you can't take back marrying your ex and splitting up with him. And I know you wouldn't want to take back Ayden for anything in this world. I respect that. In fact, I admire that about you. God gave me a second chance, but I don't have an Ayden. My Ayden is in Heaven. God gave you a second chance. So, I'm trying to say I've been praying about all of this, and if God gave me and you second chances, why can't I give you a second chance? Why can't I step up to the plate and potentially be willing to be a father to a son I could have had but didn't. I could just as easily be in your shoes. I could be a single father praying for a good woman to marry and be a stepmother to *my* child. I'm not naïve; I know that if my girlfriend and I had that child, we probably wouldn't have stayed together. We might have tried, like you and your ex, but I don't think it would have worked. Eventually she would have left, and if I knew her as well as I think, she would have left our little one in the same place she left me."

By now I picked my head up and stared into Emily's eyes with a passion I hadn't felt in years. As a swarm of seagulls gathered, begging us to toss scraps their way, I wanted her to see the honesty in my words and know without a doubt they came straight from my heart. "Now, I have another choice to make," I declared. "Actually, I've already made it. My choice is you—and Ayden." Suddenly, I felt relieved, like a football player taking off his shoulder pads after an intense game. "And don't feel like I'm trying to rush things, Emily, because I'm not. I simply want you to know that if you want to have a relationship with me and be more than just friends like I want to be more than just friends, I know what I'm getting myself into."

I stopped there knowing there was nothing else to say; I said it all. I poured out my heart and soul and left everything on the table. If Emily thought us being just friends was best, then so be it. If she wanted more, then so be it. Either way, I could accept it now.

Emily loosened up as I revealed my secret and now sat closer than ever to me. "I appreciate you sharing your past with me. I know that was difficult, but before I answer your question, there is something else I need to know."

I figured she might want to know what girl I impregnated,

thinking chances were she knew her or at least could place her by name or facial recognition. The area we grew up in was relatively small. "Sure, anything," I replied, ready and willing to be completely transparent during these moments of total honesty. Then I remembered I explained that my girlfriend was from college. Instead of wanting me to share a name, Emily brought up one that immediately sent chills down my spine.

"Who is Mindy Lane?"

13

ho is Mindy Lane?
    This was not the question I anticipated, and I didn't have an answer that I thought Emily would want to hear. I watched closely as a look of disappointment settled on her face. *A friend*, I considered saying. Then I imagined Emily's response: *A friend like I am a friend?* Then she might ask: *Is she your backup plan? Or am I your backup plan?* I hadn't looked at it that way until now, but I would be lying if I said I hadn't thought about what I would do if Emily told me today that she only wanted to be friends and nothing more. I'd be devastated in so many ways. Still, if that were the case, I probably would decide to get to know Mindy better, and for some reason I felt guilty for thinking that.

This whole situation with Emily and Mindy was one I never wanted to get into in the first place, and I'd been kicking myself for letting it drag out this far. I was used to being on the other side of decisions like this one. Unfortunately, it seemed that the woman of my interest would choose the other guy for whatever reason.

The pigeons and seagulls became more courageous and impatient, and I imagined Emily was also becoming impatient. She asked a question, and she deserved an honest answer.

In a valid attempt to give her just that, I recalled my conversation with Mindy late last night. On my knees praying in my bedroom I suddenly knew I needed to talk to Mindy. I called her, and when she discovered the urgency in my voice as soon as I said, "There is something I need to talk to you about," she asked me to come over so we could talk face to face. I felt like I owed her that much, so I got into my car at eleven o'clock, drove through the blinking stoplights above the downtown streets, and ended up in her apartment sipping on a cup of cocoa.

"Is everything okay?" Mindy asked first, obviously concerned about my disposition.

"I think so," I answered simply. Then I went on. "Do you remember the night we met?"

"Yes," she answered, almost hesitantly, and I could tell she wondered where the conversation was headed.

"It was a little awkward, wasn't it?" I acknowledged, forcing a laugh.

"It was," she agreed, "but so is this," she announced.

"After the initial shock of meeting my first blind date," I paused, "and her parents, and after one of the most interesting dinners I've ever been a part of, I ended up having a really nice time with you. Not only are you attractive, but over the course of that evening, I found out that you are sweet, funny, and full of energy. I knew instantly that I could see myself dating you and wanting to spend time getting to know you."

Mindy's shoulders seemed to relax just a bit as she sat on the couch across from the rocking chair I settled into soon after she opened the door. I watched her take only the second sip of her cocoa.

"I had a nice time too," she responded as she touched her lips with the mug.

I didn't let her say anything more. "Mindy, I have to be honest with you, okay?"

"Okay?" Tense again.

"I could see myself with you, and I don't just mean the two of us going out on a date every other weekend to fill the emptiness in each other's lives. I mean, sitting in the living room on nights like tonight, just talking for hours over hot chocolate and a crisp fire."

She glanced around the room and smiled. "Sorry that I don't have a fireplace," she shrugged.

I smirked.

"We could build a bonfire, though," she suggested, and the funny thing was that I knew she was as serious as a heart attack. Her spontaneity was another trait that made Mindy such a likable person.

"I could see us doing that too," I admitted.

Mindy's apartment building was in the historical part of town and had been around for quite some time. If my memory serves me correctly, my dad once told me he lived here as a little boy, well before the units received a makeover. Actually, he lived all over downtown Morehead City. His impoverished family bounced around from place to place, depending on where his grandmother could find the cheapest rent.

Since Mindy welcomed me in, I heard footsteps coming from the apartment directly above hers, and I couldn't help but wonder how insulated the walls were between each unit. My dad said he remembered feeling really cold indoors in the winter, almost as cold inside as being outside. Thankfully, the Crystal Coast doesn't know cold like Maine, New York, or any other northern states know cold. Between December and February we experience a little of what they go through for twice as long, but we rarely see snow. Flurries occasionally fall, but barely any white stuff blankets the ground. Our average annual snowfall is around one inch, and I can't remember the last big snow we saw. If we get between four to eight inches, we think blizzard conditions. I remember having weather events like that and being out of school for over a week.

My buddies and I built streets in the snow and rode our go-karts through it for fun. The school buses weren't equipped for such conditions; they didn't have chains or snow tires, and the city had no need to invest in a snowplow. We kids sure did think we were ready for it until one of us plowed down the neighbor's white picket fence after figuring out go-kart brakes don't work the same on snow and ice as on dirt and grass.

When a loud thump shook the light fixture above us, Mindy and I both cringed. Our eyes darted to the ceiling, waiting to see if it might cave in at any moment, wondering who or what might come crashing through. When it didn't, Mindy began to fill me in on her neighbors.

"That is a good noise compared to what I'm used to," she offered.

"Oh, really, that would freak me out, especially if I were here alone late at night."

Our conversation veered off track, but I decided that would be okay for now. It would give me more time to build up the nerve to say what I came to say.

"Usually, the newlyweds up there are moaning and groaning, and their headboard is pounding against the wall."

"Oh, that's not good," I replied, raising my eyebrows. "Not for you, anyway," I laughed.

Blushing a little, Mindy shook her head and took another sip. "I absolutely hate it. When it happens, I go to the kitchen, get my broom and start beating back on the ceiling."

I continued to laugh, almost hysterically now, as I pictured her with a broomstick in her hand, stabbing away at the ceiling. "Do they stop?"

"Not usually." Another sip. "Well, eventually they do, but not until they're done, if you know what I mean."

"That sounds annoying."

"It is. Then I see them in the parking lot the next day, and they act like nothing ever happened. They say hey, smile, and go on their merry little way."

I knew I shouldn't say what I was about to say; it was so far from what I came to say, but the moment caught me, and I said it anyway. "Want to pay them back a little?"

Mindy's brow furrowed, and suddenly I knew I should have been more specific, knowing her mind was probably floating where my mind would have if she said the same thing. "How?" she asked quizzically.

"Mess with them," I explained.

Her eyes lit up. "What are you thinking?" she asked, setting down her cup before scooting to the edge of the couch to wait for the plan.

"Let's go to your room, jump up and down on the bed, and make a bunch of sensual noises."

Mindy laughed so loud I thought a snort might come out. "That'll be awesome," she responded as jubilant as a child in a candy store. She immediately hopped up from the couch, grabbed my hand, and hurriedly led me down a short hallway to her bedroom. Her finger switched on the light as we plunged through the doorway, and then she leaped onto the bed. I followed and felt like a kid again as my feet triggered the mattress springs while we pounced around like monkeys in a bouncy house. Without any rehearsing, moaning noises filled the air, and we tried to hide our laughter as we wondered what the couple upstairs thought. Mindy said they were in their early twenties.

"Oh, Luke," Mindy howled after a few bounces as if I began to satisfy her deepest desires.

I wasn't prepared to hear those words, but I couldn't help but laugh, and then I covered my mouth to conceal the sound.

"Mindy," I responded in a passionate tone of my own.

We tossed sexual phrases back and forth for the next few minutes: "Yes!" "Again!" "Oh, my goodness!" "Right there, that's the spot!" My mother would have been beyond embarrassed.

Upstairs became eerily silent. No broom banging. No shouting. Not even the loud footsteps we heard earlier. Exasperated, Mindy and I collapsed onto her bed and whispered to one another, wondering if the neighbors enjoyed our charades.

"Gross," we both uttered simultaneously.

"Hopefully not," she added.

At first, lying in Mindy's bed with her felt awkward, but when we began to talk, the jitters slowly faded. She shared stories about her day at school, and I told her about my time at the office. Booger boy had been up to his normal tendencies, only this time he stuck one on the tour guide at the Pine Knoll Shores Aquarium where the entire first grade went on a field trip. As always, I laughed a lot as she shared the story. Another one of her kids had not simply touched one of the harmless rays but actually attempted to lift the creature out of the glass case. Mindy said that when he dropped it back into the shallow water because it was too heavy for his little arms, the splash reached nearly everyone in the class. My day wasn't quite as interesting, but I talked some about Russ and Mary without mentioning names due to client confidentiality, and Mindy seemed interested in how I spent my day.

It was getting late. I knew I should get back to why I came over in the first place. Even though I enjoyed our fun in Mindy's bedroom, I mentioned returning to the living room to finish our cocoa.

"It's probably cold by now," she noted as we headed in that direction. "I'll fix us a new cup."

I didn't argue. The first cup had been to die for.

"What I was going to say earlier before your friends upstairs interrupted is that I think you were right about me from the first night," I announced.

"What do you mean?" she asked, a wrinkle forming between her eyes.

"Well, you said I was too good to be true." I paused, and I could tell she didn't like the sound of that comment. "I haven't been completely transparent with you—"

Mindy cut me off. "Oh, my God. You're married, aren't you?" She looked at my ring finger when she spoke.

I couldn't help but chuckle. "I'm not married," I assured her. Still, I didn't want to have to tell her the reason, but I needed to. I had to. "There is someone else," I admitted.

"What do you mean? Like you have a girlfriend or a fiancé, and you are cheating on her with me?"

"Not exactly." I spent the next ten minutes explaining to Mindy how I ended up having two dates in one weekend for the first time in my life. She didn't seem too agitated about it initially, but the more I tried to explain the predicament I faced, the more frustrated she looked. "Emily and I have been friends for a long time," I finally shared. "We even dated in high school for a short time. The bottom line is that I want to give us, Emily and I," I made sure to clarify, "a shot at being more than just friends. I owe it to her and to myself." *I owe it to Ayden too*, I thought.

When all was said and done, I touched my second cup of hot chocolate about ten times and brought it to my mouth repeatedly, but I never drank a single sip. Mindy seemed to understand my decision, and when she walked me to my vehicle, she surprised me with a short, sweet kiss on the lips, which seemed to linger for hours after I left. Since it was so late and dark outside, I stood against the car door and watched her, with her head drooping a bit, walk back toward her apartment. I kept my eyes on her for safety's sake, but I also wanted to remember what it felt like to hurt a very special person. At that moment I knew I never wanted to make a choice like this again. Even though I was a licensed therapist, I couldn't think of one way to make her disappointment disappear. The truth was my heart hurt even as I spotted the upstairs neighbors peeking out their blinds. Still, I couldn't stop myself from laughing under my breath as I wondered what they were thinking, yet hoping they wouldn't see me chuckling. I certainly didn't want Mindy to hear me and get the wrong impression. If she did, she would probably never speak to me again.

14

ho is Mindy Lane?

Emily was still waiting for an answer.

"Do you want the entire truth?" I asked, knowing her response before posing the question.

"Nothing less," Emily clarified.

From the other side of the triangle, I told Emily the exact story I shared with Mindy last night, about how I went on the blind date with Mindy on a Friday evening and then the next night I spent with her and Ayden at my brother's house. I let Emily know I talked to Mindy this week and that I believed she was a great person but that she—Emily—was who I wanted to be with. "That is the same thing I told Mindy," I said honestly. I wanted Emily to know that Mindy wasn't my backup plan, and releasing the truth made my conscience feel as clear as the sky above.

The day was beautiful for lunch in the park, and now I could only hope that it would end as well as it began. I found myself praying that when Emily and I rose from this table, I could hug her and tell her I would call her later. I hoped our plans for tomorrow night would still be on, and we could act normal, maybe even a new normal around each other at volleyball tonight.

I was so glad I figured out that I wanted to be with Emily and was willing to open my eyes to the possibility of one day being a stepdad to Ayden. Now, everything hung on how Emily responded to what we spent the last thirty minutes discussing. I had no idea what she was thinking based on her facial expression; it was almost blank.

"Luke, what you've shared with me today," she started, "is a lot to process. You can't expect me to have an answer for you right now."

"Okay," I agreed. That made sense even though it would help me breathe a little easier if she would give me one. "Can I ask you one question, though?"

"You just did," she pointed out, smirking for the first time since our conversation turned serious. "Sure," she added.

"How did you know about Mindy?"

"It's a small town, Luke; people talk."

"What people?"

"You didn't get permission for a second question," Emily teased, and I threw my crumpled up straw paper at her. "All of them," she answered.

"What did you hear?"

She held up three fingers. "You're pushing your luck." She paused. "Just that you might be seeing someone." She waited for another question, but when I didn't ask, she asked, "Is that all, Mr. Investigator?"

"Did you say anything to Emily about Mindy?" I asked Colleen on my way back to the office. I picked up the phone as soon as I pulled out of the park, and even though I didn't think Ben or Colleen would spill the beans, I wanted to be sure that nothing slipped out in conversation.

"Of course not," she confirmed. "It's not my place to share your personal business."

"Emily and I met for lunch today at the park, and somehow she knows something about Mindy and me."

"Luke, I promise we didn't say anything," she insisted. "We didn't think you were doing anything wrong because your time with Emily on Saturday wasn't officially a date. Also, you said you hadn't committed to Mindy to date only her anyway."

"Thanks, I believe you. I just wish I knew how Emily knew about Mindy."

"I think I may know," she uttered.

"What?"

"I believe I know how she knows."

I pushed down the brake pedal and pulled off onto the shoulder of the road. "How?" I asked.

"Didn't you say that Mindy lives in the old apartment complex downtown where your dad used to live?"

"Yes, but what does that have to do with anything?"

Colleen hesitated for a moment. "I think I recall Emily saying someone she works with moved into one of the units there not long ago; maybe her coworker knows who you are and has seen you there."

Crud. "What is her coworker's name?"

"Rachel, I believe."

That told me nothing. "I don't think I know her."

"I don't know her either, Luke. I just now remembered Emily mentioning that to me. It was probably two months ago, and I only remember her coworker's name because it is the same as my mother's."

All of the unknowns bothered me the rest of the afternoon, to the point that I hardly accomplished anything at the office. Thankfully I didn't have sessions scheduled, or else I probably would have had to offer them at no cost to the clients. I would have been absolutely no good to them. *Rachel.* Who was Rachel? Did I know her? Had I seen her at the apartment complex? Or better yet, had she seen me? Either way, Emily knew about Mindy. But how much? Did she know I kissed her? Why did that even matter to me? People kiss on dates; that's not something I had to reveal. There had been a handful of people in the parking lot both nights when I'd been at Mindy's. Granted, it was late and dark, but they could have made me out beneath the pole lights. Usually, I was pretty aware of my surroundings; it came with the career. I noticed people. How they walk. How they dress. Their height. Their weight. If they are alone or with a group. But I'd been somewhat preoccupied when I'd been at Mindy's. I saw people moving to and from their cars and the apartment building, but they were a blur in my memory.

How could I find out?

I caught myself picking up the phone to call Mindy, but I put it down as soon as I touched the first number. What would I do, ask her if she knew Rachel? Knew which apartment she lived in? That would be awkward. She would think I was a stalker like her ex. Not a good idea, I decided. I tried to quit thinking about it. Maybe Emily would tell me more tonight at the volleyball match. Perhaps I would even ask about Rachel. Or maybe I wouldn't. Like Emily said, we lived in a small area. Anyone could have seen Mindy and me together Friday night. A lot of people had, actually. I hadn't specifically noticed any people Emily and I knew from volleyball or high school. However, that didn't mean someone who knew her and also knew who I was hadn't seen me.

It seemed like an eternity passed between lunch and the volleyball match. When I pulled into the empty spot next to Emily's car, she and Ayden stood near the opened trunk. As soon as my tires came to a halt, Emily let go of Ayden's hand, and I smiled when he ran in my direction.

"Luke," he exclaimed, burying his head in my stomach.

"Hey, little man."

"Whet's race," he suggested. "Right now, come on," he insisted, tugging at my hand.

"Is it okay if I grab my bag from the vehicle first?"

"No," he responded. "Whet's go now. Mommy can bring it."

He was a little upset when I made him walk with me to the back of my Range Rover, but his demeanor changed slightly when I asked him to carry one of the balls.

"He's excited to see you," Emily announced. "We've been talking about you," she added with a wink.

"Is that right? Good things, I hope."

"Mostly." She paused looking at him before speaking again. "I told him that you are going to start spending more time with us," she shared with an unforgettable smile.

We were halfway to the court, and I couldn't help but stop in my tracks and smile as widely as a carnival clown. "Really?" I double-checked.

"Really," she replied.

That was the answer I prayed for, but I guess a part of me thought that the Mindy aspect of the equation might throw things off, and if it had, I probably would have beat myself up over it for quite some time.

The game seemed different that night. My competitive nature dwindled a bit although I still dove in the sand for balls and moved intensely at every opportunity. We won the match, but I spent more time flirting with Emily than checking the score. We shot each other looks back and forth the entire night. During timeouts and between sets, we chatted about the date we planned for Friday night which we termed "official" after the first match.

Ayden beat me three times when we raced to the far court, but in my defense his mom held me by my hips once. He thought it was the greatest thing in the world, and he made sure to announce it to the entire team. Twice. The little fellow definitely couldn't be categorized as shy. He would always talk to any of the players or spectators even while his mom was playing. When we took a break, she sometimes apologized for Ayden talking their ears off. Of course most players didn't mind conversing with him, and the ones who would rather watch the match than focus their attention on him, they just pretended to listen.

In the parking lot after volleyball, Ayden watched me hug his mother. At first I thought he would get upset, but he ended up saying nothing. His brow furrowed just a tad, and I assumed he wondered why I hugged his mother twice in one week.

With Ayden strapped into his booster seat, Emily shut the door to allow a moment of privacy. "Are you sure six o'clock will be okay?"

"That's perfect," I remarked. "I understand you have a lot of cleaning to catch up on at the house. You have a seven-year-old, after all."

"Are you sure I can't bring anything?"

"Just that smile." In that instant the one on my face grew wider.

Emily and I talked with anticipation as the parking lot began to clear. Although we weren't the last people to leave, it was nice to have a few minutes to chat without having teammates around to overhear our every word.

"Will that devil child be coming back to this neighborhood anytime soon?" was the question Dr. Nesbitt greeted me with as soon as I stepped onto my driveway. The ride home had been so pleasant, I thought as I shut the car door and moved toward my neighbor.

"Excuse me?" I questioned my eyebrow cocking just a bit.

"This neighborhood has always been peaceful, Mr. Briggs."

"Bridges," I clarified clearly and with a little extra tone.

Nesbitt began to wave his hands as if swatting at a swarm of bumblebees. "Briggs, Bridges, it's close enough," he assured me.

For a moment I considered becoming a devil child myself, saying something I was sure to later regret. But the last thing I wanted to deal with was Dr. Nesbitt and his community watch buddies. They might patrol my house even closer on their golf carts, stop by frequently with a ruler to measure my grass, or make sure I didn't install anything without proper approval.

Devil child? Was he talking about Ayden?

I asked.

"I don't know the kid's name," he stated. "The one with all the loud noises, sounding like a hyena."

Did he only sound like you, or did he also look like you? I almost asked. *Community patrol*, I kept thinking. *Remain calm, and breathe deeply for a few seconds between every statement.* That's how I would have advised a client dealing with a situation like this.

I played dumb. "I'm not sure what you're talking about." I furrowed my brow to add effect.

"Are you deaf?" he asked but didn't wait for an answer. "I was reading the newspaper Sunday night, in the middle of a good story, I might add when suddenly I heard sirens." He paused, but not long enough for me to get in a word. "Not the sound of the vehicles of the fine men and women who serve this town on the police department and fire department," he clamored as a politician at a podium might. "No, Mr. Ba-ridg-essss," he enunciated, "the sound of an unruly child yelling at the top of his little lungs is what I'm talking about."

He was definitely talking about Ayden, and he just struck me the wrong way. I held my tongue long enough I decided. "I'm sorry, Mr. Nesbitt. I didn't realize you had to wear your hearing aid when you read the newspaper." *Good job*, I said to myself; I chose the funny insult over the mean one that also entered my mind.

After he bore a hole through me with his eyes, it appeared as though he was trying to look at his ears.

I shot him a funny glance which only added to his rage.

"Ha," he gestured. "Just because I walk with a cane," he said, touching it to the ground near my feet causing me to step backward, "doesn't mean that I wear a hearing aid or have dentures."

"And just because you heard the sounds of an excited child doesn't mean you have to come over here and complain. Isn't there something better you could be doing with your time?"

He studied my uniform, glancing down and then up. "I guess I could be playing volleyball," he snarled sarcastically.

I could have responded in many ways starting with a comment on the flannel pajama suit with a waist strap that his great-grandmother must have hand sewn for him. Instead, I decided to cool it with the jokes and spent the next five minutes listening to him bicker. I learned that was typically the easiest way to get people to shut up, aside from punching them in the nose. I decided long ago that Dr. Nesbitt was way too old for me to knock out. Mostly I just nodded my head. In his mind, the neighborhood was going downhill, he explained. Most of which happened to be my fault, he thought, since I was the one who allowed the so-called devil child to enter holy grounds, which made no sense at all. Ayden had been to my house once and made a few siren noises. He was a kid. Kids made noise, I explained to the doctor, but *he* wasn't listening. I remembered seeing him at Russ's and Mary's house a few times complaining like he was doing now, but I never asked them any questions about those encounters. It wasn't my business. Now I knew the conversations likely involved Colton's cap guns or the noises he made when playing outside with monster trucks.

Maybe I could get Colton and Ayden together one day. They could run around the yard making all kinds of noises was what I thought as I walked up the steps to the sound of Mr. Nesbitt's cane echoing off the deserted street. I snickered and then opened the door to a dark house.

15

There is no other aroma quite like the one emitted by an old-fashioned charcoal grill. I call it by that name because most people replaced charcoal with fancy gas grills. There's nothing wrong with modern technology, but I prefer charcoal for a few reasons, mostly the undeniable taste of a charcoal-flame-cooked hamburger and steak. Not to mention a charcoal grill is less dangerous, in my opinion. I had nightmares about a gas grill blowing up in my face. Both types of grills involve fire and flames and could obviously cause injury, but charcoal seems more controlled. Although I must admit, I scorched my arm hair a few times with the grill I stood over at this very moment.

Today I was a little more careful than when those mishaps occurred, primarily because of the thought of Emily staring at a splotch of singed hair on my arm all evening. It was way too warm out to wear long sleeves. I went that route once or twice during the winter months. My grill never shuts down, not even during the cold season. Whether we have one of those in Atlantic Beach is up for debate.

Mention wintry conditions at the Crystal Coast to a northerner who moved down here from Connecticut or New Jersey, and they'll chuckle. Nonetheless, I grill regardless of rainfall, freezing temperatures, or even that rare snow. However, I won't wear the outfit I picked for tonight: a pair of navy blue nylon shorts and a burnt orange t-shirt, probably the nicest in my closet. The aforementioned precipitation is the reason I purchased the blue tarp currently folded and stored beneath my deck. I pulled it out a number of times and tied it between the roof of my house and the poles on the far end of my deck. Works like a charm to keep me and the grill dry.

Emily was scheduled to arrive soon, and I wanted to be sure I had the area smelling like fiery charcoal when she opened her car door. I fetched the bag from the garage and sprinkled in enough black coals to cover the bottom pan of the grill. I then dressed them nicely with lighter fluid. Before striking a match, I went back into the house, allowing the liquid time to soak into the dry coals properly. I pulled a covered dish from the refrigerator and sat it on the counter. When I pulled back the tinfoil, there sat the two ribeye steaks I began marinating last night before going to bed. I dashed some homemade seasoning onto the meat, and when I stuck a fork in them, I was pleased with the tenderness. As long as I didn't burn them, I knew they would be delicious.

I left the steaks sitting on the counter and lit a match, using my free hand to shield it from the steady breeze blowing off the ocean at my back. In a millisecond, flames shot into the humid air, and it didn't take long for the aroma I imagined to come to life. It quickly filled the backyard and even followed me into the kitchen. I purposely left the sliding glass door open while waiting for the fire to calm. The living room was nice and neat from the cleaning I did last night, and I took a seat near the front window so I would be sure to see Emily pull up.

For the next ten minutes, my eyes darted among the magazine in my hand, the clock on the wall, and the empty driveway behind my Range Rover. Should I call Emily I wondered when I realized it was ten minutes after six. My mind began to wander anxiously.

Maybe she wasn't coming. That was a silly thought I quickly convinced myself. Why would she not come?

The hands on the clock continued to move in a circular direction. Maybe Emily rethought what happened between Mindy and me—nothing in the grand scheme of things—and changed her mind. Had I told her everything? I began to question myself. I peeked at the time again. Had Emily found out something more from her coworker or some other anonymous individual, and I would later find out that I was being stood up tonight? Would that be my payment for going on a date with two women in one weekend? In a way, I felt like that decision was careless, and I wanted more than anything to make it up to Emily. It was nice to know that my attention could now be set on her and only her. Tonight would hopefully be the beginning of something beautiful. It would be our first official date and a chance to spend significant time together alone.

I didn't want to seem impatient by calling to check on her, so I sat in the quiet for a few more minutes and could feel my forehead beading with sweat. Eventually, I breathed a sigh of relief when I watched Emily's car ease into the driveway as if right on time.

Rather than wait at the door with a cheesy grin, I decided to let her ring the doorbell. As I watched her walk toward the house, I couldn't tell if she noticed the charcoal aroma. However, I did take note of the burgundy top that fit her nicely, as well as the khaki skirt and two tanned legs that caused the fabric to sway as she made her way up the sidewalk.

When our eyes met, I could hardly control my breathing. Emily was stunning, a real knockout, and that is all there was to it. I felt like a little kid in a candy shop. I wanted to put my hands all over her, but at the same time I was just as content standing in awe with glazed eyes.

She smiled. "Hey, handsome."

The admiration must have made me light up even brighter. My

lifted cheeks caused my eyes to squint, and I felt my face freeze until I uttered a compliment in return. "You look—" What word would fit, I wondered, racking my brain for something worthy of Emily's beauty. "Charming" is the adjective I uttered in a voice just above a whisper. Elegant would have been too dressy. Beautiful would have been too easy.

"Something smells good," she noticed as I made room for her to walk through the doorway and into my house, hoping she would never leave.

I dabbed a couple drops of cologne on my neck earlier that afternoon, but I was more excited to realize the reference pertained to the grill. "Hope I'm not too late," she added, and I watched her glance at the clock I'd been staring at for fifteen minutes.

"Just in time, actually," I assured her. "The grill is nice and hot, and the steaks have been begging me to put them on."

"You talk to your steaks?" she teased.

"No," I laughed, "*they* talk to me."

Emily snickered.

Once in the kitchen, Emily didn't waste any time offering to help. Actually, I don't think she even asked. I walked toward the pantry to grab a pair of tongs, and when I turned, the steaks were heading for the grill. In the back of my mind, I could hear my dad's voice saying, "Son, a woman should never come between a man and his grill." But at the moment it didn't seem to bother me. I was just glad Emily was here, between me and anything.

I poured us both a glass of sweet tea, and we enjoyed the view from the comfort of my deck as the meat simmered on the warm rack. On my grill, there was only one way to cook—slowly. I warned Emily in advance that it might be seven o'clock before dinner was ready. Thankfully, she didn't seem to mind.

"I could sit out here all night," Emily mentioned when I reminded her of my grilling technique.

"We can eat outside if you like," I offered. "With the breeze coming off the ocean, mosquitoes and other bugs aren't usually an issue." Another perk of living at the beach, I reminded myself as if I needed one.

"That sounds perfect," she responded.

"If you get cool later, I have blankets inside that we can bring out." As I spoke, my eyes traveled to her crossed legs once more. I normally never glare at any part of a woman's body; I believed a quick glance was a compliment while a lengthy stare was disrespectful. Of course some seem to dress for prolonged gazes and loud whistles. These are often the same people who complain about unattractive men looking too long and letting out loose comments. Emily didn't dress the part, though. Her natural beauty and the skin leading to what I couldn't see made my mind wander which was way more fascinating to me than a woman in a miniskirt.

The temperature was perfect for sitting outside. A slight wind caused the sea oats to dance for us as the ocean's music ebbed and flowed in the background. We watched the scene like a Broadway show as we chatted, and I found it comforting that Emily found the natural movements as fascinating as I did. There had been many evenings when I sat out here in solitude and watched people walk along the beach as the sun set and the sandpipers frolicked and flew about. I'd even been known to pick out one particular bird and note where it started and where it ended up five or ten minutes later. Something about the journey was relaxing.

"I've been watching that one," Emily pointed out after I mentioned my bird meditation practice. "It started out over there in the dunes, then flew down to the water's edge, and now it's floating up there in the air without a worry in the world."

Nodding my head, I smirked. I wanted to say something insightful, but nothing came to mind, so I kept quiet and began to watch the same sandpiper with her.

Emily's feet were propped up on a small table she'd moved from between our chairs. The steaks smelled better and better as time passed, and I fought off the sounds of hunger in my stomach that seemed to want to talk to the beautiful woman sitting next to me.

As soon as I felt my stomach about to growl, I got up and checked the grill to make enough noise so that Emily wouldn't hear. For some reason I'd always been embarrassed by that sound. In school. At church. It seemed there was no way to hold it in. Sometimes if I tightened my abs that would help. Other times I found that pushing my stomach out muffled the sound.

Finally I wised up and retrieved a bag of chips from the pantry.

"These are good," Emily declared.

Sun Chips have been one of my favorites since I was a kid. When I told Emily that, she was surprised.

She held the bag up, and her eyes grew. "You're telling me these things have been around since we were kids, and this is the first time I've ever eaten them?"

"You must have lived a sheltered life," I teased. Then I pointed to the grill. "Have you ever tasted steak?" I added, causing her to laugh.

"Remember, I'm a country girl. I've eaten my share of steaks."

"That's right. I forgot you grew up on a farm and wore pigtails."

"I did not." She threw the bag of chips at me. "Well, kind of," she admitted as I picked a few loose chips off my lap. "My grandmother had chickens and goats."

"And what else?"

She laughed as she added, "Pigs and cows."

The bird had made its way back to the dunes, and we continued to watch it off and on as Emily talked about spending time on her grandparent's farm and with the animals.

"Did you ever have pets?" she inquired.

Just by listening to her talk about the animals at her grandparent's farm, I knew Emily loved animals deeply. Which was great. I remember a man saying to me once, "Beware of anyone who doesn't like animals." It was a basic saying, but it made so much sense. How could anyone not like animals?

"I had a dog when I was a kid. His name was Lassie."

A familiar look appeared on Emily's face. "His?" she asked, as so many others had.

"My parents let me name him, and I didn't know any better." Thinking about it, I laughed. "I loved that show when I was growing up. I watched the new episode every week and reruns every day in between." I paused as I caught a glimpse of the bird flapping its wings out of the corner of my eye. "By the way, don't tell that to the kids at school," I warned.

"I guess you did that."

"My first fight happened because some kid was teasing me about watching Lassie. We wrestled around on the playground, tore holes in our jeans, and threw a couple of lousy punches."

"Did you win?"

"It was like most fights; we both lost. He was the one who cried to the teacher, but by the time I got home I realized I ruined my favorite shirt and bruised my wrist when I missed punching him, and my hand ended up slamming into one of the bars on the swing set."

"Did Lassie comfort you when you got home?" Emily asked, laughing at me as she spoke.

"I wish. Daddy comforted me with punishment."

"Ouch," she uttered.

"The funniest thing about my Lassie might not even be that he wasn't a she. He wasn't a collie either," I admitted.

"Oh, yeah?"

"He was a mutt with no hint of white or tan on his entire body. He was pitch black and ugly to everyone except for me. We did everything together. Played catch in the yard. Walked to the river. He was a good dog much like the real Lassie in many ways."

Emily furrowed her brow.

"His character, that is," I explained. I glanced at the grill, immediately realizing I probably could have pulled the steaks five minutes ago. I jumped up and forked them onto a clean plate. One of the nice things about slow cooking is that it is difficult to burn anything unless I fall asleep while tanning. That's a story I have to tell Emily another time. The Lassie story was insulting enough for one night.

We pulled our chairs up to the patio table, and I sat the steaks in the middle with the bag of chips.

"I imagine you probably expected to find that I fixed mashed potatoes and green beans to accompany our steaks, but, believe me, once you bite into this steak, you will immediately realize you wouldn't want anything else on your plate."

"You sure are setting the bar high," Emily realized. "You better hope this steak is as good as it is big."

We sat down. I said grace, and then she took a bite. I waited for a response. I watched her lips move as she chewed, and I could tell she was purposely holding a neutral expression. She glanced up at me then back down. She took a sip of tea, said nothing, and cut another piece off the steak. I didn't want to continue to stare in expectation of a response, so I picked up my knife and cut a bite as well.

"It's killing you, isn't it?" she asked, smiling slightly.

"I'm not sure what you are talking about," I responded.

"Bull," she said, calling my bluff.

I pretended to have just caught on. "Oh, you mean the steak."

"No, I mean the mashed potatoes and green beans."

I laughed with her and enjoyed it very much. It was nice to have a woman sitting on my deck with me, eating dinner, and flirting.

"I might have been waiting to see what you thought about the steak," I finally admitted.

"I'll say this—"

I waited impatiently as if her input determined whether I would get into Heaven.

She continued, "If counseling doesn't work out for you, you might consider opening a steakhouse."

I couldn't hold in the smile that instantly overtook my facial expression. As our dinner on the deck continued, I was at ease at how quickly our conversations would go from teasing to serious and then right back to the other. The steak *was* delicious, but the company was even more delightful. We chatted further about the animals we each grew up with and talked about volleyball. I told her about my neighbors, making sure to exclude what Dr. Nesbitt said about Ayden. I imagined she would march over there and cause him to wet his pants if I shared his comments. It would have been funny to watch, but I didn't think it would be for the good of the neighborhood.

16

Shining through cartoon-looking clouds, the sunset painted the sky shades of oranges, pinks, and blues as we finished dinner. I already didn't want the night to end.

"Would you like to go for a beach walk?" I asked Emily. I planned everything I could think of to have her at my house for as long as she was willing to stay. Thankfully, she seemed to enjoy our time together and was excited about having the dessert we discussed during dinner. We both agreed to indulge later once our food was settled.

"Yes, I would love to," Emily answered, biting her lower lip gently.

"Perfect. We can chase the sunset."

Emily's eyes lit up. "That sounds fun and beautiful," she announced, staring at the sun falling into the ocean.

"Let me run these dishes in first," I suggested.

She grabbed a plate and the bag of chips. "I'll help."

Emily's purse sat on the kitchen table. As I walked past it, the sound of her phone ringing startled me, and I nearly dropped everything in my hands.

She glanced at me and then toward her bag. "I should probably check that," she said and then put the contents in her hands on the table. "It might be Ayden."

I nodded my head in agreement.

"Hello," she answered.

Emily was quiet for eight or ten seconds, so I assumed she was listening to the person on the other end. I placed the dishes from my hands into the sink and then grabbed the ones from the table that Emily set down. Her eyes darted in my direction a couple of times as I moved around, and then she excused herself to the living room using a hand gesture.

Respecting her privacy, I walked back outside to grab the rest of the remnants from dinner and then remained in the kitchen to straighten and clean a few things. I decided to move the dishes from the sink to the dishwasher but didn't start it because I knew we'd be having ice cream later. With only one person living in the house, it usually took days, if not a week, to fill the thing up. That's why I barely even used it. Most of the time, I just washed my dishes the old-fashioned way. It was quicker, and I didn't have to listen to the noise the contraption had been making for about a year.

At first, I couldn't make out any of the words from Emily's conversation in the living room. She wasn't whispering; I was just far enough away that her voice didn't carry to me. But then, as I wandered around the kitchen, finding random tasks to occupy my time, I noticed her tone change. All of a sudden, I could hear every word. Clearly. What had happened? She wasn't shouting, but her voice became stern, and I grew curious.

It quickly became apparent that she was talking to her ex-husband and was upset about something that happened with Ayden. I wondered if he was okay. Had the guy done something to hurt him? I didn't want to jump to conclusions, but the fear in her voice made it hard not to. I fired up a missile prayer.

"Why do you even call me to tell me these things?" I heard her say.

I leaned against the counter and tried to remain calm, but my hands became fidgety. I started picking up things in the kitchen for no apparent reason. A fork. A salt shaker. A pencil on the counter. As quickly as I picked up the random items, I put each down and replaced it with another.

"Just do whatever you need to do," was the last thing I heard Emily say before she slammed the phone down a bit aggressively on the coffee table.

I figured she would come into the kitchen and tell me if she needed to leave. I waited there, somewhat impatiently, wanting to give her the time and space she might need to cool down. After a few minutes passed, I stepped into the living room to check on her.

Joining Emily on the couch, I handed her a box of tissues and made sure not to say anything cliché, like *Is everything okay?* It wasn't. I knew that. She was upset. An angry countenance enveloped her, and I realized there probably wasn't anything I could say at that moment that would change it. I couldn't make her smile or laugh. I couldn't tell her I would love for her to be my girlfriend. I couldn't even ask if she wanted me to beat the guy up. So I did what I thought was best. I sat quietly beside Emily and waited for her to say or do something. It was then, as if I clicked the remote in front of us, that she put her hands to her face and wept into them.

For a long time Emily cried, and I just sat with her. I'd seen plenty of women cry over the years, but Emily's tears seemed different. I knew I was in the middle of something I'd never experienced this closely. I once dated a woman who cried every time she left my house. Every guy wants a woman who misses him; it makes us feel special; but this girl was a bit obsessive. Needless to say, that relationship didn't last very long. I watched my mom cry occasionally, most recently on her front porch when she and I talked about Dad's health. It bothered her to no end; she had been holding in many words she needed to speak. The two of us sat on the porch swing for an hour as she poured out all the thoughts pent-up up inside her.

Crying was also a job hazard in my industry. Enough tears were shed in my office to flood downtown Morehead City.

When I least expected it, Emily scooted close to me and let her head drop onto my shoulder. I felt the weight of all the anger she tried to release, and at that moment I reached my arm around her, comforting her as best I knew how. For what reason in particular, I still wasn't sure. It didn't matter. I was content being there for her whatever the issue might be.

Eventually, she leaned back against the couch, so I let my arms pull away giving her some space again. In time, she spoke. "Can we go on that beach walk now?"

"Of course," I agreed.

I grabbed a handful of tissues and stuffed them into my pocket. In the silence of Emily's tears, we walked through the narrow sandy path that led through the dunes to the beach. I left my flip-flops on the deck, but Emily kept her sandals on.

"That was my ex-husband," she uttered as we made our way toward the ocean's edge.

I already knew that much but didn't mention it.

"He thought it would be considerate to call and let me know that he and my seven-year-old son were just leaving a party—" She paused to let out a few more tears while I waited for her to continue. "He's drunk, as usual," she shared almost casually.

"And driving?" I inquired. If so, with Ayden in the car, I would certainly be willing to drive around until I found him, and then he and I might roll around in the grass. Staining my jeans wouldn't matter because he would go home with stains of his own for driving drunk with a helpless child. No, not just a helpless child, Ayden, a child who meant a great deal to me. I had absolutely no compassion for drunk drivers. It didn't matter if they were one smidge over the legal limit. If you drink, you ask somebody else to drive or stay put. That way you know you won't kill someone on your way home.

"No, thank God. That's the other part of it though. He said I wouldn't have to worry about Ayden because this really nice woman was driving them to her house. Someone he just met tonight." She smiled sarcastically. "He was so drunk that he even said, 'you never know, Emily, she could end up being his stepmom one day so don't be so freaking upset. This will give me a chance to see how she will be around him.' He's so careless," she claimed.

As we walked along the shoreline, a group of sandpipers journeyed with us. Overhead, seagulls soared toward the sunset.

"Can't you go get Ayden?" I knew she probably couldn't, not legally anyway, but I asked the question regardless. It was the logical thing to think. No child should have to be put in such a situation.

"I wish, but I talked to my lawyer about it and he said that people drink. Good people even. They get drunk from time to time, and the court wouldn't see it the way I see it. Some kids from environments like this turn out just fine, they'd say. So if I rescue my child from his irresponsible father, he could charge me for kidnapping or some mess like that."

"So why did he call?" I wondered aloud.

"Because he knows it pisses me off."

"Why wouldn't he want to keep that kind of stuff quiet so that you don't have something against him if you end up in court again about custody?"

"He did for a while, but then he found out Ayden came home and told me everything anyway. So now when something like this happens, he calls and tells me himself. I think it gives him some kind of power trip."

Emily continued to cry off and on as we made tracks in the sand. I handed her a tissue earlier, and she had held it in her hand ever since, dabbing at the tears as they fell on her cheeks. Tissues, I learned, only erase the tears on the surface; they can't touch the ones that fall from our hearts. Those require God's help.

I hated that Emily had to deal with this. I wanted to pummel her ex. We had been having such a nice night. It didn't matter that our conversations would likely be completely different because of the phone call. It didn't even matter if our plans changed and Emily decided to leave. What mattered was *who* messed it up, *why* he messed it up, and *how* he messed it up. What mattered the most were Emily and Ayden. Neither of them deserved such treatment. This guy was a jerk. I tried my best not to form an opinion of him, but what kind of idiot would take his seven-year-old child to a party, get drunk, meet a woman, and go home with her. What a piece of crap. I had a good mind to grab her phone, call the number he called from, and tell him exactly that. But, what good would that do? None. It would only make matters worse.

"I'm sorry you have to deal with this," I offered wholeheartedly.

"I should be the one who is sorry," she responded.

"What? Why?" I asked unsure what she meant by that statement as a shell cracked underneath my foot. Thankfully it was thin and didn't hurt.

"This is our first real date—probably not what you had in mind. *You* shouldn't have to deal with this. It's not your problem."

I cut her off to let her know where I now stood on this issue. "Hey, don't think that. I would rather you be here talking to me about this than for you to be home by yourself."

"That's kind of you to say, but I know you have to deal with this stuff at work daily. I'm sure it's the last thing you want to bother with at home."

"Really, it's okay," I assured her while the ocean to our left churned. "You are a friend not a client. This is what I am supposed to do, what I want to do—not what I should do *just* because I am a counselor."

I watched Emily smile as best she could, and for the first time since she started crying, she realized her makeup had run all over her face. Somehow she remained unbearably attractive. Even more so than when she walked through the front door, all put together.

Continuing to walk, we talked for nearly an hour about Ayden's father, the parties he dragged his son to, and the horrific things Ayden witnessed at such an early age. I knew it wasn't good for him. No kid needs to see drunkards falling all over the place, slurring words, and treating others poorly. Emily mentioned that hard drugs were likely involved too, which caused even more concern. I asked her about his custody rights, and she told me Ayden's father got to have him every other weekend. It doesn't seem like much, but I knew how one weekend at an irresponsible parent's house for an entire childhood can damage a child immensely. I saw kids from those upbringings turn out okay as well, but most dealt with emotional and mental scars for many years if not their entire lifetime.

While standing under the pier closest to my house, wooden and tattered from being beaten on by storms and hurricanes, Emily admitted a secret that made me thankful I told her about the abortion in my past. Otherwise, confiding in me might have felt too vulnerable. She shared that she developed some pretty destructive habits when married to this loser. She admitted that getting pregnant with Ayden was the only reason she stopped doing drugs.

"I was going down a dark road," Emily confessed. "Then God let the only thing that could pull me out of that world happen." Somehow amid her thoughts and tears, she smiled. "He gave me Ayden, my little angel from Heaven, and I put it all behind me eventually including my husband who wouldn't give up that lifestyle, not even for his own flesh and blood."

We talked about her past a bit longer, and I made sure not to judge her for the mistakes she made. I prayed she would never judge me either. When we walked back through the path between the dunes, the sea oats greeted us as they always do, and then we went inside for ice cream.

"Are you sure you like chocolate?" I asked for the second time since making our way to the couch. "Because I have vanilla in the freezer too, you know."

"You also have strawberry, cookies-and-cream, and chocolate chip cookie dough, and if you ask me again, I'm going to throw this scoop at you just like I did those chips," she threatened holding the ice cream in the air with her spoon like a catapult.

When I picked out the ice cream yesterday at the grocery store, I knew all of it most likely wouldn't get eaten at my house. I figured I could always take a carton to Ben and Colleen, and Mom and Dad, and I knew Colton loved cookies-and-cream. Plus I wanted to have Ayden and Emily over once she got him back. I was sure my little buddy would be more than happy to help eliminate some of the ice cream.

"If you sling that ice cream at me, I'll have to ask you to wash my clothes," I declared.

"I have a feeling you know how to wash your own clothes, Mr. Bridges."

"I do; I just can't seem to get out the tough stains like greasy potato chips and chocolate ice cream."

"Maybe you shouldn't start so many fights, then you wouldn't end up rolling around on the grass on playgrounds with little boys, and maybe you wouldn't have chocolate ice cream slung at you by your—" Emily stopped in her tracks and peered down. The air grew awkwardly silent. *Girlfriend* was the word I hoped she almost let out.

While we ate ice cream and laughed with each other, darkness settled outside. It felt like the perfect time to watch a romantic movie, but just before suggesting the idea, Emily posed a question.

"Are you interested in setting out a blanket on the beach and stargazing?" she asked as we added our empty bowls to the dishwasher.

"Of course," I answered. Stargazing sounded even better than a romantic movie. "While I was watching the sunset earlier as we were walking, I thought about how relaxing it would be to sit out there at nighttime."

Outside, the smell of charcoal gave way to fresh salty air. The temperature fell with the sun, and the cool sand comforted my toes as we walked to the spot we decided to claim. No other humans were within shouting distance, but we could see flashlight beams dancing a few hundred yards down the shoreline.

Lying flat on our backs with the quilted blanket beneath our warm bodies and the beach basically to ourselves, we admired a perfect view of the sky. The nearly full glowing moon was the centerpiece, and a vast array of twinkling stars surrounded it as far as the eyes could see.

Earlier, I was surprised Emily decided not to go home, crawl into bed, and cry herself to sleep, but I sure was glad she stayed. I got the impression she dealt with this type of behavior from her ex-husband way too often. Even though it caused her a great deal of pain each time it happened, she seemed to know she couldn't allow it to control her life. For that, I was proud of her. Many people would let it overwhelm them. They enabled their exes, who controlled them during the marriage to continue manipulating them even from a distance which was exactly what this guy tried to accomplish.

I rolled over on the blanket for a sip of sweet tea. "Do you want yours?" I asked Emily. I learned to bring beverages to the beach in insulated cups; otherwise, they often got turned over on the blanket or in the sand. When I mentioned this to Emily earlier as we poured them, I joked I was doing it this time so she wouldn't have to wash my clothes if she spilled tea all over me.

"I'm good," she replied, talking slowly as she stared at Orion's Belt. "This was such a great idea."

Stargazing on a blanket near the ocean hadn't been on my

agenda for the night, but I certainly was elated it turned out this way.

"It's getting a little cool out here," Emily said after pointing out several constellations.

"I can run inside and grab another blanket to use as a cover," I offered.

She shook her head from side to side. I waited a moment and then scooted close to her.

"That's what I hoped you'd do," she admitted.

I wasn't sure if she also hoped I would roll onto my side, gaze into her deep blue eyes, run my fingers through her soft hair, and then gently kiss her shivering lips—but that's exactly what I did next.

Beyond us, waves rolled one over the other; the seabirds called out through the gentle breeze; and ships sailed in the distance.

Emily's thin lips tasted like perfection, and I found myself caught in a moment more intimidating than anything I had done in a long time. I felt her body flush against mine, causing my insides to tremble ever so slightly. Our lips moved together, slowly and passionately, as if dancing to the most romantic song the Universe ever played. Before I could think about what was happening between us, I realized her arm caressed the back of my head and her leg wrapped around my thigh.

I desired this moment for so long even longer than I realized. To touch her soft skin and to sense the tiny movements between our bodies felt good. Her perfume tickled my nose as I kissed her neck. She turned slightly, and I continued to navigate my way across her collarbone with my lips. At the same time she rubbed my back with her hand barely digging her fingernails into my skin causing me to want more of her. Yet this was just enough. Kissing her. Touching her. *This* was intimacy.

What was happening between Emily and me at this very moment meant way more to me than any encounter I talked myself into on lonely nights. It was real, and I think it meant as much to her as it did to me. I could tell this by how our eyes locked every time we looked at one another. Even though we kept our clothes on as we rolled around on a blanket by the sea for nearly thirty minutes, I felt as though I already made love to Emily Beckett.

17

aving Emily and Ayden sitting nearby in beach chairs watching me play volleyball on the first breezy Saturday morning in June was a treat. Over a week passed since the blanket episode on the beach, which ended up lasting until 2 am, and I couldn't stop thinking about Emily since.

This morning, I picked them up from her place early around sunrise, and we made it to Myrtle Beach a little after nine o'clock. The highlight of the trip so far for Ayden was that there happened to be a playground next to a random local breakfast restaurant we found with good reviews. My first match wasn't scheduled to start until ten, so we let Ayden play after he consumed what he called his "shausage" biscuit.

Emily and Ayden had been over to the house twice this week, and both nights Ayden and I took a chunk out of the carton of chocolate chip cookie dough ice cream. Being his favorite flavor, he wouldn't even consider the others. Emily ate one bowl of the chocolate on Tuesday night, and on Wednesday I made my delivery to Mom's and Dad's and Ben's and Colleen's for their ice cream. Ben teased that I should have turned on my ice cream truck music so he would know I was coming.

When Ben mentioned it, I suddenly realized how much I

missed the ice cream truck. As far as I knew, our area didn't have one anymore. Every kid deserved the experience. Nothing is quite like sitting on the front porch steps in the summertime racing against the heat to see if you can lick more of the ice cream off the stick than what melts onto your shorts. I suddenly wondered if Ayden had ever picked out ice cream from a truck.

As I watched Ayden play this morning, I couldn't help but remember how he'd been forced to see his dad guzzle down one beer after another this past weekend and bring some random woman home to fulfill his selfish desires. "Daddy likes to wrestle with women," Ayden told Emily when he returned home. "But for some reason when they wrestle, they make a lot of noise." Shocking, I thought sarcastically when she told me on Thursday at volleyball what Ayden said.

Once my first match started this morning, it didn't take long before I began sweating from all the moving around. The air wasn't hot yet, and the sand was relatively cool, but the forecast called for high eighties, so the playing conditions would become more demanding as the day moved along. After my team scored our ninth point, I glanced at Emily while waiting for the ball to be returned for our next serve. With a smile, she held up a Body Armor bottle and jiggled it, a reminder that I needed to stay hydrated, I was pretty sure. During a timeout I jogged over to where she sat.

"You look like you might need this," she suggested, smelling like the sunscreen we rubbed on each other earlier. Ayden played nearby in the sand with a dump truck and tractor he brought from home.

"Thanks," I replied appreciatively while grinning boyishly.

By the time my team finished our second match, I'd guzzled down two sports drinks and some water. During a break, Emily, Ayden, and I ordered hot dogs—probably not the best meal when playing in an all-day volleyball tournament—from a food truck parked for the event.

"You guys are really good," Emily complimented as I rested in my chair that sat empty next to her most of the morning.

"We've played together for a long time which helps. We all know what the other guy is going to do." I took a sip of water, figuring if I was going to eat a hot dog I better drink the healthiest beverage possible. "I'm sure you could tell that the last team we played against was made up of very talented players, but all they did was argue with one another the whole time. Every one of them wanted to do things his own way. Being on the same page makes a big difference in these tournaments. Our bodies scream at us for pushing them so hard, and people's tempers get short if they're not prepared especially when the weather is a factor."

I couldn't say I hadn't been aggravated a few times myself this season. Hot summer days will do that to a person. I was tired already from playing today, and we still had at least four more matches if we made it to the championship.

"I overheard one of the wives telling some of the other ladies that her husband—the really tall guy who spiked so hard—played volleyball in the Olympics at one point."

"A lot of the guys out here played professionally at some level, and many played in college although as you probably know, men's volleyball isn't as popular as the mainstream sports." It didn't take long for me to point out a few of the professional athletes. "At most tournaments, we see the same guys and teams; we even hear the same stories."

"How many colleges have teams?" Emily asked.

"I think there are close to two hundred and fifty," I vaguely recalled. "There are a handful in North Carolina. Most of them are Division II colleges."

"Our coed league is competitive, but the competition here is noticeably at a higher level," Emily admitted.

"Some of the best beach volleyball players never played in college or any other professional league." I laughed thinking of a story I probably told too many times. "Last year there were some guys from one of the North Carolina college teams vacationing in Atlantic Beach, and of course they came out to The Circle to play. They were beating every group they played because there were just random people out there of all talent levels playing pickup volleyball. So, one of the guys from my team did what most competitive athletes would do—he challenged them to play us. The next day we beat them five matches in a row, and the most points they scored on us was sixteen."

Emily chuckled. "I bet they came away with a newfound understanding of beach volleyball."

I nodded my head up and down as I took the last bite of my hot dog.

Ayden was back playing in the dirt with his vehicles not paying us any mind. Obviously, he was used to being at volleyball courts. There were people all over the place, some talking, some relaxing in beach chairs, some throwing balls, some running, but he didn't seem to notice any of them. He just had the time of his life in the sand beyond the blanket Emily sat on earlier.

"Ayden, are you going to finish your hot dog, buddy?" Emily asked.

The question didn't even seem to reach his ears. He continued to make buzzing and beeping sounds for his cars. A few incidents this week caused me to notice how Ayden didn't mind quite as well as he probably should. Sure, he was only seven, but he seemed adamant about following his own wants rather than his mother's guidelines.

"Ayden," Emily called out again a bit louder. This time the little guy looked up but continued playing.

"I'm not hungry," he finally responded.

"You will be thirty minutes after I throw this hot dog away." She picked it up to show him and then set it back down.

"No, I won't."

I watched quietly as they went back and forth.

"It's going to get cold."

"I don't care."

"Okay, but I won't buy you another hot dog." Emily turned to me. "I knew I shouldn't have let him eat those chips earlier. That's what he does at his dad's house," she whispered. "He fills up on junk food and then wants to do the same thing when he's with me. Sometimes I find myself caving into his requests."

"I'm sure it's hard not to; he's so cute."

Emily finished her hot dog and let Ayden play for a while longer rather than making him eat. It was almost time for my next match, so I left the two of them and headed back toward the net. Each time my team moved to a different court, we moved our chairs, blanket, and Ayden's toys to give Emily the best view. A handful of courts were being used for this tournament, and I think twenty teams were participating. Most likely it wouldn't conclude until well after dark.

Before Emily committed to coming, I asked her if it was okay for Ayden to stay up that late, and she promised me it would be fine for one night. "He'll fall asleep on the blanket," she reiterated while we were enjoying the lunch break together. I reminded her that I kind of felt guilty about bringing him out here to endure such a long day. "Believe me, he will be worn out after he plays out in the sun all day. Like I mentioned on the ride here, I'll take him to some of the shops along the boardwalk during the heat of the day to let him cool off, and he and I can swim some too. This isn't somewhere I would take him every weekend, but one time won't hurt him," she promised.

I wondered if that was a reference for the future. It made sense, I guess. If Emily and I were in a relationship, I couldn't expect her and Ayden to accompany me every other weekend while I played because that would be selfish. Who knows, I might even decide to cut back a little. I would definitely want to spend time with the two of them on weekends.

With my bag over my shoulder, I checked the tournament bracket displayed near the food truck to double-check the time of our next match. I was right; it was scheduled to start at 1:30 pm. I found some of the other guys, and we warmed up together. The hat turned backward on my head was lined with sweat, and after the last set my shorts felt nearly as soaked as if I dropped them into a bucket of water.

When I trotted onto the freshly-raked court to start the first set, I waved at Emily. She waved back and blew me a kiss. Like a teenager, I jumped into the air and pretended to catch it like a ball thrown at me. I would be lying if I didn't admit to looking around as soon as I made the motion hoping no one else saw what I just did. Thankfully the other players were doing their own thing. Stretching. Jogging around. Chatting amongst each other. It was just like me to act silly, but if the other guys saw me catch a kiss from Emily, I would definitely receive an earful of teasing.

The newness of our relationship was still as fresh as the scent in a brand new vehicle or the vinyl of a freshly installed swimming pool, two smells I loved. Since our first kiss—the longest and probably most intoxicating—we fell into each other's embrace several times whenever we could slip away from Ayden's view for a moment to ourselves. Emily wanted to be sure he didn't see us making out anytime soon, and she even hesitated about a short kiss goodnight.

When I walked her to her car the first evening they came to the house together this week, she whispered, "I think it would be best if we just hugged."

Of course I wanted to kiss her, like every other minute of each day this week, but I respected the decision. He was seven, and it would take a while for him to get used to Mommy spending time with me even though he knew me. I imagined he would most likely become jealous at some point, and he did. When I wrapped my arms around her that night, he yelled out like parents who caught their teenager going too far. "Get off my mommy," he demanded.

Startled, I stepped back. I wasn't sure what to say if anything. Emily peered into the car, and I sensed she dealt with this before. "Ayden," she said, "does Mommy tell you not to hug your friends?"

Valid point I thought. His countenance didn't change. He didn't like it, and he wanted me to know it.

"I don't want you hugging him. He was my friend first." The latter part of the sentence kind of shocked me. He was jealous of me, but he was jealous of her too. Or maybe he was just brilliant.

"We can talk about it on the way home," she responded. Through the opened window, she touched my hand. "I'll talk to you later," she said.

That night we talked on the phone for nearly an hour. I discovered that Patrick Mahomes was her favorite NFL football player, and she was a big fan of his team, the Kansas City Chiefs. She shared that if she could pick one professional game to go to, it would be the Chiefs. That night wasn't the only night we talked so long that I switched ears several times throughout the conversation. One hand would grow tired and then the next. I tried propping the phone on the pillow on my bed, but that only worked temporarily. I made a mental note to buy earphones but still hadn't gotten around to it. My phone fell off the bed a few times, and a few other times I almost fell off. To talk until one, two, or even three in the morning and then get up for work was challenging. Emily agreed, but we were so exuberant about each other that we continued our bad habit.

"We have the rest of our lives to be responsible," she mentioned once.

I chuckled, and she returned the chuckle later in the week when I asked if I could fall asleep to the sound of her on the other end of my phone. Something about the presence of her being there, even if we weren't talking or touching, comforted me. I felt close to her, but at the same time when she wasn't right there next to me, it felt like she was on the other side of the Atlantic Ocean.

On Monday morning Jackie Jones asked me several times why I was yawning so much.

"I just didn't sleep much last night," I offered.

"Talking to a woman, huh?"

How did she know?

"Other women know these things," she informed me without my asking.

I suddenly felt like I was the one being counseled. I made it a priority not to share my personal life with my clients, so I just laughed and changed the subject. A couple other clients asked similar questions. Some commented on the yawning and others on changes in my behavior. More smiles. More energy. By the way, how was it possible to be yawning and at the same time be more energetic than when you got a full night's sleep? It was fascinating how the human mind and body worked with and against each other.

I leaped as high as possible and spiked a ball through the outstretched arms of the other team's tallest player and then heard Emily and Ayden clapping for me in the background. "Good one, Wuke," Ayden hollered at the top of his little lungs. Emily shook her head and giggled. It sure felt nice to have a fan base. In fact every feeling in my body right now was positive. Things were going so well with Emily; we seemed to be on cloud nine so to speak. She only told me how happy she was fifty times in the past week, and I was beyond content with how things were progressing. It seemed we were falling in love already, and it was so much more fun than the last time I fell in love or any time before that. I thought of her constantly. I wanted to see her, talk to her every second of the day. My heart and soul yearned for more Emily Beckett, even amid how much I consumed in the past eight days.

She was such a pleasure and so was Ayden. I cherished being and doing things with them. I liked helping Ayden get in and out of the car. I enjoyed playing on my living room floor with him, and it didn't matter if there were so many Army men lined up that we had to make paths around them to get into the kitchen. I took joy in holding one of his hands while Emily held the other and on the count of three, finding out how high we could swing him into the air. Ben stopped by the house one night when Emily and Ayden were over, and Ayden asked Ben and me to do the same. After the third swing, we asked if he wanted to try a super duper high one. We warmed up, swaying him backward and forward gaining momentum with each motion. On the count of three, we flung him high into the air, and while holding tightly to his hands, we flipped his body all the way around. He landed on his two little feet and screamed, "Again, again!" I lost count after the tenth flip.

What would come next? How would the rest of the afternoon and evening go? I wondered as I stopped for short moments here and there during each match and in between. I caught myself looking forward to the three hour trip back to Atlantic Beach. Ayden would probably be asleep allowing Emily and me time to get to know each other better. I felt like I knew her so well after all of the conversations we had lately, but at the same time I learned more and more every day. It was exciting. We just seemed to click. We liked many of the same things which made for interesting conversations.

After every play, I turned toward Emily and Ayden just to see what they were doing. I found them wrestling on the blanket once, her chasing him a time or two, and she was on the phone the last time I looked over. The conversation seemed intense, like the one with her ex at my place last weekend. She wore an angry and concerned expression on her face. She wouldn't look up at me, and I thought that was odd. I prayed everything was okay while trying to pay attention to the match simultaneously. I wanted to jog over to her chair and ask what was happening, and I decided to go during our next break.

It worked out perfectly; I tracked down a ball in the far corner of the court and saved the match for my team. We needed one more point to win and scored it on the next volley. Otherwise, our backs would have been against the wall.

After brushing the sand off my bare chest and stomach, I shared high fives with my teammates and then planned to make a beeline for Emily. I knew I would have time between matches to listen to what happened and maybe be able to encourage her in some way.

But when I looked at our setup, everything was different. The chairs were packed in their respective bags, the blanket folded and put away, and Ayden's toys were in his hands. He stood next to Emily with an unhappy look covering his face. For some reason, I saw him first, but then my eyes climbed Emily's body and discovered a facial expression that stopped me dead in my tracks. She was staring directly at me. I never saw her look so angry, not even when she was upset at her ex the other night.

I felt my heartbeat pick up and imagined my face was turning red. As I approached Emily, the sand felt more like a field of deep mud. Everything seemed to move in slow motion, and then I heard four words that shot an arrow through my chest.

"We need to leave," she mumbled with a fiery pitch.

In unison with my heart, my mind began to race. Had someone died? Been in a car accident? Suffered a heart attack? What could it be? I wanted to ask, but at the same time I was almost afraid to; her anger seemed to be directed at me for some reason.

I stepped close and asked, "What happened?"

"I don't think you want to talk about it right here," she acknowledged, glancing at my teammates, who noticed something was wrong. Word seemed to spread from one to the next like a virus. By the time I asked Emily if we could walk to a more private area, the entire team was trying not to stare, if you know what I mean. My lips began to shiver. I suddenly felt like a kid in an elementary school classroom who got caught doing something wrong and was asked to come to the front.

Emily made Ayden sit on a wall near the outdoor showers and asked me to walk far enough away that we were out of reach of his little ears. That's when she asked me a question that sent a lightning bolt through my body. I wasn't sure why it shocked me as much as it did, maybe because she demanded an answer as if she already knew the outcome. I realized I was on the spot and could do nothing except tell the truth.

With glowing eyes and flaring nostrils, she waited for me to respond to her question, which felt more like an accusation: "Did you sleep with Mindy?" she interrogated. "Why didn't you tell me you had sex with Mindy?" she added.

This wasn't good. Not at all. What had she heard? Why did I feel as if I'd already been proven guilty in the court of Emily?

"No," I answered hastily. It was as simple as that. I thought.

Her hands darted to her hips, and she planted her right foot on the ground, reminding me of a raging bull ready to charge at the slightest movement. "I'm going to ask you one more time, and that's it. This is your chance to look me in the eyes and be totally honest with me. "Did you?" she asked again, this time being more specific, "have sex with Mindy the night before you told me you were not going to see her anymore and that you wanted to be with me?"

"No," I promised, knowing I hadn't had sex with Mindy.

Having sex is like being pregnant. Pardon the pun. Either you are pregnant, or you are not. You can't be partially pregnant. In the same manner, you either have sex with a person, or you don't. I would have remembered having sex with Mindy. Of course I didn't say it that way; if I had, I could have guaranteed it would have come out the wrong way. *What do you mean you would have remembered? Was it that good?* I could hear Emily saying just before slapping me in front of all my teammates who still had eyes on us.

I could feel the temperature of my body rising, and I felt like giving off a little steam of my own. Why didn't Emily believe me? I had been transparent with her. I told her everything she needed to know about Mindy. "No," I replied again, this time more sternly while staring intently into her eyes. I hoped she would see the truth in tune with the spoken answer I gave for the second time.

"You're a jerk," she claimed. "Why can't you just be a man and admit it?" she quizzed but didn't allow me to respond. "I want you to take Ayden and me home right now. I don't care about this stupid volleyball tournament. I don't care about anything except getting home and being as far away from you as possible."

I blew out a sigh of frustration. "Emily—"

She grabbed my arm and squeezed tightly. "You don't understand, Luke." *Don't understand what?* I wanted to know. "You can get your bag and we can leave. Or else I'll find another way home."

I could tell she meant that with all of her being. As for me, I wanted to know exactly what was going through her mind. Why was she so convinced I had sex with Mindy? She wouldn't let me ask; she wouldn't let me get a word in. The last thing I wanted was to start a big fight in the middle of hundreds of people already whispering about us like we were a nighttime television drama.

"Give me a minute to gather my things and tell my teammates I have to go," I uttered disgustedly and nearly in tears.

I didn't want to turn around. I didn't want to face anyone right now. I wanted to settle this. But I knew I had to leave. It was the right thing to do. We could discuss this issue in the car. Ayden would probably fall asleep fifteen minutes after we started driving, giving Emily and me a chance to talk.

As I gathered my stuff and politely requested to be replaced, not one soul asked why I was leaving, and I didn't offer a reason. We always brought a few extra players to these tournaments so everyone could have a break here and there and just in case someone got injured or had to leave abruptly like this. It happened in the past, but it was never me. No one else, however, had been demanded by their girlfriend or wife to leave during the tournament, in the middle of a match, nonetheless. I wanted to ask Emily if I could finish the match, but I knew she was serious when she spoke the words "right now." By the time the last set ended, I knew she would be on the highway hitchhiking.

Feeling like a scumbag for reasons I didn't quite understand, I walked the plank toward a sea of eyes that still tried not to stare. Apparently they even held off the next match for me. I was mad, very mad.

When we reached the car, Emily dashed my hopes even further as she closed the door after buckling Ayden. We stood as close as we had earlier. "Not one word. I don't want to hear you say a single thing, and I'm not going to either. I am so sick and tired of excuses. I put up with it for too long in my marriage. I won't start a relationship built on a lie."

I watched her turn away swiftly and stared at her as she circled my Range Rover. She didn't look at me, not even a quick glance. I got in the vehicle then cranked the ignition, and Emily and I didn't speak one word to each other from Myrtle Beach to Morehead City. The only things that were said were said to Ayden, the first of which was, "Ayden, we're going to play the quiet game all the way home," Emily explained, meaning it. He didn't ask why or argue. Even at seven, he could tell something was terribly awry, and if he wanted to know, I guess he knew not to ask.

As the miles passed, I glanced in the mirror, expecting to find him asleep eventually and planning to break Emily's protocol once Ayden's ears were no longer a barrier. However, he played games on his tablet for three hours straight.

18

With my phone beside the pillow and tears in my eyes, I sprawled across my bed praying for Emily to call. Hoping for an opportunity to explain whatever misinformation she had been fed. It was midnight now, and my screen showed five missed calls—all from teammates. Three left a voicemail, but I wasn't in an emotional state to return the messages, not tonight. I was embarrassed and upset.

I dropped off Emily and Ayden at her place at six o'clock. She slammed the door, and I couldn't help but wonder if it would ever open for me again. "Don't call," she insisted. Between then and now I began to dial her number several times, but something kept telling me it would only make things worse. She'd made up her mind, and my only chance was time. In time she would calm down and maybe then she would allow me to talk to her. That is what I would advise a client to do. Wait. Let the other person settle down. There are verses in the Bible about patience and giving our anxiety to God, but I didn't feel like opening the book right now even though I knew I should.

What made me the most upset was her not believing the truth. Mindy and I had not had sex. We kissed, but that was all. Nothing more. So why was Emily so sure we'd been intimate? That is what I ached to figure out.

As the sky darkened outside, I replayed every moment Mindy and I spent together. It all started with the stupid blind date. I wished I never agreed to it. But that didn't matter now. I couldn't go back and change things. What had been done was in the past.

I recalled that we went out to eat and then walked around downtown. I took Mindy home afterward and things heated up in the car as we said goodnight. What began with a simple kiss led to her front door but that was where it stopped. I said "No," to her invitation to go inside. I probably could have had sex with her then, I realized again, but I didn't, which made me even more upset now. It wasn't just that I hadn't had intercourse with Mindy; I likely had the opportunity and refrained. Had I done that for Emily? No, I reminded myself. I made the decision for myself, and in the end I liked to think that it meant the same thing. I had not been intimate with Mindy. The only other time I saw Mindy was the night I went to her apartment to let her know I was interested in someone else. *The night Emily referred to earlier at the volleyball tournament*, I suddenly recollected. I went in, Mindy fixed us hot chocolate, and then . . . *Oh my.*

All of a sudden this all made sense, and I couldn't believe I hadn't thought it through before now. Emily's coworker, who apparently lived in Mindy's apartment complex, had to be the connection. She was the upstairs neighbor. *Oh my* . . . The neighbor who *heard* Mindy and I having sex, not literally, of course. However, if I had been in the apartment above where Mindy and I jumped up and down on the mattress, released sensual noises, and called out each other's names in groans of pleasure, it would take more than O.J. Simpson's lawyer to convince me otherwise.

My mind began to race. *How can I explain this to Emily? I can call her and tell her the truth, the whole story. I can admit to pretending to have sex with Mindy.*

Immediately, I snatched up my phone. After clicking on the

recent calls list while breathing heavily, I found Emily's name near the top. I stretched my pointer finger toward the call button, but then reality struck me hard. This wouldn't work. The story would sound like a ridiculous cover-up I concocted over the past six hours. I was screwed. There was no way out of this one. If I had thought of all this the moment Emily accused me, maybe then my true story would have sounded plausible although still unrealistic, I'm sure.

The only thing that could get a person out of a hole like this was a mountain's worth of trust. Trust that Emily didn't have in me, especially since I hadn't been totally upfront with her about Mindy in the first place. There was no way she would believe the truth now. If I were in her shoes, I doubt I would either. Who would? You would have to be a complete idiot to believe my story. It had *B.S.* written all over it. I'm sure plenty of guilty people would pay me for a tale as good as the one I could share about Mindy and me pretending to have sex. They would love to use it to convince their significant other that they hadn't cheated. *No, honey, we were just pretending to have sex to get back at the neighbors.* That would go over well.

I grabbed the phone again. What could it hurt? All she could do was not believe me, right? Heck, she already didn't believe me. I touched her name, and the call symbol popped up. I stared at it momentarily. *It's the truth*, I kept telling myself.

A moment later my phone hit the floor with a loud crash, and as soon as it did, I couldn't help but wonder if I broke it. Technically it didn't slip out of my hand; I purposely threw it across the room without intending to throw it so hard that it struck the wall. My anger got the best of me.

Now, I couldn't call Emily and there was no need to hope she would call me. She wouldn't, and even if she did, my story would still be the same. It would be unbelievable. Unless . . .

What if I convinced Mindy to tell Emily? Surely she would

believe her. What reason would Mindy have to lie? Actually, she would have a reason to lie in the other direction to get back at me for choosing Emily. But if she didn't, if she chose the path of truth, Emily would have to believe her, right? It was worth a shot; my only hope, I convinced myself. I wanted to be with Emily. I wanted to be a father figure to Ayden. I needed them in my life. I wanted them in my life. I had no other option.

I hurried out of bed in my boxers and collected my broken phone. I wouldn't be calling anyone; my device confirmed that when I pressed the power button several times. Not Mindy. Not Emily. Not until I went to the mobile phone store tomorrow and paid a small fortune for a replacement. Of course I didn't have insurance on this one, now completely shattered. The mere sight of it caused me to want to break something else: the lamp illuminating my bedroom, the volleyball trophies on my dresser, my knuckles against the wall.

I slipped on a pair of green mesh shorts, the ones on top in my drawer, and grabbed the first t-shirt I could put my hands on. Then, I snatched my keys off the nightstand where I flung them before diving face-first into my bed upon arriving home.

This was it. This was my plan. I was going to Mindy's. I was going to straighten this out. All of it. Tonight. Right now.

I cranked my vehicle's ignition and put the gear shift in reverse. By the time I reached the end of the driveway, I wised up. This was a stupid idea. Right where I punched the brake, only a few feet from the asphalt, I turned off the engine and let my head collapse onto the steering wheel. If I went to Mindy's, I would only dig a deeper hole. It would be my luck that Emily's coworker would be awake, probably in the middle of wild sex with her husband, and she would call Emily immediately. *Guess where Luke has run to?*

I was back to the same conclusion: I was screwed.

I knew tonight I wouldn't be singing in the shower or anywhere else. Instead, I played the saddest country music songs I could find until I dozed off in the front seat of my Range Rover surrounded by pitch black and the sounds of bullfrogs in the ditches. I didn't have the energy to walk back inside, nor did I have the willpower to drive my car off a cliff. One of the songs mentioned doing just that. Another one was about living the rest of your life with a dog, but I didn't have a pooch. Maybe I could get one. An old mutt that I could name Lassie II. My mind raced in circles, yet a resolution never came.

I went to church the following morning even though I didn't want to be there. I slipped in late to avoid talking to anyone before the service. Mom and Dad sat near the front as usual, and I noticed Mom scanning the sanctuary for me. Ben and Colleen were a half dozen rows behind my parents, and I was in the back near some teenagers. Like I did when I was their age, they were sitting in the last row chewing gum and chatting. They had no idea what they were missing. But who was I to think that? I struggled to listen to the preacher's message too. My mind was elsewhere, and I hadn't felt like singing during worship.

When the pastor began the final prayer, I quietly slipped out of my seat at the end of the row and cautiously opened the door that led out of the worship center trying my best not to disturb anyone. If somehow yesterday hadn't happened, Emily would have been here with me this morning. Like last Sunday, we probably would have sat with Ben and Colleen and gone out to eat after the service. Instead, I was going home alone. Everyone would try to call me, but I wasn't planning to answer. Not just because I didn't want to talk, but like an idiot I broke my cell phone. I didn't feel like replacing it today and wasn't even sure if the store opened on Sundays.

I knew I should get over myself and spend time with my family. They would be good company and help keep my mind off this situation with Emily as much as humanly possible. In the past, they had been there for me after breakups, and I knew they would be here for me now if I would allow them. Maybe tomorrow, I told myself, I will tell them what happened.

I held the door handle until the heavy door closed all the way shut. Thirty minutes later, I was home in more comfortable clothing sitting on the couch and watching television. The first thing I did after putting my keys down and changing clothes was grab a bowl and a spoon from the kitchen cabinet. I dropped in four scoops of chocolate ice cream, wiped the carton's condensation from my hands onto my shorts, and turned on the TV for some baseball.

This was more of an appetizer than lunch I decided. I didn't feel like cooking, and I drove home aimlessly, not even thinking of grabbing fast food. Maybe I'd run out later whenever I felt hungry, I considered. I flipped back and forth between random games because the Braves weren't playing yet. Ordinarily, Ben and I, and probably Dad, would be watching baseball together on a day like today. They probably even tried to call a few times to see if we were all getting together.

Watching the games helped get me through the afternoon, but then it seemed there was nothing to do except think about Emily. I wondered what she was doing. Had she gone to her regular church this morning? What did Ayden and she do for lunch? Did they order delivery from Bella Pizza & Subs like I had? Hopefully, they had more of an appetite than I did. I only ate one slice compared to my usual two or three.

The clock on the wall told me the time was precisely seven when my doorbell rang. I jumped up hoping to find Emily standing on my front porch. Why do people in shoes like mine often set themselves up to be let down? It wasn't Emily, but I was surprised.

Mom, Ben, and Colleen stood there with all kinds of desserts in their hands. I reached for the pan of brownies in my mother's hand and sniffed in the aroma as I welcomed them into my house.

"What are y'all doing here?" I asked, and at the same time I remembered it was Sunday night—our traditional family game night. In the midst of everything that happened this weekend, I forgot all about it. This week was Ben's and Colleen's turn to host game night. So why were they at my house?

"When you didn't show up at Ben's and Colleen's, we got concerned," Mom confirmed.

Ben took a turn. "We've all been calling you all day."

"We were worried," Colleen shared. "You weren't at church; you haven't returned our calls—"

I guess none of them noticed me in the back row.

"Is everything okay?" Mom asked.

The concern written on their faces nearly brought tears to my eyes. "I'm fine," I fibbed. "I had some things to take care of today."

"Is it okay if we have game night here?" Ben asked. Colleen already headed for the kitchen where I assumed she planned to find a spot for what looked like a plate of cookies.

"Sure," I agreed. I would have said no to almost anyone who showed up at my door tonight uninvited but not my family. Sure, I avoided them at church this morning, but there was no way I could turn them away when they were standing on my porch. "Where's Dad?" I probed.

"Where do you think?" Mom responded by asking the same question with her facial expression.

"In his recliner watching the news?"

Mom and Ben nodded their heads in the same direction.

Colleen opened the game box in the kitchen and scattered the Scrabble tiles on the table. They danced across the wooden tabletop, clattering like little pieces of wood chips. We each picked out seven letters and let Mom have the first turn. As usual she took her time. She rested her elbows on the table and held her chin in her palms, analyzing. Ben grew impatient and began to give her a hard time; Colleen told him to leave her alone; and I sat back quietly and appreciated the moment as much as possible.

Last week game night took place at my parents' house, and they invited Emily to join us. Surprisingly, Dad also sat at the kitchen table with us, filling up every chair, although he didn't play. I think he graced us with his presence because Emily was there, and once the two of them started talking about the Bible, his eyes lit up. I never knew someone who could speak longer and get more excited about God's Word than my father. He would discuss it with anyone: a neighbor, a friend, a stranger, probably even a dog or a cat or a tree.

I remember Emily asking him if he thought a person could lose their salvation—a controversial question even amongst the Christian church. Dad didn't hesitate. "Did you do anything to earn it?" he asked.

Emily pondered. "No."

Nonchalantly, Dad replied, "If you didn't do anything to earn your salvation, what makes you think you can do something to lose it?" She commented, "But I had to ask for it through faith and believe in Jesus, the cross, and the resurrection . . . what if I quit believing and I asked for God to take it away?"

Dad grinned. He didn't have a degree in theology but always seemed to have the best answers to questions like this. "Read Romans 6:23 and Romans 11:29. These passages tell us that salvation is a gift from God and that His gifts are irrevocable. This message is woven throughout scripture. There is no one or nothing that can take away your salvation, not even you, and more importantly, God won't."

Profoundly said, I thought to myself. Emily agreed out loud.

This was the first day in quite some time that I hadn't bothered opening my windows, and as we sat at my kitchen table, I realized I missed the sound of the ocean. I tugged at the sliding glass door, and immediately we felt the breeze float in through the screen.

Mom finally wrote a five-letter word and then came the question I dreaded: "Where's Emily?"

Ben and Colleen didn't seem too curious, but I knew that was an act. Thinking I missed church was one thing, but when I didn't show up tonight at their house, I was sure that raised a major red flag. I didn't want to go into details, especially about the sex part, at least not with my mom present.

"Emily is upset with me," I answered honestly.

"Why?" Colleen inquired. "If you don't mind me asking?"

"She thinks I did something I didn't do, but I can't prove to her that I didn't. It's a big mess."

"Have y'all talked about it?" Mom asked.

"A little but Emily doesn't want to hear my perspective, at least not right now."

"I'm sorry," Mom replied. "Is there anything I can do to help?"

I forced a smile, genuine in my heart but not on my face. "I'll be fine."

Ben didn't ask any questions or respond to anything anyone said. I knew he realized I was taking it hard, and I'm sure Mom and Colleen did as well. It was obvious. My house was messy; my clothes didn't match; and I hadn't flashed a natural smile since their arrival.

"How's Dad?" I changed the subject attempting to occupy my mind with something other than my current dilemma. It bombarded my thoughts all night last night, which was why I was already sleepy, although it wasn't even eight o'clock yet. Normally I wouldn't go to bed until ten or eleven, but tonight I figured I would knock off as soon as everyone left.

"He was acting kind of strange today," Mom announced.

"What do you mean?" I probed. "Was he not feeling well?" Lately, I worried about him constantly.

"Not that kind of strange," Mom confirmed, and I felt a sigh of relief. "All day he has been really sweet and affectionate. He made breakfast this morning." In all the years I lived at home with my parents, I remember my dad making breakfast for my mom once, which was on their twentieth wedding anniversary. I should say *trying to make* instead of *making*. He burnt the pancakes and spilled milk all over the kitchen floor. It was hilarious. Ben and I laughed so hard that we almost passed out. Mom ended up cooking eggs and grits that morning because there was no more milk for pancakes. "He took me out to lunch after church." Mom paused for a moment, realizing she forgot something. "By the way, he said he missed seeing you at church today and having you eat with us afterward. We went to Cox's, your dad's favorite. He wanted you to go and even tried calling you although you know he hates talking on cell phones." It took years for Ben and me to convince Mom to get a mobile phone. Dad hated the thing though. He wouldn't use one unless in dire need. I furrowed my brow, surprised that he tried to call me. "He left you a nice, long message," she informed me. I found myself wishing I could hear his message right away. She finished with, "He hugged and kissed me a lot today. It was nice," she said with a big grin. It always made me happy to see my mother cheerful. "Maybe he's turning a new leaf."

"Maybe he wants something," Ben chimed.

"You've got him confused with yourself," Colleen jabbed.

We all laughed, knowing it was true.

Whenever my turn came around, I wrote the quickest word I could conjure up. My intentions weren't to hurry my family out; I simply didn't want to think. In all honesty I was tired and hoping to sleep better tonight. Even though I hadn't eaten much today, the desserts seemed to go down much smoother than normal food. I warmed up the cookies and a brownie to make them softer.

Around nine-thirty, I flipped on the porch light and waved bye to my family a couple of minutes later. When I pushed the door shut, the house instantly became lonelier and part of me wished they all stayed for a sleepover. When I was thirteen and my first girlfriend broke up with me, my big brother stayed up with me into the wee hours of the morning, listening to me cry and complain. He would have done it tonight if I asked, but I put on my adult mask and chose to handle this by myself.

I sure missed Emily. It had only been one day since I last saw her, but it felt much longer. I knew it would get better eventually, but the guilt emotion crawled all over me right now. Tomorrow it might be anger or sadness. Who knows, I thought to myself as I opened my bedroom windows to let the ocean air in and then pulled back the sheets on the bed and fluffed my pillow.

I imagined that tomorrow morning I would go to work and my clients would notice a drastic personality shift. I would attempt to hide my feelings, but concealing raw emotions is like trying to shelter the entire beach from the sun with a single umbrella. It's not that I cared what my clients thought; I didn't mind them knowing I was hurting or upset and simultaneously furious with what happened this weekend. I just didn't want to have to deal with it. I didn't want to talk about it or be asked questions. That sounds kind of backward since my work requires me to be there for people in similar situations. The difference is they come because they want someone to talk to. The only person I wanted to talk to tonight other than Emily was the Man upstairs.

I fell to my knees and made sure to tell God everything that was on my mind even though He already knew. I explained how much I wanted to be with Emily. How much I missed her. And how much I missed Ayden. I reminded Him over and over that my heart hurt, and I even screamed at Him a few times. Not loud enough for Dr. Nesbitt to come knocking on my door, but the walls echoed my voice a couple of times. I told Him it wasn't fair, and I heard the words I'd spoken so many times: *life isn't always fair.* I knew that, of course, but it didn't make my pain any less real or my face drier. God promptly answered my last request: *please help me fall asleep quickly so my mind can rest.* I rolled over, and the last numbers I remember seeing on the clock told me it was ten.

19

I was in the midst of what felt like a deep sleep when a loud, pounding sound suddenly startled me awake. Opening my eyes, I questioned whether the noise was in a dream or reality. A moment later, the answer came. It sounded like someone was trying to beat down my front door. My heart began racing and I jumped out of bed faster than I ever remember moving.

What was happening?

Before leaving my bedroom, I grabbed my pistol from the fingerprint lock box in my top dresser drawer but prayed I wouldn't have to use it. I had no idea who or what I would find as I hurried down the hallway to my living room. My initial thought was that someone was trying to break into the house.

I counseled people who shot intruders, and I felt compassion for their posttraumatic stress. They did what was required to protect their lives and sometimes their family, but nightmares haunted many afterward. Some became afraid of things they never feared before, such as the dark, unexpected noises, especially at night, and continuous worry that someone else would break in. Others feared retaliation from the intruder's friends or family members; criminals typically run in dangerous circles.

The number of lives saved by personal protection is beyond

staggering, a fact I didn't know until I researched it thoroughly. I now understood why people slept with a gun nearby. For safety reasons, I always encouraged everyone who did to make sure the firearm was locked up securely but with a method of quick access for the responsible party.

As I entered the living room, the beating stopped. I tiptoed cautiously toward the door I locked earlier. When I reached for the light switch that controlled the outdoor bulb, the pounding started again and caused me to jump back a step or two. I gripped the pistol and pointed it toward the floor in the direction of the disturbance.

I could feel my heart speeding up with every knock. One. Two. Three. Four. Five more bangs—loud and consistent. Somebody either wanted in or wanted me awake. The thought of calling 911 popped into my mind but a split second later, I remembered my cell phone was broken. At that moment, I realized if the person on the other side of my door wanted to rob me, the police wouldn't make it here in time to help. All I could do was wait inside and defend myself to the best of my ability.

I crept around the couch and slowly reached for the curtains carefully pinching the edge of the fabric with my thumb and pointer finger. I pulled it back ever so slowly, hoping whoever was out there wouldn't notice the movement. Then I tilted my head and squinted.

Through the tiny opening I created, I could see the silhouette of a figure, but I couldn't make out much. It appeared to be a man. Tall. Average build. I wanted to get closer, but my hand and every other part of my body were trembling nervously. I began to look for the person's hands, wanting to know if he had anything in them. A gun. A bat. A knife.

It was too dark to tell.

My brain began to rummage through a list of people who might wish to harm me. For some reason, Emily's ex-husband came to mind. He was the jealous ex who I warned so many of my clients about. It was evident from some of the conversations I had with Emily that he still wanted to control her life. Maybe he was here to try to scare me off. Thinking of clients, I remembered they didn't always walk away happy in my line of work. Even though I hadn't been practicing all that long, I already had a couple of death threats. What's to say this wasn't one of those folks hoping to carry out a promise?

The beating started again. Whoever it was, they were persistent. My right hand gripped the pistol; my finger neared the trigger; and I released the safety. Finally, I grew the nerve to flip on the porch light. I could reach it from my current position, still able to peek out the window. I stretched my arm upward trying not to make any noise whatsoever.

When the porch area illuminated, I watched the figure back up, startled by the light. I thought he might run, but he didn't. Then, for the first time, I heard him talk.

"Luke," he barked.

Recognizing the voice, my heart leaped out of my chest. Why was he here? Beating on my door at . . . I was pretty sure I remembered the clock next to my bed showing 10:29 pm when I was jolted awake.

I slid the pistol into my pocket and reached for the knob, frightened at what he would say when I opened the door.

I immediately noticed his eyes filled with tears. His car was parked crookedly at the driveway's edge as if he slammed on brakes there. The driver's side door remained open, and there was fear written on his face and worry in his words. "It's Dad," Ben cried. "He had a heart attack."

20

The ride to Carteret General Hospital seemed to take ages even though our vehicle was one of only a few on the desolate roads. Ben pushed the pedal nearly to the floor. Thank God we didn't have to pause for any stop signs or stoplights. As Ben drove, he explained that Mom found Dad lying on the living room floor just after he and Colleen dropped her off at home. Within a few minutes of them pulling out of her driveway, she called Ben, short of breath and barely able to speak, and told him Dad wasn't breathing. No one knew how long he had been unconscious. She hadn't been able to pull herself together enough to call the paramedics, so Ben called as they sped back to her house.

As I watched the blur of buildings outside the passenger window, I wondered if this was it? Had I seen my dad alive for the final time? A single tear ran down my cheek. I couldn't even remember the last words I said to him or that he spoke to me. Ben was crying too. He performed CPR on Dad, but it hadn't worked. He said he went through the motions just like they practiced in a recent class he and Colleen attended, but he couldn't elicit any response. He told me how Dad was just lying there, motionless. His skin was tinted blue, and his eyes weren't visible.

As Ben continued driving, I prayed. I asked him questions to which he didn't know the answers, like "Has the medical staff said anything about Dad's condition?" Colleen drove Mom in one of my parents' vehicles, and they followed the ambulance to the hospital. Since Ben couldn't reach me on the phone, he came straight to my house. Now I was even angrier with myself for breaking my device last night.

My dad turned sixty-nine on his last birthday, and I couldn't imagine him not being with us for his seventieth this November. Sure, he had some health issues, but this wasn't supposed to happen. I wanted to be at the hospital *now*; I wanted to hold my mom. I knew she was crying and frightened. I couldn't do anything for Dad right now; I realized that. He was in the hands of the medical professionals who were in God's hands. But I could be there for Mom. I reminded myself that I could have already been there if I hadn't thrown my dumb phone against that dumb wall.

Why had I done that? And why had I not talked to Dad at church this morning? More buildings: Restaurants, shops, office spaces. This ride never seemed so long on a normal day, even at regular speed. I kept thinking about how I could have spent one more day with my dad if I hadn't been so selfish. *Stupid. Stupid. Stupid. Calm down*, I told myself; *he's going to be okay. He has to be.*

When we reached the hospital, I ran through the parking lot and into the emergency room. I found Mom and Colleen sitting in the corner where the floor filled with tears. I didn't know yet if Ben scurried in behind me; I hadn't looked back since I opened the car door. I didn't even know if I shut the door, but things like that didn't seem to matter right now. What was important were people.

Mom glanced up but didn't stand. Her movements reminded me of a sloth. Right in front of her chair, I dropped to my knees like I did so many times to dig a volleyball nearing the sand. I embraced my mother tightly and subconsciously expected her to squeeze me back. But she didn't. She couldn't, I soon discovered. Her body felt limp, and I suddenly realized this situation was so overwhelming to her that she couldn't even wrap her arms around me. She didn't have the strength. Out of the corner of my eye, I could see her arms dangling loosely at her side.

The floor beneath my knees was cold and hard. Still, I remained in that position for what felt like an hour, and it reminded me of the many times I prayed at my bedside. I hadn't noticed if there were other people in the blue, padded chairs scattered throughout the large room on the back right corner of the tan and white brick hospital. I didn't care. Nor did I care that I was crying in public or wearing ragged clothes. My dad was somewhere in the hospital, maybe alive, maybe—dead, I realized.

I didn't want to consider that word, but it kept seeping into my thoughts. I wanted to ask for the latest news, but part of me didn't want to know. I feared the worst. I wondered where Dad was now. What were they doing to him?

"We are going to have to perform open heart surgery on your husband," a tall man wearing a green lab coat with the name Dr. Bobbett stitched on the chest pocket said to my mother. She heard him but didn't react or utter a word in response. Didn't even look at him or acknowledge his presence.

Our family had been moved to a room adjacent to the ER waiting area. We were alone with six empty chairs and four taken chairs. We knew family and friends would arrive soon, but it was just us for now.

Ben asked the question bubbling in each of our minds. "Is he going to make it?"

Holding Mom in one arm, I watched the physician closely, noticing immediately how he didn't want to speculate.

"Your dad is in great hands—"

We waited for the *but* . . .

"It's just too early to tell." Dr. Bobbett paused. It was apparent he had this conversation many times. "He went a long period without oxygen. That's what concerns me most at the moment, but let's focus on what we can do right now: repair his heart."

The doctor spent as much time with us as needed, and I was refreshed that he didn't talk above our heads. He answered every question honestly and showed concern for my dad. That meant a lot, and so did the fact that he made eye contact with every person in the room. He didn't glance off to avoid our pain or look at his watch to see how long we'd been talking.

"We are going to wheel him to surgery," he informed us, "and you are all welcomed to walk with him."

We did. I stood on the right side of my father's bed, and Ben stood on the left as the wheels turned, squeaking every ten feet or so. An oxygen mask was affixed to his mouth and nose, handling his breathing for him. My mother was holding Ben's hand, tightly I noticed, and we were all talking to Dad. "You're going to be okay," we said at different times. "We are right here," we informed him. "We love you," we reminded him. I think we spoke the same phrases over and over. His eyes were shut tight, and his forearm was cold. Still, he felt as strong as an ox. He'd always been strong, not lifting weights strong but hard-working strong. Anytime I grabbed a hold of him, I remember thinking that my dad was the epitome of a man; it didn't matter if I thought back to age six or twenty-six. Dad was a tough man. He could handle anything. Overcome any obstacle. Even this. Even a heart attack at sixty-nine years old.

We turned the final corner and reached the door where we would have to say goodbye, and that is when I felt God, really felt God, for the first time tonight. I watched my father's eyelids slide open for a fraction of a moment, just long enough for his eyes to roll toward the side of the bed where I was standing. In that instant, I felt life pause. Our eyes connected, and my heart leaped. In the quiet that took over all the noise of a busy hospital—pagers buzzing, doors opening and shutting, nurses moving frantically, intercoms sounding, elevators dinging—we shared a conversation. No words were spoken, but it was more real than any talk I ever had with my father or any other human being. Relief poured through my body, and it seemed God somehow miraculously intertwined my mind with my father's. *Everything is going to be okay*, I heard. The voice didn't sound like one coming from a burning bush or a bright figure standing in the heavens. Instead, it sounded like—my dad's.

21

It amazed me when family and friends began showing up at the surgery center waiting area so late at night, faces that simultaneously brought smiles to my lips and tears to my eyes. The first to arrive was my Aunt Suzie, my dad's sister. She and Dad were close, always had been. Growing up, they were so poor they didn't have toys to play with. They had each other, and that was it, and enough for that matter.

Aunt Suzie quickly found my mom and stayed by her side for quite a while. A few years back, she lost her husband. So I knew she would have a good idea of the many directions my mother's mind must be racing as we watched the clock tick as slowly as honey dripping from a spoon.

The next person through the door surprised me. I'm not sure how the pastor from our church found out so quickly—although Colleen and Ben had been sending texts and making calls—but for some reason, it relieved me to see that his hands were empty. He often admitted he didn't carry his Bible in the hospital. "The best-selling book in the whole world, by far, intimidates some people," I heard him claim before. "Especially the people who desperately need to hear the message I devoted my life to spreading." He didn't look like a preacher, but I think he memorized nearly the entire Bible. His easy mannerisms complimented his Hawaiian shirt and boater's shoes, and his presence had a way of setting people at ease. His arms around me brought comfort to a difficult situation, and I expressed to him how grateful I was that he came here so late at night.

I experienced another wave of comfort when Larry walked in the door. His disposition alone spoke volumes, and he seemed to have the right words to say to everyone. I realized I was again learning from my mentor, this time in the trenches, as he poured out his love. Larry spent time with each of us and gave Mom, Ben, Colleen, and Aunt Suzie his personal number and told them to call him anytime, day or night.

As others arrived, I couldn't stay still. I paced the room. I figured out it took twenty-one steps to get from one side to the other. In the corner, a small television anchored to the wall broadcasted the news, but no one seemed to be paying attention. I noticed some people looked in that direction at times, but I think mainly to avoid conversation. Friends and family continued to show up, and each initial encounter basically mirrored the one before. That individual would hug the first person they came to and then go down the line. Each person sitting would stand then sit, and fresh tears spilled with every new person.

I wished Dr. Bobbett had been the one to bring us the news regarding the outcome of Dad's surgery, but he wasn't. As the emergency room physician, he handed over the care of my father to Dr. Reynolds, who introduced himself to our family as the surgeon who spent the last few hours of his life performing the triple by-pass surgery on my dad. He was a slender gentleman with a scraggly white beard who spoke in a monotone voice.

"The procedure went as I anticipated," he relayed with confidence. His words gave us immediate hope. What surgeon in his right mind would anticipate an operation going poorly or ending tragically? "Mr. Bridges came through the surgery successfully. His heart is as strong as an ox." I choked up when he used the exact words that slid through my mind earlier in the evening.

What now? Everyone wanted to know. Those who were not immediate family stood or sat in the background as we huddled around Dr. Reynolds.

"Now it's a waiting game, unfortunately," he uttered almost remorsefully. The tension in the room seemed to heighten. "We have to monitor his brain function. Tomorrow morning a neurosurgeon will evaluate Mr. Bridges. We will know a lot more then. But for now, let's focus on the good news: a successful surgery."

Good news and bad news, I thought to myself. I wanted my father to be better now. I wanted to have a conversation with him. I wanted to watch him breathe on his own. But it wasn't going to happen, at least not tonight, and I had to come to grips with that realization. I would have to wait; we all would just like the surgeon stated.

22

Spending the night in the hospital isn't fun or comfortable. After the surgeon told us the news, I found the drink machine and slid cash from the wallet in my back pocket into the slot. Until that point adrenaline kept me alert. The first Pepsi I drank rejuvenated my body, keeping me wired for about an hour. I didn't want to fall asleep. At least not until my mother did. I made that pact with myself and asked Ben to wake me if he caught me dozing off. He nudged me several times when my head bobbed, and I did the same at his request. People who weren't immediate family headed home before the surgery ended to sleep in their own beds. Still I knew many would be back tomorrow which made me feel better.

Mom fell asleep on my shoulder just after I finished a second Pepsi. Even though my position in the padded chair made my back ache worse than it had since injuring it while playing high school baseball, I didn't move an inch until my eyes opened the following morning. I didn't want my mom to wake up until her internal alarm clock went off. She looked peaceful for the first time tonight, and I knew she needed the rest. Tomorrow we expected a long day.

When I woke up, I couldn't believe who was occupying the chair next to mine. I wondered how long she sat there. She hadn't tapped me on the shoulder to let me know she arrived or said a word; she just waited for me to wake up. For a moment, we didn't speak to each other. I held her gaze. The last time I saw her, she hadn't said much to me, and I guess we both knew that a certain distance grew between us. Nonetheless, I was relieved to see her— shocked but still relieved.

"How are you?" I finally uttered, glancing at the clock on the wall, reminding me I hadn't slept much. The little hand pointed toward the seven and the long one nearly due north; I figured I might have slept a few hours total, if that.

"How I am isn't important right now," she whispered, placing a gentle hand on my forearm. "How are you?" she wanted to know.

I appreciated the words she chose. "I'm here," I admitted, issuing the phrase with a double meaning that I think she understood.

As I asked my pastor last night, I wanted to know how she found out about my dad but figured I would save that question for later.

"Can I get you anything?" she asked.

She always had an accommodating and compassionate heart.

"More sleep," I mumbled sluggishly yet trying to muster up a laugh.

She smiled simply. "Anything else?"

I didn't answer the question. "Thanks for being here," I replied instead. "It means a lot."

I hadn't seen or talked to Kate Johnson in years. We had a fight and broke off our engagement, then life went on for both of us. I heard she moved to Portland not long after we broke up, but I had no idea what she did with her life or how she ended up back here. We hadn't kept in touch. I wondered if she was in town visiting her parents. As that thought crossed my mind, another interrupted. For the first time since opening my eyes, I realized the chair to my right was empty. Where was my mother?

In a near state of panic, my eyes darted around the room searching for my family. Kate noticed the sudden change in my behavior, and I watched her eyes follow mine to the older couple sitting across from us watching the news. I didn't know them, nor did I recognize the teenage girl sitting near the door and wearing the black hoodie and earpods mouthing the words to the song playing in her ears.

Kate realized what was happening. "Your mom is in the cafeteria." She hesitated knowing that was the information I needed. "Ben and Colleen are there with her. They were hungry."

I was too, I suddenly realized. Along with an empty Pepsi bottle at my feet, I noticed the remnants of the last thing I ate, a small bag of Doritos.

"I told them I would sit with you while they went down for breakfast."

"How long have they been gone?"

Kate studied the clock for a moment. "I think I arrived at six-thirty; they must have left about ten minutes later."

That meant Kate had been by my side for thirty minutes, waiting for me to wake up just watching me sleep. Impressive, I thought, after glancing at my shirt to make sure I hadn't drooled on my sleeve. Not that she hadn't witnessed that bad habit in the past.

"You weren't snoring either," she clarified.

She'd always been as sharp as a tack, which inevitably was one of the reasons we'd taken different roads. My life was here in Atlantic Beach with my family, and Kate had other dreams and ambitions. She wanted to move to a big city and practice law. I tried to convince her to live here and join one of the local firms, but it wasn't what she wanted in the end.

"Did anyone say anything about my dad?"

"There haven't been any specific updates regarding your father's condition," she informed me. "However, the neurosurgeon is supposed to be in around nine o'clock."

"I think I'm going to go find my family," I stated and stood as the words spilled out.

"Okay, I'll walk with you," she replied, as though there wasn't any other option.

I didn't mind. It was nice to have company as we trekked through what seemed like the barest hallways of any building I ever stepped foot in.

A few minutes later, we found Mom, Ben, Colleen, and Aunt Suzie sitting at a round table in the buzzing cafeteria. The food smelled surprisingly delicious. We zigzagged through the tables and chairs to join my family. I noticed none of their plates were empty, but all except Colleen had dropped a napkin on top, signaling they weren't eating anymore.

"Kate said the neurosurgeon isn't here yet," I stated.

Mom looked as beat as a rug slapped against the corner of a brick house. Ben and Colleen didn't look much better, and the bags around Aunt Suzie's eyes told me she slept about as well as the rest of us. Kate, it appeared, was the only one who had a good night's sleep, but I couldn't fault her for it.

Kate and I worked our way through the breakfast buffet line, and although everything smelled delectable, I didn't really want any of it. I finally picked out a biscuit and scrambled eggs then grabbed a carton of milk from the cooler near the register. Kate reached for an apple juice in the same cooler to go along with her bowl of oatmeal and fruit. The cashier rang up my food, and then I motioned for her to add Kate's.

"Luke, I can pay for my own."

"I'm sure you can," I acknowledged, "but the least I can do to share my appreciation for you showing up here this early in the morning is buy you breakfast." I had no idea how long she would stay or how long I would want her around.

Just after we sat down, Mom informed us that she wanted to return to the waiting room. She was tired of being around people she admitted. As if following an unwritten rule—for as many people as possible to stay with Mom at all times—Ben, Colleen, and Aunt Suzie accompanied her. It broke my heart to see my mother like that as though she could collapse onto the floor at any moment. I'd never seen her so weak and helpless.

"What are you doing these days?" I asked Kate, thus creating small talk to occupy my mind.

"I'm living in Denver," she shared.

"I thought you hated cold weather."

"They sell coats in Denver," she replied sarcastically but with a grin.

I was glad to see she still possessed a sense of humor. I thought momentarily about making a risky statement—one I definitely would have made when we were together—about us not having enough name brand stores in our area that carried nice coats, adding something about us having a few thrift stores instead. But I decided to let bygones be bygones.

"Are you a lawyer?"

"Yes, I am."

Her outfit, I realized for the first time this morning, played the part—black dress pants, high heels, and a black jacket with a button-up white shirt peeking out the top. Elegant would be and always had been an excellent word to describe Kate. She took terrific care of herself, and it pleased me to find out she practiced law in a big city and seemed happy.

"Are you in town for business or pleasure?" I asked.

"Both."

"Working remotely?"

Her answer surprised me. "Actually I have a case in Beaufort. I am licensed to practice law in three states," she enlightened me, "one of those being North Carolina."

"What case is worth coming to North Carolina for?" I wondered aloud.

She sighed. "My cousin got into trouble, and I am trying to help her out."

"Pro bono, huh?"

"Pro bono."

Kate quickly and lawyerly changed the subject from her case to my father. "What happened?" she asked. "I mean I know he had a heart attack, and Ben told me about the surgery, but how—." A woman I assumed was never at a loss for words in the courtroom suddenly began to choke up in the cafeteria. For the first time today, I felt the space between us implode allowing us to close the gap and fall into each other's arms as if that's where we were supposed to be.

Kate knew my dad well. She respected and loved him, and even though she hadn't been a part of my life or his in years, I could tell she was concerned and hurting in her own way. We both broke down in the midst of dozens of random strangers. None of them seemed to notice because most probably worked at the hospital and encountered similar scenarios daily while the others were likely dealing with something challenging as well.

We stayed physically connected for over a full minute. I felt her tears rolling down my neck soaking into the cotton inside my shirt. At that moment when the first tear touched my skin, I realized I wanted someone like Kate here with me and longed for that person to be by my side for all of life's unexpected moments.

23

When the clock struck eight, I remembered today was Monday, a regular workday, where five counseling sessions filled my calendar. "Oh, no," I uttered.

"What?" Kate asked, furrowing her brow.

We were walking side-by-side toward the CCU. I wasn't sure what the abbreviation stood for until I studied the sign outside the heavy, partially-glassed door where bold letters spelled out the words Critical Care Unit. I found out it meant my dad needed around-the-clock care. The first thought I had when realizing the state of being most people in the unit were in was that this was the hospital's version of death row. That thought scared me to death, no pun intended.

"In less than an hour, a couple will be standing at my office door expecting me to offer profound advice, but I will not be there."

"Would you like me to call your office and have your assistant reschedule your appointments?" Kate asked while reaching into the leather bag beneath her arm to pull out her phone for the first time since we'd been together.

"That's the thing, Kate, I don't have an assistant."

"Oh."

In the middle of the hallway, we stood in silence for a moment as I thought, and it looked like Kate was also thinking.

"Do you have the phone numbers of your patients?" she queried.

"Clients," I corrected.

"I'm sorry?" she questioned.

"Clients," I said again. "They are my clients not patients."

The correction didn't seem to faze Kate, but I suddenly felt silly for making a big deal out of semantics. "Do you have your clients' numbers? I can call them for you," she offered.

Now leaning against the cold, white brick wall, I ran my fingers through my hair. "My planner is at home and my client list is at the office. Both have client contact information." In frustration I slapped the wall hard enough to make a noise but not with adequate force to injure myself. Been there, done that, got the t-shirt. "I am going to have to go home."

"Luke, you are staying here with your mother," Kate demanded. "Give me your keys, and I'll go." Her eyes traveled up and down my body. "You need fresh clothes too."

I had no idea what Kate's plans had been when she got out of bed this morning. I hadn't even thought to inquire when I handed her the keys to my home and office and thanked her in advance for calling my clients. Suddenly, I felt selfish. I would have to make it up to her somehow. Kate's favor enabled me to spend time at the hospital with my mother who, at the moment, reminded me of a zombie. She hadn't moved an inch since I plopped down in the seat next to her and intertwined my arm with hers.

Our family was the only one in the waiting area which was much smaller than the surgery waiting center. I hadn't counted the seats, but it seemed about a third of the size at first glance. The same blue padded chairs lined the outer wall, and another group of seats facing ours formed a square in the center of the room. Small tables sat in the corners with a larger one in the middle; each table stocked with magazines and Kleenex boxes. Like the other waiting space, the corner featured a small television where the news played silently.

Aunt Suzie stepped out for a cigarette; Colleen was three seats down reading a tattered edition of Glamour; and Ben sat on Mom's other side resting his head against the wall. We had all been in to see Dad together for about fifteen minutes even though, technically, the hospital allowed only two people to visit at a time.

The nurse on duty was one of the friendliest people I ever met. Kevin was how he introduced himself, and he had been more than generous with his time by answering every question we fired his way. He explained that my father probably couldn't hear us but said only God and my dad knew that for sure. Kevin was honest which is what I liked most about him. He said Dad was in critical shape, reminding us he went a long time without oxygen, but he assured us that angels seemed to be frequent visitors of this hospital. I hoped they would bring the neurosurgeon with them because as I watched a tear fall from my mother's pale face, I didn't know if any of us could take one more minute of not knowing the answer to the big looming question: Did Dad have any brain function left?

My mind recalled a mental picture of Dad lying there with tubes and IVs surrounded by various machines. I was unable to erase the image nor quit thinking about what it meant. I had some knowledge of the function of the instruments attached to my father, but I hoped the nurses at the station in the middle of about ten patient rooms knew them inside and out. Kevin explained some of the devices to our family; however, my mind moved in so many directions I forgot everything he said.

When we were in there, my father didn't look like he was in any pain, which meant a lot. I wondered how much he suffered during the heart attack. Had he cried out for my mother? For God? For his children? Had he thought he was going to die? Had he died? Was he already in Heaven? Were we all here just waiting for the doctors to tell us that the signs of life we were witnessing were all brought about by life support?

When is the moment I wondered when a human's soul escapes his earthly body and reaches the afterlife? Around the times of actual death experiences, it seems most everyone hopes for Heaven although I have come to believe both places are as real as this earth is to us while living here. I find myself praying that God will give everyone grace, but that's out of my hands. I certainly don't want anyone to live in a place absent from God which seems to be the true reality of the dwelling some perceive as thermal. Does the soul float away when the heart stops beating? I considered the possibilities. When the brain stops functioning? When a person can no longer breathe on his own? I knew no one other than God had a definitive answer to any of these questions. If I asked a hundred doctors, they would all have an opinion; some might even categorize their own as truth. Others might be honest like Kevin.

He slipped into the waiting room and informed us that the neurosurgeon called and was en route to the hospital. I felt my heart leap. We were all anxious and afraid.

"Can I get you anything?" Ben asked Mom after Kevin disappeared through the door.

She shook her head but said nothing.

"Are you sure? I know you must be hungry."

Out of the plates on the cafeteria table this morning, Mom's was the one that looked like a bird had only taken a few pecks at it. I learned that Ben made it for her against her will and tried his best to get her to eat. Aunt Suzie told her it would help her feel better. Ultimately, Mom said she couldn't eat. She didn't have an appetite and was afraid she would throw it up.

"How about something to drink?" I asked.

Again she shook her head. At that same moment, two people I thought I might never see again suddenly appeared at the room's entrance. I looked twice to ensure a lack of sleep hadn't caused me to imagine things. Crazy things. These two people, here together; I had to be hallucinating, I concluded as my breathing sped up. The last thing I needed was a scene. I wouldn't put up with it if it happened. I would have security kick Emily and Mindy out if they said one negative word to each other, me, or anyone in my family while at this hospital.

They continued to stand in the doorway. I wanted to jump up and head things off, just in case something awkward might happen. At the same time, I didn't want to startle my mom. She didn't seem to notice Emily or Mindy. Of course, she hadn't met Mindy. I glanced at Ben then at Colleen. Colleen was engrossed in her magazine, and Ben just shrugged his shoulders.

"I'll be right back," I whispered to Mom.

When I got up, Colleen peeked her eyes over the top of the pages.

"Hey," I whispered, speaking to both Emily and Mindy with one word. I didn't want to play favorites. Each of them returned the formality, and as I neared them, I pointed toward the hallway.

There, I knew we could talk without everyone else overhearing our business. However, I wasn't sure what all that would entail. Obviously, the two of them weren't here to cause a scene even though that ridiculous thought initially popped into my mind. Neither seemed to have that sort of bone in their body. What I didn't know yet was if either of them knew who the person standing next to her was? Had they just happened to arrive at the hospital at the same time? Ride the same elevator up to the second floor maybe? Had they talked? Exchanged pleasantries?

I imagined Emily and Mindy standing next to one another at the visitor's desk downstairs, and one saying, "Hey, I'm here to see the Bridges family" and the other adding, "Me too." As we walked a few steps in silence, I realized that probably wouldn't have meant anything to them. Just because they were here to see someone from the same family didn't tell them they were the two women I entangled myself between like an idiot. Unless one asked, "How do you know the Bridges family?"

Well out of earshot, I had to ask the question when we stopped: "Have the two of you met?"

Emily glanced at Mindy, Mindy at Emily, then both at the same time back at me.

24

In the distance the clinking of high heels echoed through the hallway. As the sound grew louder and closer, I waited for Emily or Mindy to speak. The diversion, in a way, was appreciated. It gave me time to study their facial expressions.

"Yes," Mindy finally announced.

"We met this morning," Emily added.

The tension in my shoulders suddenly dropped to the ground. *God is in this hospital today*, I thought, knowing I needed to wipe the sweat from my brow. This news saved me from a very awkward introduction.

Or did it?

In black high heels, Kate appeared from around the corner just down the hallway, and I felt every drop of tension jump off the floor and back onto my shoulders. *God, come back*, I begged.

The clanking slowed when Kate spotted the three of us standing along a row of large glass windows, offering a picturesque view of Morehead City featuring the Bogue Sound in the background. The change of pace caused Emily and Mindy to look in her direction. I realized I hadn't told Kate anything about the current state of my affairs. Given her keen observation abilities, I was sure she noticed I wasn't wearing a wedding ring. I was also confident that, at this moment, she was wondering if one of the two women standing before me was my significant other in some form or fashion.

Feeling the cold glass against my back, I wondered if I could escape out the window and avoid one of the most awkward situations I'd been a part of in the history of my twenty-six years on this earth. Kate made it to where we stood. Now, three women I had been romantically involved with at one point in my life—some more so than others—made a semi-circle around me.

"Here are your keys," Kate offered, seeming as though the presence of the other two women didn't strike her as odd in any way. "And a change of clothes."

Emily furrowed her brow, and I couldn't help but notice how Mindy's eyes shot toward Emily—waiting for some sort of reaction I assumed.

I held up my hands. "Okay, this is the most awkward situation I've encountered in the history of my twenty-six years on this earth." I wasn't sure if the words were verbatim to the thought from moments ago, but they sounded like the best way to start this conversation. I had no idea what would come next.

Along with Emily, Kate furrowed her brow.

Mindy and Emily had apparently met, but now I needed to introduce Kate to them and them to Kate.

Or not. "I'm Kate," Kate offered. "A friend of Luke's from the past," she added. She reached her hand toward Emily first and then shook Mindy's. They returned the introduction without adding any titles to their names. As the three of them met, I couldn't help but notice that Kate checked both of their hands for an engagement ring.

Kate took a swig of the coffee steaming in her left hand. Mindy dug her hands into the pockets of a pair of tight jeans. Emily crossed her arms at her chest, covering the small window into the purple polo she wore. All three of these women were beautiful, each in her own way.

"Luke, when you said awkward," Emily announced, "I thought you were going to tell us that she," referring to Kate, "was your girlfriend."

Kate nearly choked on her coffee, and with the sudden movement, the cup danced in her hand causing a small brown splash on the tiled floor. Everyone seemed to notice, but no one seemed to care.

"That's funny," Kate responded. "I thought he was going to say the same about one of you."

I held my hands up again. "Okay, let me clear this up right now." I had to. It wasn't going anywhere good. I figured I would start with Kate. "Kate is my ex-fiancee." It seemed very strange to introduce her that way for the first time in my life. Nonetheless, I went on. "Mindy is a friend." I figured I would leave it at that. Emily already knew the rest of the story. However, she didn't believe I told her all of it, and I couldn't think of any reason why Kate would need to know anything further about Mindy. I took a quick breath. Last but not least. "And Emily is—" *What do I say*? I thought to myself. *God, are you back yet*? "Emily is a very important person in my life whom, until Saturday, I was dating."

That was a great starting point, I decided. It would probably take a few more minutes to clear things up, and we could all just get along. Maybe. Hopefully.

No one else got a chance to speak because Kevin called out my name when I finished. He was walking quickly. "Luke, the neurosurgeon is here, and he would like to speak to your family."

25

"**B**ased on the information I have gathered, I believe Mr. Bridges's brain has little or no function."

Those weren't the first words the neurosurgeon spoke when we met him in a room that now seemed to be collapsing on us, but they were the last I heard. He continued to rattle off more medical terminology as my mind drifted to the times I spent with my dad. Suddenly, childhood memories I hadn't thought of in years surfaced as if they happened yesterday. I vividly remembered my dad carrying me on his shoulders through a crowd at his company picnic. I was probably Ayden's age, and I thought it was so cool how I could see the tops of everyone's heads as my dad let me direct him to the Ferris wheel. If we needed to go right, I would pull his right ear; if we needed to go left, I would tug on that one. I thought that was hysterical. The wind blew fiercely off the sound, sweeping through the crowd and blowing our hair like a hair dryer. Mine was shaggy and all over the place, and I just had my picture taken with a clown whom my brother had been terrified to glance at.

My mind shifted gears; I remembered my dad helping me buy my first car. *Helping* isn't really the appropriate word since he paid for ninety percent of the vehicle. He did all the talking to the people in buttoned-up shirts and ties. I merely picked out which car I liked best and then watched him work his magic. I had never seen anyone talk down a salesman like my dad could. When we sat at the sales manager's desk, finalizing the deal, the price suddenly rose by one hundred dollars. *That's not much*, I recall thinking to myself as I watched my dad's face turn red. His hairstyle was still the same as at the company picnic. "You promised me the final price, including tax and tags, would be—." I'm still unsure why I did what I did next, a reflex, I guess; I kicked my dad's leg. Thankfully, ever since that day, Dad and I had laughed about me kicking him underneath the table. I wanted that car desperately and knew if the salesman said the wrong thing, we were walking out of the glass door behind us, and we weren't coming back. The kick had been hard enough to get his attention but not bruise-worthy. It turned out the salesman did say the wrong thing, and we did walk out that door even though he followed us all the way to my dad's car and ended up saying he would do the deal for three hundred dollars less. I learned an important lesson from my dad that day: Not that many salesmen are dishonest although I've since learned way too many are, but that a man's word is more valuable than three hundred dollars.

Sure, I was a man now and could take care of myself. I didn't need my dad to walk or talk for me anymore, but I still needed him in so many other ways. I needed his love, advice, and positive outlook on life. Those were the things I would miss the most if the neurosurgeon was right. Kevin told us already that if a person loses brain function, he lives the rest of his life in a vegetative state if the family chooses life support.

My family collectively walked out of the room with heads down and eyes leaking like broken faucets without a sink to catch our tears. How do you make a decision to pull the plug that will end your father's life? My mom made it clear that she wanted Ben and me to make the call if it came to this. She said she couldn't live with the not knowing part, wondering if she let the machines breathe for him for five more minutes maybe things would have turned around. Ben and I didn't want to decide, but we had to. Mom was between us now, and it took both of us to keep her off the floor. In a word, she was a wreck. In a sense, we all were. Even Colleen, who wasn't blood kin, took it as hard as the rest of us. Aunt Suzie was still in the waiting room. She hated doctors and said she would rather hear the news—good or bad—from us instead of someone she didn't know. People—doctors, nurses, patients, visitors—were all around but I can't remember one face from when we left Dad's room until the end of the hallway where we pushed a button on the wall to walk through two automatic doors. The CCU required a swipe card to enter or you pressed the intercom button to reach the nurse at the desk inside to let her know who you were there to visit. I'm unsure if she pressed the button to open the doors for us or if Ben or Colleen pressed it. Maybe it was Kevin; I finally noticed him walking with us.

When the door opened, I saw Emily, Mindy, and Kate standing in the same spot I left them. I noticed that their conversation abruptly stopped when they looked in our direction. To be honest, I forgot they were even out here. My mind became overwhelmed by anxiety as soon as we walked into the CCU. Then, when the neurosurgeon informed us of Dad's current state of mind, some other emotion took over. The one question I asked the doctor before we left the room still occupied my mind: "What if you are wrong?"

26

I could tell by the way the neurosurgeon's eyes squinted when I asked the question, as though he was thinking through them, that he believed himself to be a man who rarely made a mistake. I knew by the manner in which he presented himself to that point he would be tactful enough to dance around the answer that was obviously blaring in his mind as I would have if I was in his shoes. "It never hurts to get a second opinion," he offered graciously.

Surprising us all, my mother spoke up. "Yes, we want to do that." Ben and I agreed. In this situation, a second opinion couldn't hurt. Kevin and the neurosurgeon confirmed that Dad was in no pain; physical pain is the realm in which they spoke. The pain I was concerned with was beyond the physical body. What if my dad could hear every word being said in that room? What if he knew we were considering taking him off life support? Is that not pain? Emotional pain? That is my dilemma with doctors and scientists; far too many work only in the manmade world of the five senses. They say if something can't be tested by the five senses—touch, taste, smell, sound, sight—it can't exist. Where does that leave love and hope and faith and anger and pain and grief—emotions experienced by every member of my family in the past two days. Where does that leave God? It doesn't; it takes him out of the picture. The problem with that is a photographer can leave anything she wants out of her image, but that doesn't mean what she left out doesn't exist. She hid, neglected, or chose not to include it in her photograph.

No doctor, scientist, or photographer could take hope out of my life. I hoped my dad would wake up and walk out of this hospital one day soon. I hoped Emily, as I walked in her direction, would believe that every word I told her had been the absolute truth. That even though it might not be able to be tested by the five senses, it was indeed real. With Kate on her left and Mindy on her right, I reached my arms around Emily and told her that her being here meant the world to me. I hid my face in her neck and held on for dear life knowing that behind me—out of my sight but not out of my mind—my mother was doing the same thing on Ben's shoulder.

When Emily whispered into my ear, I cried even louder. "I am sorry I didn't believe you," she confessed. At that moment, somehow, I knew everything would be okay, just as the message in my dad's eyes had spoken. I knew that God was in this hospital today.

"Mindy told me exactly what happened between the two of you. She told me about you and her jumping on her bed like a couple of monkeys," Emily revealed. I was relieved to hear a snicker at the end of the sentence. "She said that occurred on the night you came over to tell her you wanted to be with me. She said that when you did, she was so jealous and wanted to rip my hair out." I furrowed my brow, wondering how Mindy hid her anger so well that night. "This morning, though, after we talked, she said she thinks I deserve you, but if I let you go one more time, she would be there to catch you when you fall." Emily paused for a moment. It was just the two of us now sitting on the floor in a desolate hallway near a utility elevator. Close enough that my family could find me if they needed to but far enough away for privacy.

In the twenty minutes we sat in this spot, only two people walked directly past us: A candy striper wheeled a cart loaded with food out of the elevator heading for patients' rooms, and a maintenance guy wearing the name Ed stitched on a pale brown shirt whistled while hurrying to the elevator.

"Luke, I promise I will trust you from now on," Emily affirmed. "I need you. First, for me, and second, for Ayden."

In that same conversation, I found out Kate had pretty much told Emily everything there was to know about the relationship between Kate and me. About how we met, fell in love, got engaged, and stayed together for far too long, each knowing we wanted different things out of life. I was surprised to hear Kate told her I was the greatest guy on planet Earth and that she would have given anything other than her career to spend the rest of her life with me. I wasn't sure whether to take that as a compliment or an insult; I found there is often a fine line between the two.

All in all, Emily spent about an hour talking to Kate and Mindy. I was shocked to see the three of them standing there when I walked out of the CCU with my family. When I headed to see the neurosurgeon and my dad, I was afraid they would talk enough to walk out together, but I guess I did the right thing in the end. I had been honest with each of them.

Prior to this conversation with Emily in the hallway, I said goodbye to Kate and Mindy. Maybe one day, I could repay each of them for the kind things they said about me. For now, I let my eyes close long enough to utter a silent prayer, thanking God that they all came to the hospital today to check on my loved ones and me.

When my eyes opened, I thought back to when my family and I huddled around my father in hope that he would once again become the dad I knew and loved but now feared I would not know again on this side of Heaven.

27

I wish I could say the second opinion turned out differently than the first. I prayed it would. However, when further tests came back, and another specialist interpreted the results, she confirmed my dad would never live life the way we hoped. If kept alive, he would be confined to a bed in a hospital, nursing home, or possibly at his own house, needing around-the-clock care. He would most likely never show any sign of life again. He would never talk to me, remember my name, or open his eyes to look at the blue eyes he passed down. He couldn't wrap his arms around me or tell me he loved me.

Even more heartbreaking, my mom would never again feel his lips press against hers as they said goodnight, not even one more time. She couldn't tell him to turn the television down so she could hear herself think. Her companion, her soul mate, her best friend had lost his life, and she let her two sons make a decision that no human being should ever have to make. But in life, sometimes we are forced to choose between two roads. Some prefer the path less traveled, and others opt for the seemingly easy road. We chose the path that led my dad straight to Heaven. However, something told me he was already there.

❧

I spoke at my dad's funeral. Through a flood of tears and a downpour of sweat hiding beneath an uncomfortable black suit coat, I told two hundred people what my dad meant to me: everything.

Honestly, I didn't know what I would do without my father. It showed as I stumbled over nearly every word I read from a white sheet of notebook paper, which was covered with more splotches than words by the time I finished speaking.

Ben spoke too. His fond memories brought smiles to my face and tears to my eyes, which reminded me of when rain clouds are pouring out, but somehow the sun is shining through.

One of Mom's friends sang "How Great Thou Art" and "I'll Fly Away," my dad's favorite songs. Mom cried the entire funeral and had to be physically supported throughout the ceremony. Tears were also plentiful in the audience, from the front rows to the back, where there was standing room only.

Once the pastor spoke the final prayer at the graveside service, I felt a slight sense of closure. I experienced something similar at the hospital when we walked out as a family just after Dad passed. I was beginning to learn firsthand one of the lessons I taught my clients: closure comes in layers.

Mom spent the next two weeks at Ben's house before returning to the home she and my father built together nearly thirty years ago. She would swing by *their* house occasionally during the day to take care of things like watering plants and checking the mail, but she never went alone. Ben or I would take her and help with whatever was needed. She hadn't driven since the morning Dad suffered the heart attack. He asked her to drive to church—a rare request—because he wasn't feeling quite himself. A red flag, maybe, but no one noticed.

Mom and I spent an entire day in my parents' closet sorting through Dad's wardrobe. She wanted to donate most of them to The Salvation Army, but first, she smelled each article of clothing one last time. I cried with her as I watched her hold every piece flush against her face, tears streaming onto the fabric and memories clouding the small space. Dad's clothes were on the left side of the walk-in closet and Mom's filled the right. In between on the carpeted floor there was just enough room for us to sit with our legs crisscrossed.

Below the hanging attire on a rack were shoes and above was a shelf for sweaters and jeans semi-neatly folded by my father the last time he helped with laundry. He always liked folding clothes; towels were his specialty. It made Mom anxious to watch as he stacked them as high as possible erecting a monument reminiscent of the Leaning Tower of Pisa. I think it was a random thing he did one time early in their marriage to be funny, and it made my mom laugh. As time passed, it irked her as well. Dad made a tradition out of one of those nagging things people complain to their friends about regarding their spouse. But I learned that when a widow comes home on a Friday afternoon to wash clothes and her husband is not there to build a tower, she thanks God for every stack he ever made and cries relentlessly wishing he were there to make just one more.

Ben, Colleen, Emily, and I almost skipped going to the first volleyball match after Dad passed, but Mom convinced us he'd want us to be out there playing doing what we loved. She came to watch, and although she rarely showed emotion, I noticed a smile on her face occasionally when I glanced over to check on her. I knew it was beneficial for Mom to be around people even if she wasn't talking much. I felt good inside when Ayden played in the sand near her feet. At seven he didn't wonder what he should or shouldn't say to someone who just lost their spouse, he just spoke to her like normal, and I think she talked to him more than everyone else combined during our Thursday night sets. We won the first week and lost the next but playing was therapeutic. I somewhat forgot what was happening off the court during that short time.

I hadn't taken it personally that Mom always left with Ben and Colleen and that she asked to stay with them instead of at my house. However, I would have loved to have her there, especially since I lived alone. It certainly would have made it easier for Emily and me to stay at our respective dwellings where, as a professional therapist, I would have suggested we each remain during such an emotional time early in a relationship.

However, during those first couple of weeks on the nights when Ayden went to his dad's house, Emily stayed at my place. Like my mom, I found it hard to be alone especially once darkness pushed the sun out of the sky. On the other nights, I would sleep over at Emily's apartment leaving early in the mornings before Ayden crawled out of bed in his Spiderman pajamas.

This routine continued even after the early stages of grief. We became comfortable together and enjoyed having each other close. However, there was a dance to it because we didn't want Ayden to see us sleeping together. Before my dad's heart attack, Emily and I agreed to try our best to wait until marriage to have sex. Even though we slept in the same bed every night, we had somehow been able to keep our clothes on, at least most of them. One night early on, certain articles started falling to the floor, and our hands and bodies discovered new places on each other's map, mainly south. Then a few more nights happened just like that. Somehow, though, one of us was able to draw the line each time, usually right before we made it to the land of no return.

I found it hard to get back into the swing of things at the office and to pinpoint my clients' challenges while personally experiencing the stages of grief I often discussed with many of them. Larry reached out a lot and encouraged me to have a session with him to talk about my dad, but I declined, preferring to chat on the phone for short amounts of time. For some reason, I found it easier to talk to Emily, maybe because she lost all three of her immediate family members when we were younger.

In the beginning as I sorted through life in my head, I questioned whether Emily returned to me based solely on the fact that my dad had suffered a heart attack. I felt I knew better but still couldn't shake the thought. Then as the weeks passed, I wondered if we were staying together because our new life became a coping mechanism for me. It was nice to have a beautiful woman to come home to, fall asleep next to, and wake up close to every morning. There is glue in repetition, and I couldn't help but let my mind travel that road too. What if she wouldn't always be by my side?

There were nights when I thanked God we were basically living together. Like the first time I experienced her having a migraine, and I was able to give support rather than be on the receiving end. On the way home from work, she started seeing splotches, and as soon as she walked in the front door, she asked if I would take care of Ayden. From her viewpoint the room spun in circles, and I literally had to help her walk as her feet fumbled to the bedroom. There, I watched her bury her head in a pillow.

I thought about taking Ayden out for dinner or to the town park but decided it would probably be best for us to remain home in case Emily needed me. I ordered a pizza from Bella's, and we played video games while we waited on the delivery driver.

When our meal arrived, I checked with Emily to see if she wanted to eat, but she said no. The only thing she wanted was a caffeinated beverage which I grabbed from the refrigerator while Ayden cuddled with her for a few moments. I could tell she appreciated him being by her side, but our presence kept her from the one thing she said would eventually help her migraine go away—sleep.

After dinner, I sat with Ayden at the kitchen table while he did his homework which was a bit of a struggle, but he finally got through it.

We played cars on Ayden's bedroom floor for a while then returned to video games. He constantly wanted to switch activities.

"This is awesome," he exclaimed. "It's like a boys' night."

I could tell he was happy to have me there, and I couldn't help but wonder what things were like when Emily had a migraine on a night when it was just her and Ayden. He had been sympathetic when I explained that his mommy's head was hurting very badly, but after the short time we spent in her bedroom, he seemed to forget. Thankfully we were far enough away from where Emily slept that I didn't think the noise would travel to her. I purposely kept him in his bedroom with the door closed almost all night. I knew it was nearly impossible to keep a seven-year-old quiet, especially after I let him drink half a Mountain Dew.

As I watched Ayden sip from the can, I recalled Emily's comment when we first started dating about his dad letting him guzzle soda like she did water. I hoped my choice would be a happy middle ground. I wanted to treat the little guy but didn't want to get us both in trouble.

I'd been around a few times when Ayden's dad picked him up or dropped him off, and I could tell he wasn't fond of my presence. The first time we met, he squeezed my hand as hard as he possibly could. He pretended to be kind to me, but it was obviously a show for Ayden, Emily, or maybe all of us. The next time I saw him, he asked if we could talk. He proceeded to let me know that if I ever laid a finger on his son, he would see to it that I never took another breath. I understood the fatherly protective spirit, but it felt more like a threat than a genuine concern for his child's safety.

After getting Ayden into bed and ensuring he fell asleep, I quietly crawled onto Emily's mattress beside her. She didn't even budge. I prayed that was a good sign, but it also made me nervous. For a few moments, I lay there as still as possible to make sure I could hear her breathing.

The following morning Emily shook me awake. "Luke, you're still here," she clamored.

I opened my eyes and realized daylight was peeking through the curtains. In the past I always left before the sun rose, but last night I'd been afraid to set an alarm because I didn't know if Emily needed to sleep in. I quickly explained this to Emily who seemed groggy but much more coherent than the last time we spoke.

"When Ayden came in to kiss you goodnight, you barely budged, so when I tucked him in last night, I told him I would make a bed on the couch and sleep there in case either of you needed me."

"But you're not on the couch."

"Well, I did tell him that if I wasn't on the couch, I was probably in here checking on you," I explained. I thought this through as best as possible as the evening hours passed. "Honestly, I had no idea what you and Ayden needed, but I knew I wanted to be here for you two."

I wasn't sure how Emily would respond to the news of this decision I made without her, but I didn't have another option since we couldn't have a conversation last night.

"It was sweet of you to go through the trouble of making a bed on the couch," she mumbled with a smile.

I returned the gesture. "Do you need me to wake Ayden up and take him to school?"

"That's okay, I'm used to this; I'll be fine to get him ready."

After the briefing, we both got out of bed relatively quickly so Ayden wouldn't catch us lying next to each other. Looking at the clock, I realized Emily slept for over twelve hours. When I confessed about the soda I let Ayden have with dinner, she placed her hands on her hips still wearing her work clothes from yesterday.

"I can't believe you let him drink Mountain Dew and eat four slices of pizza!"

I played my best sad face, and she began to let me off the hook. "It's okay this one time," she decided, pulling me close and kissing my lips. I was so happy she was feeling somewhat better as she explained that the morning after a migraine feels like a hangover. "Thank you for taking care of Ayden. I guess I owe you something, huh?" We kissed again. "What would you like?" she asked tugging slightly on the rim of my shorts, bringing our bodies together.

"Oh, I don't know," I responded, "I'm sure I can come up with something."

"Wait, one more thing? Did you make sure he brushed his teeth thoroughly after drinking that Mountain Dew?" I furrowed my brow. "If you don't watch him, he'll goof off the whole time."

Teeth? I knew I brushed my teeth before bedtime but couldn't vouch for Ayden.

"He did brush his teeth, didn't he?" Releasing my shorts, Emily took a step back. "Tell me you had him brush his teeth, Luke."

"I helped him with his homework," I pointed out, searching for credit elsewhere.

"Are you serious?" she wanted to know.

"He didn't mention it." *Why did I say that?*

"Of course he didn't mention it; he's seven. Before he goes to bed, he has to brush his teeth just like you do. He also needs to change into his pajamas, use the bathroom, and he likes to have story time."

"We did—" I hesitated.

"All of that?" she quizzed with her head tilted.

"Most."

"What did you leave out?" I knew this wasn't good. "Please tell me that he used the bathroom."

When Emily went into Ayden's room and pulled back the covers, she found out he *had* used the bathroom—the half can of Mountain Dew was now a stain on his white sheets. Oops.

The night had been chaotic and a little scary, but I hoped we could laugh about it later. Emily smiled at me when we walked into the living room and saw the makeshift bed I created on the couch.

Thankfully, I was able to make it out the door without Ayden seeing me, so even though he knew I was staying the night, we hadn't crossed paths this morning. Emily said she'd still let him know I stayed over to care for them, but she'd let him assume I slept on the couch.

As I drove away, I sensed for the first time what having a family of my own might feel like.

28

After the night of the migraine, Ayden started asking every evening if I could spend the night.

"Mom, it was so much fun having Luke to play with," he professed.

I smiled thinking about how most evenings before that night, I'd been there until his bedtime and played with him often. I think the difference was that all of my time was devoted to him during that particular evening while his mom slept off the headache.

Still, we started caving to his requests for me to stay overnight for some reason. It was as though we needed his permission all along. Every night I would make the pretend bed on the couch by covering the cushions with a sheet and then adding a blanket and a pillow. I'd even lain on it for a few minutes to make it look like I slept there. Some nights Emily and I would fall asleep on the couch watching a television show or movie. Eventually, we made it to her bedroom. In the mornings I always returned to the sofa to put on the show when Ayden entered the living room.

I started helping with breakfast, preparing Ayden's lunch, and even taking him to school some days. When Emily's ex-husband learned about the living arrangements, he became irate which we found interesting given that random women spent nights and weekends at his house with Ayden present. Nonetheless, I could see why he wouldn't be fond of the situation, but I didn't appreciate how he talked to Emily about it. He called her a few choice names on several occasions, and I eventually confronted him about how he spoke to her. I could tell he didn't like me stepping in at first, but after I stood up to his bullying technique, he changed his tone with her.

Emily and I met for lunch often. When we ate in Morehead City where we both worked, we liked to go to Cox Family Restaurant which offered an extensive menu with delicious vegetables. It was akin to eating at most any Grandma's house in the South. We also enjoyed dining at Taste of Napoli which serves some of the best Italian food I've ever tasted. When we wanted to enjoy warm, sunshiny weather, we sat at what became *our picnic table* at the visitor's center and watched the boats pass by on the Bogue Sound.

When we had time to drive over the bridge to Atlantic Beach, we ate at Four Corners Diner which served typical diner food; Shark Shack where orders are taken at a window and the only seating is at outdoor tables; and El Zarape which I made sure to confess to Emily is where Mindy and I met on our blind date. The first time Emily and I dined there, I told her about the crazy first date that included my mentor, his wife, and Mindy's parents. Thankfully, Emily wasn't jealous. She seemed to let everything go regarding a situation that both of us had blown out of proportion in different ways.

I recalled this example many times as I explained to clients how we all blow things out of proportion from time to time. It's important to reflect on those events later and discuss how they weren't as problematic as we made them. This exercise serves as a positive reminder when new issues arise. One of the goals is to think: how might this affect our relationship a week, month, year, or even ten years from now? Often, the answer is . . . minimally.

On the days when Emily and I didn't have lunch together, I ate with Ben, Mom, or both of them. Ben and I always looked for opportunities to get our mother out of the house which seemed to be swallowing her in some ways. Sometimes she didn't feel like being around people, and we tried to respect that. On other days we kind of dragged her out hoping to help her avoid a deep depression.

After losing a spouse, it's nearly impossible not to go through a depressive state. I am more concerned for the widows and widowers who aren't overcome by grief than those who are. A heart hardened over the years is often the culprit for the ones who seem to move on without their spouse more easily—often true in divorce as well—but I realize that the loss eventually catches up with these people who pretend to be stronger than other human beings. They then also have to deal with their heart problems that have been an issue all along. Sometimes it stems from trauma experienced within the marriage which was never resolved during their life together. Other times it's a selfish perspective they chose in the relationship trying to protect themselves by not fully giving their heart to their mate. These people almost always end up regretting being more afraid to be codependent than self-serving. In marital relationships becoming one with another person while still maintaining individuality is one of the key components of a happy life. When a human being loses either one, the balance is off but longs to be found.

Ben liked to eat at Ioanni's Grill and Morehead Burger Company. Mom often picked Red Fish Grill near my office or Pita Plate offering Lebanese, Mediterranean, and Greek dishes.

On volleyball nights we all went to eat before or after playing depending on the time. Sometimes we grabbed takeout and ate at the beach while another match took place. Most summer evenings were beautiful for outdoor eating, but we made sure not to feed the seagulls who were always begging. We won more than we lost and often jumped in the ocean to celebrate and share our sweat with the sea.

On the weekends when Ayden was at his dad's, Emily and I felt as free as birds. We stayed at my place where we could step out the back door and walk across the short path leading over the sand dunes to the wide-open beach. We enjoyed long strolls beside the Atlantic Ocean early in the morning, late at night, and anytime in between because we talked for hours and learned thousands of details about each other's lives. I was surprised to hear that Emily worked as a bartender during college. I think it shocked her that I once thought of pursuing a career as a professional cuddler.

"Are you serious?" she asked with a smirk.

"Not really," I confessed, "but it is a real thing."

"I'm not sure I believe you," she contested.

"Look it up," I encouraged.

We spent fifteen minutes talking about how a person who would choose cuddling as a profession as well as the individual who hired one would most likely need therapy.

"They'd be better off seeking counseling before taking either path," I observed.

When we weren't walking on the beach, we would ride our bicycles all over the island. We peddled to parks, shops, restaurants, the grocery store, and sometimes simply for exercise. We often visited Fort Macon State Park and rode on the nature trail. On other occasions, we parked our bikes and walked the path hand-in-hand, taking our time to focus on the little details like the songs the birds sang, the miniature cacti plants, and the playground of trees formed by the hands of God. When Ayden ventured down the trail with us, he liked to climb the branches while pretending to be Spiderman. Emily and I enjoyed climbing with him. A few trees looked more like benches, and when Emily and I walked alone, we often became lost in conversation at one of these resting spots.

The trail connected the beach access area to the actual fort at the end of the barrier island. Emily and I walked through it occasionally but enjoyed it most when Ayden was with us. He thought it was cool that Fort Macon was constructed after the War of 1812 as a station of defense from foreign invasion. "It's older than Mommy," he liked to tease.

He said the fort looked like it was basically built into the ground beyond the sand dunes. The heart of the fort was a large open grassy area entirely surrounded by whitewashed red-brick walls with many open entrances. Doors led to various rooms that were once officers' quarters, kitchens, artillery storage, and much more. These rooms almost all connected, so it was fun to walk from one to the next to explore while feeling like you were in a secret underground tunnel.

The three of us liked to play hide-and-seek at the fort. In many of the indoor areas, the lack or absence of light added intrigue to the game and made finding each other more challenging. Ayden always accompanied one of us, and we took turns being the hider and the seeker. The walls echoed making it a great place to play Marco Polo. We just had to make sure to wear old shoes because due to the sunk-in area where the fort was created, the ground was often wet, and sometimes water stood in certain rooms.

In the courtyard a couple sets of brick steps climb to the top of the fort. A grassy area allows access around the entire highest point of Fort Macon which overlooks the Atlantic Ocean. The cannons placed atop the wall are set up to allow for visibility of approaching ships or any other danger during the period the fort was used for protection. Beyond that wall is another twenty to thirty foot drop—just as on the inside—circling the fort's inner portion and another wall with a grassy area built as the outer layer of protection.

Ayden loved to pretend he was a soldier on the grounds. After hearing and reading tons of facts about Fort Macon, he made up how he thought things were during the early years when the structure was in use. He called the trail we walked on from the Fort Macon beach access to the actual fort the dusty road. He said that was where the soldiers rode their horses before there was a paved road.

Along the dusty road was where I realized I'd fallen in love with Emily Beckett. As she and I stood atop a sand dune surrounded by sea oats, salty air, and a breathtaking view of the Atlantic Ocean, I decided to tell her.

29

I wrapped my arms around Emily, and as the wind whipping off the ocean blew her hair sideways, I hugged her tightly. The warmth of her body felt perfect against mine.

After a few moments, I pulled back from the embrace just enough to view her face fully. I wasn't sure how she became even prettier since we first started dating, but somehow she turned into the most attractive woman I'd ever known. Every time we gazed into each other's eyes, I felt our souls connect.

"I am in love with you, Emily Beckett," I declared with sincerity as I felt the magnetic pull of her eyes.

Emily didn't flinch. Her eyelids didn't blink. She just smiled from ear to ear. "I love you too, Luke Bridges," she professed.

It seemed the whole world stood still as the words we shared soaked in slowly and tenderly.

The ease with which we articulated what I believe to be the most powerful sentiment on earth made me feel as though we spoke the phrase to one another thousands of times. We held each other tightly for what seemed like hours and then kissed passionately. Her lips tasted like sea salt, her breath smelled like the beach, and her eyes glistened with the words I heard her utter confidently.

"I've been falling in love with you for a long time," I admitted with a sideways smirk.

"Falling in love with you has been the most magical experience of my life," she replied.

⤜⤙

Emily and I began saying "I love you" all the time starting with the moment we woke up in one another's arms each morning. While we were getting Ayden ready for school and ourselves off to work, we mouthed the words in the kitchen with grins covering our faces. Before leaving in separate cars, we kissed and professed our love. We sent each other texts during the workday. When we went out for lunch together, we said "I love you" as we embraced at arrival and again when we departed. Upon coming home, we repeated it. The words came out randomly during our evenings together whether riding bicycles, eating dinner, walking on the beach, or brushing our teeth. The last three words we spoke to one other each night were "I love you."

Our love grew as we experienced life together. I would be lying if I said there weren't moments where Emily and I felt like we didn't like each other, but love prevailed every time. We bickered about our differences. We said things we shouldn't have said and stormed out of rooms when we should have stayed and talked.

Relationships were hard. Life wasn't easy. I often reminded others of those two truths and did so for myself as I continued to deal with the loss of my dad while trying to comfort my mom and ensure she had everything she needed.

A couple of times Emily suggested I babied my mother which was something I intended to identify for my overbearing clients, not hear my girlfriend say to me. Ultimately, I stepped back and analyzed her words. We talked. We talked more. We said, "I love you," and we promised always to be transparent regardless of how it might make the other person feel. We set boundaries. We overstepped boundaries. We made each other cry. We made each other laugh.

Every day was a new adventure. We kayaked to the Cape Lookout National Seashore which is only accessible by private boat or ferry. During the trek across the waterway, we paddled alongside a pod of dolphins, one of the most magnificent experiences of my life. It was as though they hung out with us, and we absolutely adored the cute little noises they made when playing. Once we reached the shore, we climbed the Cape Lookout Lighthouse even though it wasn't technically open because of maintenance. Emily worked with the wife of a gentleman who gave us private access and allowed us to spend a good amount of time gazing out over the Crystal Coast.

In all the years Emily and I had lived in this area, neither of us had climbed the lighthouse.

"It's surprising what we sometimes miss out on in our own backyards," I admitted.

"I'm happy to be experiencing this together for the first time," she replied.

"It was worth the wait."

We took lots of pictures of the black and white diamond patterned structure from the ground and plenty of the outward view from the top as well.

When we finished exploring the lighthouse, we visited the Light Station Visitor Center and Keeper's Quarters. We imagined how the lighthouse keepers lived out here by themselves, especially as far back as 1859 when the structure was erected.

"I bet the people who lived here had some interesting stories," Emily mentioned as we settled on a blanket on the beach with the lighthouse as our immediate backdrop.

"I'd sure love to hear some of them," I replied.

"It would have been fun to live out here with you and have this place all to ourselves," Emily daydreamed out loud.

I grinned mischievously. "We could certainly make some stories of our own on a remote island like this."

"Yeah, like what?" she inquired with a grin.

"At nighttime we could run around naked on the beach."

Emily playfully popped my arm. "That sounds fun," she said, biting her lower lip.

"I can't wait to make love to you," I announced. It wasn't the first time either of us expressed this thought with anticipation.

"One day, we can make love on the beach beneath a blanket of stars and pretend we're out here on Cape Lookout."

My eyes lit up like a Christmas tree. "I'm going to hold you to it, Emily Beckett."

"You better," she insisted.

We talked about making love for the next few minutes then the conversation drifted to how the sand out here was whiter than the sand on the beach we walked regularly. "It feels softer as well," Emily announced.

"It might be. It's obviously been far less traveled."

We spent the rest of the day wandering around the island. It was much bigger than I expected, and by the time we decided to paddle back, we ended up watching the sunset from our kayaks.

Life with Emily Beckett was so much fun. I never enjoyed being with someone as much as I did with her.

The following week we went surfing together. Pretty much everyone who grew up on the Crystal Coast surfed at some point in their lives. Emily rode my longboard because even though she surfed a little off and on over the years, she admitted she still felt like a beginner. She let me teach her techniques she hadn't learned before, and by the end of our session, she was catching and riding waves impressively.

She was insanely sexy in a bikini on a typical day. Watching her rip into waves while wearing her bikini made my heart pound even more than surfing waves twice the size we'd been riding today.

I liked how Emily didn't hide that she was checking out my body too.

"You're so hot with your shirt off," she proclaimed as we sat atop the surface of the ocean on our boards just waiting for a worthy wave. "The way your back muscles flex when you ride does something to me," she admitted.

We floated close enough together to hold hands, bobbing up and down in unison as small waves rolled beneath our boards. I pulled her slowly in my direction then leaned in to kiss her salty lips. Her hair was wet, and her eyes were closed as we tasted the sweetness of love.

Pelicans soared by; ships sailed in the distance; people strolled up and down the beach; and we just sat out there beyond the crashing waves kissing, talking, and planning our future.

Once again, we watched the sunset together. Pinks and blues subtly took over the horizon as God painted a picture that would make Van Gogh jealous.

The only other wave we rode that day was the one that took us back to shore where we packed up our things and headed in for the night. We took showers and watched a movie on the couch.

On Sunday evening, we picked Ayden up from his dad's and took him to Atlantic Beach Town Park. We played putt-putt golf and pretended to be kids as we enjoyed the swings.

"How was your time with your dad?" I asked as we soared back and forth nearly in unison.

Earlier while at the front door waiting for Ayden to come out, I noticed an array of primarily empty alcohol bottles on his dad's kitchen countertop as well as what looked like drug paraphernalia in one of the corners of the living room. Emily previously mentioned her concern with these dangerous habits, but this was the first time I saw them firsthand. However, I smelled alcohol and marijuana on his breath a few times during conversations.

"I played a lot of video games," he answered.

"Did your dad play with you?" I asked.

"No, he was sick the whole time," he relayed.

"What was wrong?"

"I don't know, but he took a lot of pills while he was drinking."

Oh, the truths kids tell us. I hated that Ayden had to be around such careless behavior. When I looked at Emily, she rolled her eyes and shook her head.

The following Saturday, we went to the aquarium and watched the otters swim, the sharks eat, and we petted the rays. We ordered pizza from Bella and then watched a cartoon movie.

Sunday morning, we went to church. We sat with Mom, Ben, and Colleen, and after the service we all went out for lunch at Cox's Family Restaurant. I ate more hushpuppies than I should have, and when we took Ayden to Flashbax Arcade, I could barely walk, which worked out well because I sat at a table with Mom and talked.

"You don't have to sit with me if you'd rather be playing games with Ayden," Mom mentioned.

"When Ben and Colleen are around, I'm an afterthought," I laughed.

At the moment, Ayden and Ben were playing air hockey against Emily and Colleen, and Ayden had absolutely no idea I wasn't there.

"I remember those days with a couple of little boys," Mom reminisced.

"Ben may have gotten caught up in the excitement, but I always knew where my mother was," I teased.

"I promise you that Ayden knows exactly where you are," Mom pointed out. "That boy really looks up to you, Luke."

Hearing my mother talking about people other than my dad was comforting. We'd all been guilty of focusing our conversations on him; it was just the way things were after the death of a loved one.

"You think so?"

"I know so. I see the way he looks at you. The way he climbs on you. I see the way Emily looks at you too."

"She climbs on me as well," I joked but as soon as the words came out, I felt a hint of embarrassment hoping my mother wouldn't take the comment as a sexual one.

"When are you going to ask her to marry you?" Mom inquired.

I figured if the previous comment sounded the way I wondered, she ignored it.

"Do you think I should marry Emily?" I asked.

"That's up to you," she said. "She seems like a good catch. I hear the two of you making all your lovey-dovey comments, and I see how you look at each other."

"She's a good woman," I declared.

I could tell Mom was really enjoying the one-on-one time, and so was I. I was happy to hear her giving me advice even if it wasn't direct.

"Just make sure you don't break that little boy's heart," she mentioned.

"What do you mean?" I questioned.

"If you decide you don't want to be a stepdad, let him down easy," she advised.

I furrowed my brow. "What?" I quizzed.

"I know you all have been staying the night with each other," Mom announced.

Even though I was a grown man, I think my face turned red. "We have," I concurred. "How did you know that?"

"Little boys talk," Mom shared.

Every week I made sure to stop by her house a few times to check in and do things my father took care of like mowing the lawn, repairing a leaky faucet, and changing air filters. Sometimes I took

Ayden with me, and he helped me or did fun activities with Mom.

"Ah, I see," I realized.

Mom kept a running list for Ben and me like she did for Dad. I felt relieved knowing she wasn't trying to do everything herself. However, she occasionally asked me to show her how to do something she never did before. Early on I told her she didn't need to learn because Ben and I could always handle these things for her, but as time passed, I knew it was good for her to take on new projects as long as they were safe. We still demanded that she not climb ladders or work the saws. I was even a little intimidated by the latter myself.

"Luke, it can be dangerous to play house," Mom stated surprising me with her bluntness.

I wasn't sure how to respond. Initially, I found myself wanting to debate her, but I knew she was right. I told my clients the same thing when they were in situations like mine. If I had been having sessions with Larry like I probably should have, I was sure he would have given the same advice as my Mom. Statistics proved that couples in serious relationships who lived together before marriage aren't nearly as likely to get married as those who live apart.

Later that night I made the mistake of mentioning to Emily that we were playing house and even quoted studies regarding the matter. In hindsight I should have thought the conversation through more before having it with her. I wasn't saying we should quit staying the night at each other's places or stop seeing each other, but it seemed she took it that way. I just wanted us to talk about the effects, but instead she quit talking altogether.

Her reaction reminded me of when she went silent on me after thinking I had sex with Mindy and subsequently pulled away from me. She didn't ask me to leave but said she wanted to be alone in her bedroom which meant she didn't want me in there tonight.

Those words hit me really hard. As I lay on the couch thinking about a hundred different ways the conversation could have been handled from her perspective and mine, I couldn't sleep. In fact I don't think I slept at all, but I'm not positive.

30

The next morning Emily barely looked in my direction and only spoke to me when necessary. While we were both at work, she didn't answer my calls or respond to my texts even though I reached out several times with apologies and professed how much I wanted to be with her and Ayden.

I found it hard once again to focus on helping my clients when I needed help myself. In between sessions I called Ben and asked for his advice. He wasn't a professional counselor, but he was a good listener who approached life with logic and reasoning.

"It sounds like you shocked Emily by bringing up the topic of playing family. Just give her a little time to calm down. Then, hopefully, as responsible adults, the two of you can talk through the best approach for moving forward," Ben suggested. "Pray. Ask God for peace in the waiting."

I often said similar things to clients, but it felt different on the other side. Although I appreciated the sound advice from Ben, I was most grateful that he listened. Listening to a hurting person allows one to sort through the thoughts and emotions trapped in one's head and determine the best pathway forward.

That evening Emily and I talked briefly about our living situation. She accused me of not wanting to be a stepdad to Ayden.

She mentioned the comment I made to Ben before she and I were dating. I promised that this wasn't the case anymore, but I'm not sure she processed a word I said. She seemed to only manipulate her thoughts to what she assumed I was thinking.

In the past twenty-four hours, she hadn't kissed me or told me she loved me. She barely touched me or talked to me. It hurt. Bad. I felt like I was going crazy. I felt how my clients sometimes sound when they came to see me—confused and afraid.

We slept in the same bed that night but only because I begged her to let me be close. She reciprocated the words "I love you," but they didn't sound genuine. Afterward she rolled over with her back to me and said she was too tired to talk.

The following day the text messages were limited but she at least responded a couple of times.

Slowly, we started talking more. Emily began to show me affection again which I strongly desired all along. I tried to point that out to her lightly, and after a couple of days, we were able to have a more in-depth conversation about what happened. She confessed that when I mentioned we were playing house, she got scared that I would abandon her and Ayden, so she did what felt right. She pulled away from me thinking I would run from her. Ultimately, Emily was trying to protect herself, but both of us were hurting in the meantime.

"I will never just run away from you and Ayden," I promised. "I will always give us every chance to talk through any obstacle and work together to figure it out."

We talked a lot that week and came to the difficult conclusion that it would be best if I stopped staying at her place when Ayden was there, which was more often than not since she maintained primary custody. She still stayed at my house, but the separation at the other end began to strain us.

It was hard when you felt you were going backward in a relationship. Still, from a professional standpoint, I knew it was what we needed, and I prayed it would ultimately propel our relationship to the next level. I still went to Emily's house most evenings because we didn't want to shock Ayden as much as we shocked ourselves. Emily and I learned a lot about each other during this time testing our patience and commitment.

When home alone at night, I thought about my dad much more and soon realized I hadn't fully processed his death. I hadn't dealt with the stages of grief as carefully as needed. Some nights I sobbed in bed alone, and others I called Emily or Ben and cried with them. I didn't reach out to Mom because she seemed to be moving forward lately while I spiraled downward.

I did something else I should have done much sooner. I began regular sessions with Larry, who accepted my timing with grace and love. I needed his profound words, ideas, challenges, and listening ear all along.

Rather than releasing the emotions that followed my father's death, I soon realized I poured all that energy into my and Emily's relationship. Those emotions were good in many ways or at the least intended that way, but anytime we allowed our feelings to be our masters rather than our servants, we ended up dealing with unavoidable consequences. Inevitably at some point, I had to face my dad's sudden death head-on. Now was the time.

I cried—a lot. I prayed. I yelled at God. I begged Him to help me through the pain and suffering. I thanked God for my mom, Ben, Colleen, Emily, Ayden, Larry, and all my family and friends. I was grateful for my clients. Without knowing it, they helped me through the most challenging days and weeks.

In life, we all identified as students and learned some of the most valuable lessons as teachers. When talking to others about grieving, I saw a mirror in their faces. I learned a lot from Ayden, and I'm not sure why I was surprised by that. All along, he asked me the tough questions about my father's death: "How did he die? What is a heart attack? Will we ever see him again? Is he in Heaven? Do you miss him?"

Kids are some of the best therapists we'll ever meet.

I tell adults this all the time, especially parents. One of a parent's primary roles is teaching their children how to become responsible adults. What is often overlooked in the process is that by instructing kids, parents learn the lessons too because children expect them to practice what they preach. When adults don't, they call us out.

As time passed and I was around Ayden's dad more, mainly at drop-offs and pickups, I began to recognize his behaviors. In addition to smelling alcohol on his breath and noticing details pointing to drugs beyond marijuana, I saw his aggression although subtle in some ways. He attempted to show me that he was the alpha male in Emily's house. He walked in the door without knocking. He wandered back to Ayden's bedroom like he owned the place. One day he helped himself to cookies on the counter. He pointed out things he thought needed repairing and offered to fix them, like a loose towel rack. He made random comments about when he and Emily were together and bragged about things he helped her with since their divorce.

For the most part, I tried to ignore him, but I can't say it didn't bother me. His words and actions were blatantly disrespectful. Emily didn't recognize a lot of his behaviors probably because she was somewhat numb to them. When she did, she would talk to him and ask that he respect our boundaries. He didn't like this confrontation. He wanted to do whatever he wanted. I ended up having to speak with him about it, and even though he pretended he was being friendly on behalf of Ayden, we both knew better.

He tried to drive a wedge between Emily and me, but I saw straight through it. I wish I could say that it didn't cause any friction or arguments between us, but it did. She admitted that she always avoided conflict with him, even in their marriage.

In time, she and I ended up on the same page and were mainly able to shut down his attempts to make things awkward. We set limits with him which made a world of difference.

I liked how Emily and I worked together to solve conflict in our relationship in this situation and in others. We continued to discuss my being careful how I phrased important topics like the 'playing house' issue, and she worked on talking to me through conflict rather than withdrawing. Compromise was one of the keys to a healthy relationship, along with trust, respect, and commitment.

As the months progressed, we built our life on these foundational values. We put God first and realized we became more connected with each other when we did. A visual Larry shared with me about this concept was a triangle with God at the top point, Emily on one side, and me on the other. The closer each of us moved to God, the closer we came together.

This way of life encouraged us to deal with issues we had overlooked or hadn't noticed before. I realized I stressed myself out by focusing too much on the accumulation of materialistic things, such as a house on the beach and a brand-new Range Rover. As I honed in on my budget, I figured out that if I didn't make a change, I would lose one or both possessions. Handing over the keys and letting go of the new vehicle aroma was difficult, but I soon found out that a used Ford Explorer got me to and from work just fine but didn't keep me stuck there to pay for it. The demands of finding new clients and booking more sessions dwindled allowing me to focus on the people I already worked with to grow my practice at a steadier pace.

Emily decided not to travel with me every weekend I played in a men's volleyball tournament. It was too much for her and Ayden. When they did come, we had a blast and found ways to make a mini-vacation out of it. We stayed an extra day or two and explored the town where I played.

Our coed volleyball team won the championship by a few points over a team that beat us twice in the regular season. Emily and I credited it to less stress in our lives which enabled us to play more freely, but in all honesty there was a lot more to it. Our entire team played well together, and we improved a lot over the season even though we started as one of the best teams in the league. Our chemistry, like that between Emily and me on and off the court, improved.

Once I found peace with my dad's death and became comfortable living alone—most of the time—again, I understood exactly what I needed in my life. I grew up a lot since Emily and I began dating and knew I was ready for the next step. I realized that the words I heard when looking into my dad's eyes in that lonely hospital hallway—*everything is going to be okay*—didn't mean he was going to live but that even without him and in large part because of him, everything, in fact, was okay. I listened to the voicemail he left me on the Sunday before he passed away. It brought happy tears to my eyes to hear his voice, to listen to him say my name, and to tell me he loved me one last time. I knew I would treasure the message for the rest of my life.

31

"Will you marry me?" Gazing into the twinkle in Emily's heaven-sent, deep blue eyes, I waited for the moment I once thought would never happen. In a way I realized this was another life on another night, and I actually had the guts to whisper those four words into her ear. We weren't at the volleyball court sporting our swimsuits and sandy bodies where I first had this thought. We were in her favorite Japanese restaurant, surrounded by a room full of strangers and the smell of Teriyaki sauce. We just finished a fabulous meal and a wonderful conversation. If she said yes, I knew this would be the most perfect proposal I could have ever imagined.

Before our meal came out, I went to the restroom and intentionally ran into our waitress.

"Do you think you can help me with something," I inquired.

When I finished telling her my plan, I thought I saw tears forming in her eyes. Maybe it was the onions on the plate balanced in her right hand, but I think she really liked my idea. I came up with this plan months ago and had been waiting for the right time. Emily and I had been talking about marriage for a while and even discussed it tonight at dinner. In fact, she brought it up.

"If you decide to ask me to marry you, how do you think you

would do it?" she inquired with a grin.

"I can't tell you that," I replied.

I wondered if she knew what was about to happen. There was no way though; I hadn't told a soul. I purchased the ring yesterday knowing if I picked it out sooner, a circular hole would burn through my pocket, sock drawer, or wherever I placed it while waiting.

"What would you say?" I queried trying to get an inkling on how she might respond. Christmas was right around the corner, and I think she hoped I'd ask her then or at least on Valentine's Day.

"I can't tell *you* that," she offered with a smile and an intentional wink.

The waitress interrupted our conversation to drop off the check and two fortune cookies. She then winked at me and said, "I'll be right back" before walking away.

Emily didn't have a clue. Everything worked out as planned. Dinner went well; I caught the waitress out of Emily's view, and in a matter of minutes I would find out if I would spend the rest of my life with Emily Beckett. With that thought, I remembered my dad's story about proposing to my mother. After dating for three months, he popped the question. She loved him and could see herself spending the rest of her life with him, but she didn't feel she knew him well enough to say yes. He asked the next week again, and she said no, giving him the same reason. My dad was a persistent man; he knew what his heart desired. His downfall, however, was patience. Three weeks later, he asked my mom a third time if she would marry him. She said yes. He waited twenty years to tell her that he planned to give up on their relationship if she said no the third time.

I wondered what I would say or do if Emily said no. I figured my odds were better than 50/50. About 85/15 I convinced myself which sounded like a pretty good chance. I knew Emily loved me and *wanted* to marry me, but she had gone through a lot in her life that caused her to second guess the idea of marriage. Her parents divorced when she was eight, and she and her ex split up relatively quickly. Whenever Emily considered marriage, the word divorce also came to mind. She wanted to marry again; she told me that, even tonight, and I was pretty sure she knew I would be there for her and Ayden to provide the stability and love they needed.

Emily and I casually debated Japanese customs all night, which I purposefully started. When she began unwrapping the fortune cookie in her hand, I informed her it was bad luck for a woman to open it before the man.

"It is not," she swore, playfully slapping my shoulder. "You made that up."

"No, this one I know," I insisted. "I saw it in a movie."

"In a movie? Do you believe everything you hear in movies?"

"Let's ask our waitress," I suggested.

"Okay, go ahead," she agreed, probably thinking I wouldn't.

I motioned for our waitress.

"Luke, what are you doing?" Emily quizzed, her face beginning to show embarrassment.

"I'm asking our waitress about the fortune cookie," I confirmed.

"Yes sir, you need more Coke?" she asked. Perfect, I thought. I couldn't have scripted this better if I had written the scene for my own film.

"No, thanks," I replied. "I have a question about a Japanese custom. Is it bad luck for a woman to eat her fortune cookie before the man with whom she's dining?"

Her eyebrows rose, and I felt like we were in the movie I made up moments ago. "Yes, very, very bad luck," she warned quickly in perfect Japanese vernacular, waving her finger like Emily did with Ayden when he asked for a Mountain Dew yesterday. "Man always open and eat cookie first. Then woman's turn."

Emily shrugged her shoulders in defeat, and I held my breath trying not to laugh.

"You eat cookie first," the helpful waitress demanded, pointing her finger at me as though she were my school teacher.

With her standing there, I peeled open the plastic encasing my cookie. The folks at the tables nearby began to stare after hearing our waitress use her motherly tone. Extra pressure, I realized, but it added suspense.

I plucked the cookie from the wrapper and read the fortune aloud: "Ask the question on your mind," the words insisted. I furrowed my brow and attempted to stare above my head as if a bubble hung there.

The waitress took a few steps back but continued to watch with anticipation.

"What question is on your mind, Mr. Bridges?" Emily inquired, tilting her head while smiling.

The mood felt just right, and suddenly I found myself wanting to pop the question at that moment, but that would mean deviating from my plan. "Let me think about it," I mentioned, waiting for Emily to follow suit and open her cookie.

"Eat your cookie," Emily insisted, pretending to be impatient. "You heard the lady; it's bad luck if you don't open *and* eat your cookie first."

Along with my fortune cookie, I swallowed my laughter before watching Emily rip the plastic around her cookie. As she did, the pen the waitress handed me to sign the check fell onto the floor between our chairs.

"What does your fortune say?" I asked nonchalantly, bending down to retrieve the writing utensil.

Emily's eyes were glued to the thin strip of paper. What happened next reminded me of Keanu Reeves dodging bullets in the Matrix. It was as if time began to slow down, just for us, and everything fell perfectly into place.

A puzzled look overcame Emily's face as I watched her whisper the words aloud: "Will you marry me?" the fortune asked. She turned to me, and I spoke the same phrase waiting on one knee for the answer every man hopes to hear. In that instant, she put the whole thing together: the made-up Japanese custom, my fortune, the pen dropping to the floor, and last but not least, her fortune. She smiled at me, her grin growing as her heart pounded, then looked at the slip of paper again, her face asking: *How did you do this?*

That I would explain later after she answered the big question. Out of the corner of my eye, I could see that most other restaurant patrons had temporarily put down their chopsticks to watch us, curious about what was happening. Some caught on, and some didn't. "What's going on?" I heard one man say. "Is he okay?" another fellow asked the waitress as if I had fallen out of my chair. "He asked her to marry him," an intuitive woman blurted out, followed by a unified "Awe."

My ears perked anxiously as Emily's lips began to move. The answer couldn't come quickly enough.

32

"Yes!" Emily exclaimed.

She became so excited I thought she might jump out of her chair. "Yes," she uttered again as if the entire restaurant hadn't heard her the first time. "I will marry you, Luke."

With trembling hands, I slid a magnificent princess cut diamond ring onto Emily's thin finger as smoothly as possible. It didn't surprise me that she barely glanced at it, maybe long enough to ensure it wouldn't fall off. She leaned down to kiss me, and as our lips met, the audience around us clapped realizing they had witnessed a proposal. Many even stood to their feet, which I hadn't expected, but it was a nice bonus.

That night we nearly made love. I wanted to, and Emily wanted to, but we agreed that we could wait a little longer. We were almost there.

⤜❦⤛

Emily and I immediately began planning our wedding which we decided would take place in May—a year from our first date. The next few months moved as fast as Mario Andretti once raced on the blacktop. We met with a handful of photographers, cake artists, florists, and, of course, the pastor who would marry us. He guided us through premarital counseling which was eye-opening and informative. I discovered things about Emily that hadn't come up in our conversations to that point in our relationship.

We talked about the little things that really didn't matter, like our favorite colors, foods, and songs, although we couldn't agree on which ones we wanted at the wedding. I jokingly mentioned the Boyz II Men classic "I'll Make Love to You" because I always liked the song. Emily explained that song would be too intimate to be performed in the presence of our guests. I teased her by telling her I knew she wouldn't have the ability to keep her hands to herself. Her first choice was an Eric Clapton piece I never heard; I'm sure it had been a hit at some point; but I didn't really want a song I didn't know sung at our wedding.

The pastor's assistant knocked at the door, and as he attended to her question, Emily and I chatted. When he sank back into the cushioned seat across from us, we began discussing men's and women's needs. He recommended a book titled *His Needs Her Needs* that tackled natural needs such as affection, sex, respect, and much more. Then he asked a question that somewhat caught us off guard: "Have you been completely transparent about your pasts? Such as any struggles with depression, drugs, alcohol, pornography, finances, anger, etc.? Also, about relationships and intimate partners? Anything that would surprise you if you found out after you say *I do,* especially if you heard it from someone other than the person sitting beside you right now?"

I shifted in my seat and uncomfortably turned to Emily knowing we discussed some of those topics but not all. I told her about the abortion, which was my biggest secret, and she shared about her bout with drugs. She knew all about my financial situation and was forthcoming with hers.

"I don't really think knowing about each other's sexual encounters is important," Emily shared.

I wondered how many sexual partners she had but never asked.

I assumed every human being wonders until they know, and some maybe even beyond that.

The pastor spoke softly. "I'm certainly not encouraging you to discuss the specifics of intimate relationships. However, on that note, if there is something regarding sex that you struggle with, the person you are marrying needs to know." He paused for a moment as if to choose his words wisely. "I've learned that being open and honest upfront can save a lot of pain and heartache down the road. It's your decision," he said, "but anything you find yourself wanting to keep a secret is something you seriously need to consider telling the person you are engaged to marry." With his hands clasped together and knees crossed, his eyes spent equal time looking at each of us. He appeared very astute, as he was. From a therapist's perspective—and this man had way more letters behind his name than I'd earned—I knew this meant even though he was responding to Emily's aversion to part of the question, the reply was for both of us. "Being transparent about the number of sexual partners is something I've noticed a lot of people aren't honest about, especially men. However, like with anything else, questions and fears begin to disappear once the truth is exposed."

Later that night, I told Emily how many women I slept with in my lifetime. I was disappointed it was even one more than it should have been on the night when we would first share an experience God created strictly for husband and wife.

"Why did you tell me that?" Emily questioned, her cheeks rising and brow furrowing.

"I want you to know everything about me," I offered.

"Do you expect me to tell you?" she asked. "And if I don't, does that mean I'm not being forthcoming with you?"

"It's up to you."

"It's up to me? That's bologna, Luke."

It was our first argument in weeks, and even though I hated to argue with her, I knew conflict was good for us. Knowing how your partner will retaliate is vital to the success of a marriage. All relationships experience fights, but the key lies in keeping them fair.

"Yes," I answered honestly, "I do want to know."

"But you didn't want to know before the pastor brought it up today, so why now?" she quizzed, her voice rattling. Thankfully, Ayden was with his dad tonight.

"It's been on my mind," I admitted.

"What if my number is larger than yours?" she asked, but it sounded more like a warning.

I shrugged, selfishly hoping it wasn't, yet curious. But why did it matter? I wondered. What was in the past was in the past. It wasn't like Emily or I owned a magic eraser and could clear our records even if desired. She slept with her ex-husband, obviously. Did I really want to know how many more, if any?

"If it is, it is," I answered, hoping it wasn't. It wasn't like I would break off our engagement if Emily had been intimate with more men than I had women, but it would bother me selfishly nonetheless. There was no sense in lying to myself about it.

"I just don't see why it matters."

"Then don't tell me," I declared, louder than intended, pressing my hands firmly into the couch and pushing my feet to the floor. I paced around the living room as she walked out and headed to her bedroom. I considered following her but then thought better.

The sound of crickets woke me the next morning, and I instantly realized it was freezing in Emily's apartment. The small blanket I retrieved from the top of the couch last night was barely larger than a hand towel, and I found myself exposing my feet as I pulled it close to my face. Frustrated, I threw it across the room and tiptoed to the bathroom. Emily's door was shut, so I assumed she was still sleeping. I used the restroom, splashed my face with water, and brushed my teeth with a toothbrush I brought over after my dad passed away and left here ever since.

Last night was the first time we hadn't brushed our teeth together or slept in the same bed. I knew I didn't want to make a habit of sleeping on the couch. I decided to crawl into Emily's bed and apologize for pushing her to answer the question from our premarital counseling session. I turned the knob, but Emily wasn't there. The plaid comforter was pulled tight, and the pillows were fluffed and positioned perfectly at the head of the bed. I searched the rest of the house but found no sign of her. Did she leave? I wondered.

When I opened the front door, I spotted her car parked in the same spot as last night. I was surprised I hadn't heard her when she got out of bed; I had always been a light sleeper. I walked onto the back porch and breathed a sigh of relief as I saw Emily's back between me and a thicket of trees.

"Good morning," I greeted my future wife.

She said nothing and didn't move either. As I stepped closer, I could hear her crying softly.

"I'm sorry-" I said, but before I could add to the apology, I heard a number come out of her mouth.

"What?" I asked, confused.

"That is the number I thought I didn't want to share with you," she clarified.

I wrapped my arms around her and let the morning breeze press against my skin until she mentioned going inside for breakfast. We ate pancakes and talked about the day we planned. Then we spent the next eight hours with my mom, shopping and shopping and shopping. I thought I would die or at least collapse in the middle of one of the dozen stores it seemed we visited.

"How can you play volleyball in a weekend-long tournament but can't walk for a few hours with us without complaining?" Emily wondered aloud.

It wasn't that I couldn't walk; the walking wasn't that bad. It was the standing as they tried on countless outfits and continued to ask my opinion, even after I asked that they not. They posed ridiculous questions like, "Does this outfit make me look fat?" Are you serious? Even if it did, I wouldn't admit it. I may be an honest man, but I'm not stupid. And why the need to try on the same blouse in three different colors? "If one fits, they all fit," I reminded Mom and Emily, and simultaneously they rolled their eyes.

We ate dinner on the outdoor patio at Sanitary Fish Market and Restaurant, a staple on the Morehead City waterfront. We watched sailboats float by and fishermen cruise along as we enjoyed our seafood plates. It was indeed lovely to relax after a long day that ended with my trunk packed with bags from stores in Beaufort, Morehead City, and Atlantic Beach. The shopping spree had been my gift to Emily and Mom. I joked that they had to pay for my dinner because I had run out of money.

The following weekend came quickly, and Emily and I chose to cater to Ayden's every need. We'd been so busy planning the wedding we hadn't been able to do as much with him as we would have liked during his past few weekends with us. He had a tough couple of days at his dad's house the previous weekend, and he eventually shared that information with us over 'shausage' biscuits at Kountry Kitchen. Early in our relationship, Emily informed me that Kountry Kitchen was Ayden's favorite breakfast spot.

"I want two shausage biscuits and a Mountain Dew," Ayden told his mom as soon as we sat down for breakfast. Emily told him to let her think about it, but he quickly showed he disagreed with that idea. "If I can't have two, I don't want any," he muttered, crossing his arms and pouting as if she said he couldn't have breakfast at all.

"Ayden, stop it. We are in a restaurant, and there are people around."

"No," he demanded, his brow crunching. "Daddy lets me have Mountain Dew whenever I want it."

Ayden's behavior was a touchy subject that Emily and I battled on numerous occasions since I asked her to marry me. I'd been upfront with her on this issue before giving her a ring. If we were going to become husband and wife, I would need her blessing to be a *real* parent to Ayden, not just a stepfather who stands on the sidelines of his stepchild's life. I didn't desire to take his biological father's place, but I wanted Ayden to respect me and expect consequences if he didn't. Since our first conversation about my feelings, I had been slowly trying to step in and help with Ayden's behavior. I knew from my educational and real-life counseling experiences that the transition was a process much like walking on glass. It wasn't that Emily didn't want her son to be a good kid, but I concluded she didn't quite know how to bring the idea to fruition. She agreed with me verbally that I should be allowed full parental rights once we tied the knot. She also acknowledged that it made sense to slowly transition into my new role immediately, but following through with supportive actions on those words hadn't been quite as easy for her.

"Ayden, not another word, or you will have to drink water and eat a plain buttered biscuit for breakfast," Emily warned, her tone intensifying with each word.

"No, I won't," Ayden sassed.

"Yes, you will."

Thus the battle began, right there in Kountry Kitchen. As I spotted the waitress headed our way, Emily made a threat which, due to previous experiences, I knew would most likely not be carried out. I recently explained to her if she wanted to teach Ayden to make sound decisions, now was the time to follow through with consequences rather than trying to tell him as a teenager he couldn't smoke, drink alcohol, or talk back to us.

Customers at other tables looked at us now. Even though none of them said a word, at least not to us, I had a good idea what they thought: *If I acted that way when I was a kid, my parents would have set me straight right here in front of everyone.* That's what was going through my mind too.

When the young waitress approached our table with an ordering pad, Emily and Ayden were still squabbling. I took the liberty to order my breakfast and then told her Ayden would have water and a plain buttered biscuit.

At those words, Emily and Ayden froze.

"What would you like, honey?" I inquired after turning to face Emily. Her nostrils flared. I didn't want to deal with this, not now and not here, but I knew I had to. We had to.

Ayden began crying again. "I don't want that, Mommy. Please don't make me eat that," he begged.

"Luke, you can at least get him a sausage biscuit."

I could feel people staring holes in my head. "I am simply following through on what you told him, Emily."

I knew Emily understood precisely what I was doing, but she didn't like it. I could see it in her eyes and figured we would discuss this later which was fine. It was part of the process. If this happened two months ago, we would have argued right here in front of everyone. She said what she said to Ayden hoping the threat would be enough, but it wasn't and it never would be. Directions without consequences, when not followed, are as empty as puddles without rain.

Emily ordered, Ayden continued crying, and then we began what I feared was a long wait for our food. In a way, I felt bad, but I knew I did what needed to be done. I helped Emily follow through on her statement: *Not another word out of you or . . .*

When we began eating, Ayden said very little. He was mad at me and at his mom. When he did speak, however, he spoke a little more cautiously than earlier. As soon as the food arrived, I offered him a chance to redeem himself. Five years down the road, I probably wouldn't make the same choice, but given that Ayden wasn't used to having to follow directions up to this point in his young life, I wanted to show him that just as there are consequences, there are also rewards. If he listened to his mom earlier, he would probably be eating a sausage biscuit and drinking orange juice. That would have been his reward. Now, I put another reward on the table.

"If you eat your plain biscuit and drink your water, and if you behave while we all sit here and eat, we will let you have a sausage biscuit." I made sure to use the word 'we.' Emily hadn't yet joined me on the 'we' side of the consequences, but I figured if I continued to include her in the rewards, maybe she would come around. The other day I told Ayden if he finished his homework before dark, we would let him play video games. He did, and we let him play.

It always intrigued me how kids can be downright mad at you one moment and then a few minutes later act like they never were. That's one of those lessons I tried my best to let kids teach me over and over, and I had been doing the same with Ayden just as I was teaching him lessons.

"Daddy pushed me down," Ayden mentioned out of left field.

Emily, biscuit in mouth, paused, and I watched the sound of those words raise her eyebrows. The red on her face told me if her ex were in this room right now, her biscuit would be shoved into his mouth, and her fist would probably be inserted right behind it. All of her frustrations with me seemed to dwindle at this new revelation. What I did to upset her was suddenly like a grain of sand on a freshly formed beach.

"Why?" she demanded, wiping crumbs from around her lips. "When?" she added. I could see her fingers shaking.

"Last weekend," he confirmed.

"Did he hurt you?"

"A little."

How much was a little? I wondered. "Were you playing around?" I asked, hoping for the best.

"No. We were at a party, and Daddy was drinking again."

Thank God kids are so honest, I thought to myself.

"Ayden, tell Mommy why he pushed you down," Emily requested.

Ayden lowered his biscuit and his head. I could tell that he knew his dad wouldn't want him sharing this information with us. In fact, his dad most likely told him not to, which was one of the issues that made parenting kids from broken homes so difficult. They are torn even if they are being raised properly in one home. His dad didn't like the idea of me being included in any instruction for Ayden. He told Emily that on the phone just a few weekends ago, moments after Ayden told him I made him clean the kitchen floor for throwing his mashed potatoes off his dinner plate.

Ayden swallowed, but there was nothing in his mouth. Emily and I could see the tears forming in his eyes as he relived the event. "He—" he paused momentarily, looking at the floor, then at the biscuit on the circular plate in front of him. He began to pick at it as if pulling beads out of a box one by one. "I was sitting on the cooler drinking a Mountain Dew, and he wanted me to get off so he could get another beer."

"So he just threw you off?" Emily barked, somewhat jumping to conclusions.

"Kind of," Ayden agreed, shrugging his shoulders and going along with his mom.

"Did he ask you to get off?" I asked.

Ayden shook his head yes.

"But you didn't?" I asked. I wasn't trying to defend his father. In the past few months, I came to realize this boy's dad had serious issues. With drinking, drugs, and fighting, the man was unsafe for Ayden to be around. In my opinion, both personal and professional, no man whose life was ruled by any of those three things was fit to parent, especially if he subjected his child to the lifestyle.

This time Ayden shook his head in the other direction.

"Why didn't you want to get off?" Emily asked, realizing we needed to know the whole story.

"I didn't want Daddy to have more beers."

Ayden's motive made me want to cry. He was trying to protect his dad. A seven-year-old boy trying to keep his father safe when it should be the other way. *What has the world come to*, I thought.

As breakfast and life went on all around us, Ayden continued, "I told him I wasn't getting off because all the beer was gone, and only Mountain Dew was left."

"Then what?" I probed.

Ayden pushed his biscuit aside. "He told me to shut up and get out of his way. I think he said a dirty word too." He paused to think about that. "Do you want me to say it, Mommy?"

"No, honey, you don't need to say it." We had a good idea of what it might have been. "Did your daddy push you with his hands or fists?"

"Hands," he answered simply. "It didn't hurt that bad." Ayden's defensive mechanisms were coming back up.

"Thank you for letting us know," I proclaimed. "We are proud of you." Emily nodded her head. "Did anything else happen?"

"Nah, not really. Dad just got more beer and got drunker with his friends."

"What did you do after he pushed you?" Emily asked.

"I cried, I think, but not for long. He didn't push me again, and he told me he was sorry on the way home."

From the sounds of it, Ayden's dad drove himself and Ayden home—drunk. We let the conversation roll into a more positive one. When Ayden finished his plain biscuit, he wanted to walk with me to the register to order his sausage biscuit.

After breakfast, we took Ayden bowling and then let him play in the park, where we stopped for a picnic lunch. The three of us fed the geese down near the water's edge and watched sailboats float by for nearly an hour. Ayden loved seeing all the boats. He even asked if Emily and I would buy one when we got married. Before heading home, we swung by the grocery store to pick up a few items for dinner. Emily and I decided to make a chicken casserole dish together, and Ayden offered to assist. Since it had been only him and his mom for so long, he enjoyed helping prepare the meals. It was more fun for him to be in the kitchen with her than on the floor rolling cars around, although he and I enjoyed our fair share of Matchbox playing in the past few months. I found out that I really anticipated the times when he and I would play. It took me back to my childhood, making up stories about life as I drove around whatever vehicles I chose to drive that day. Ayden's favorite was a '66 Camaro; mine was a '72 Chevy pick-up. He liked to pretend he had a wife, probably because he heard Emily and me talking so much about getting married.

When we finished dinner later that evening, we watched a movie and put Ayden to bed. I listened as Emily made up a story for him instead of reading one out of a children's book. Her story featured a little boy who became the head chef in his parents' New York City restaurant after they began to struggle for business. The establishment became an overnight success, but no one besides the father and mother knew the chef's age because only family was allowed in the kitchen. When two of the restaurant's nearby competitors began to lose customers because of this little boy's success, they began to pry. They would peep in the windows from the alley behind the restaurant and even disguised themselves as the city's health inspectors. They tried to have the restaurant shut down. In the end, the little chef continued cooking for the customers who grew to love his food, and the restaurant made the front page of the *New York Times* for winning numerous awards.

Not long after Ayden fell asleep, Emily and I curled up in bed and talked about how much fun we had with Ayden today. We held hands under the covers and whispered back and forth until dozing off. It had been a great day, and it would have been perfect if we hadn't found out Ayden's father pushed him off the cooler for another beer.

33

The lawyer who previously handled Emily's divorce listened intently as she upsettingly retold the story Ayden shared with us at breakfast three days prior. Emily decided I should go along for moral support. She also thought I could help recall things we learned about her ex-husband over the past few months—details Ayden shared with us as well as information that friends and relatives happened across. These things frightened Emily, primarily for Ayden's safety but ultimately for ours also.

"Were there any bruises, scrapes, or cuts on Ayden's body following the pushing incident?" probed the distinguished gentleman sitting across from us at a large antique desk.

I presumed him to be in his mid-forties, most likely married with one or two children. He wore a red bow tie around the neck of a button-up blue shirt, and his pants, which appeared to be a suede-like material, donned blue stripes down the leg. I figured he probably drove a BMW or Mercedes and lived in a house as large as Dr. Nesbitt's.

"We checked," Emily shared. "There wasn't anything noticeable."

"If there ever is, take photographs for evidence," he suggested. "You said there are other issues; what else happened that I need to know about?"

I liked how he phrased the question; it made me presume he cared about Ayden and Emily. I hoped I was right. I met many lawyers who cared more about winning cases and fattening their bank accounts than the people they represented. The fact that he looked me in the eyes, shook my hand, and said he appreciated me being there when we first arrived impressed me as well.

In the court system, stepdads or in my particular case, a *future* stepdad seemed to get trampled on. Well before I fell in love with Emily and her son, I found it unfortunate how the bad apples ruined the reputation of heroes—my view of most stepdads; men who didn't have to be fathers to children they didn't create but chose to anyway. Almost any man with a reproductive organ can be a sperm donor and contribute to a biological child. However, most men who choose to become a parent are a gift from God Almighty. The same is true for stepmoms. Counseling blended families fosters this conclusion for me. That said, I believe a healthy nuclear family is best for every man, woman, and child, and statistics prove this time and again. Abandonment rips lives apart, but unfortunately, that's part of our world. There are too many people out there who don't have their priorities straight.

"Well," Emily started. "His dad has always let him watch R-rated movies and play adult video games. He gets drunk when Ayden is with him, and I know he is doing drugs."

"Do you have proof . . . about the drugs?" the lawyer wanted to know.

"Yes, I can smell pot on him when he picks up Ayden."

"Do you know of any other narcotics?" he asked as if marijuana held an exemption. This response made sense based on the laws in our country loosening, especially regarding the drug's medicinal usage.

Emily glanced at me. I smelled weed on his clothing several times but understood where this conversation was heading. I never stood close enough to Emily's ex to smell his breath, but I thought about getting close enough to punch him in the face on a few occasions for the way he talked to Emily and Ayden. He looked at me once or twice as if thinking the same. Personally, I made sure to keep my thoughts to myself. Emily said he liked to fight, and I imagined he probably won his fair share of brawls. He stood about six foot three inches and probably weighed 225 pounds. I mentally noted the shotguns hanging on the rack in his truck and the knife he carried beside the oversized brass belt buckle he never seemed to leave home without.

"I'm pretty sure if his vehicle and home were searched, other drugs and drug paraphernalia would be discovered," I mentioned. "Ayden comments about his dad taking a lot of pills," I added.

"Again, we need proof of exactly what he is ingesting and find out whether the medication is prescribed," he acknowledged. "The latter can be found out pretty easily."

"Another big concern is we learned that Ayden's father held a pistol to a man's head at a party a couple months ago," I revealed, speaking for Emily and myself.

The attorney furrowed his brow and leaned back in his chair as if saying *tell me more*. Before coming to this appointment, Emily asked me to unveil this information because it made her cry every time she talked about it since finding out from her coworker—the same lady who thought she overheard Mindy and me having sex. In that instance she had been incorrect, of course. But this one seemed to hold more truth.

"Emily's coworker just happened to be on the court's website looking up her court date for a traffic ticket when she happened upon Ayden's father's name. He, as I mentioned, was being charged with threatening a man's life with a deadly weapon."

The attorney's ears perked up even higher. "Do you happen to know if the case has been tried?"

Emily spoke up with tears filling her eyes but not yet rolling down her face. "Yes, but the victim ended up saying my ex hadn't threatened his life, that he was only joking around even though other witnesses testified that he wasn't."

"The case was dismissed, I assume?"

Emily shook her head east to west while tears rolled slowly down her flushed cheeks. I reached across the space between our leather padded chairs and held her hand, just as I did when previously discussing this issue.

"Is there anything else?"

I could almost hear what Emily was thinking: *Really, there needs to be more!* Instead of speaking, she shook her head once again.

The attorney twiddled his thumbs. His mind seemed to be analyzing the information gathered thus far, considering what to do with it. When Emily calmed down and finished pulling from the box of tissues he passed across his desk, he asked how Ayden was doing at school. He wanted to know about his grades and interactions with other children; if his dad had been involved in extracurricular activities; if he picked him up and dropped him off on time; if he fed him properly and cared for his son's hygiene.

Thinking back to the teeth brushing incident in my mind's eye, I ashamedly hid my face. With my real eyes, I couldn't help but stare at the red bow tie.

Emily and I answered each question individually and honestly.

"We have a few options here," the lawyer stated. We waited, Emily less patiently than I. "I will start with the most severe. We can take him back to court and attempt to provide evidence that Ayden's father is an unfit parent. We can request you be granted full custody and that the father is not allowed to see his son." I knew Emily would prefer that, but I also knew it wouldn't be as simple as it sounded, as we were about to find out. "Here is how I imagine a judge will interpret the case you have placed before me today. He or she will say drinking or getting drunk isn't illegal even around a minor child. The latter is certainly unfortunate, in my opinion. It will also be stated that if we don't have sufficient evidence showing this man's involvement with drugs—for example, an arrest and conviction—this information is simply he says, she says. The judge will be forced to remind us that the case about the threat with a deadly weapon was dismissed." He pursed his lips before opening them again. "You and I know this man is an unfit parent, but the court won't see it that way. Unfortunately, there are a lot of parents out there who fall into this same category. Some love their kids and their family, and they provide for them. Some don't. Some love their kids but are too selfish to be good parents. In my opinion, it most often takes way too much evidence to prove a person is unfit to be a parent."

For Emily's sake, I cut in. "Basically, you're saying he has to have a rap sheet to be even possibly found unfit to parent."

He seemed to select his next words carefully. "There is more to it than that, but in a more political fashion, that is what the court says."

"What other options do we have?" Emily asked.

"My office can send your ex-husband a certified letter stating we have recorded everything disclosed today and will continue monitoring his behavior and parenting. We will gladly do this if you like."

Emily shook her head and took over the conversation. "No, we can't do that. That will only rile him up. He will know Ayden has been telling us what goes on over there; his father hates when he does that. Then he will take this all out on Ayden. I can't let that happen."

"Unfortunately, that does happen, Ms. Beckett," he sympathized. "Like I told you when you first came to me, divorce is often very ugly for children. I know firsthand. I thank God my ex-wife decided after our divorce that she wanted nothing to do with our two children. As much as I hated to see her move away and out of their lives, I think it was best for them." He paused, walking around his desk to get within whispering distance. "Off the record," he uttered, "the lifestyle your ex-husband lives has a way of catching up with people."

"Let's just pray Ayden isn't around if that ever happens," I declared.

Emily and I spent the rest of the afternoon at her place trying to decide the best solution to this problem. Three hours later, we concluded there wasn't a *best* solution. In fact, there wasn't a solution, only a problem that neither she nor I nor the court system could seemingly do anything about. The attorney's third option was to do nothing and hope Ayden's father's lifestyle either caught up with him, changed, or submitted to divine intervention. He seemed to hate this situation nearly as much as we did. The attorney that is, not God. Although we figured, God did too.

34

$\mathcal{E}$mily and I moved full steam ahead with the wedding plans. She did most of the work, and I mainly answered questions. She and Mom seemed to have become best friends which I thought was good for both of them. With Emily's parents deceased, she needed someone who could assist with all the things a mother normally helped with when it came to weddings. Every bride deserved a motherly figure.

Ever since Dad passed away, Mom had been saying that she needed friends. This wedding gave her and Emily a chance to connect on a deeper level, and they had really hit it off well. It seemed they spent as much time together as Emily and I these days. This gave Ayden and me an opportunity for male bonding. We went to the park, played sports, and fished, and I also taught him how to surf. Like his mom, he was a natural.

On a beautiful weekend in May one year from our first date, I watched Emily float across the sand dunes behind my house as the sea oats danced to the slowest and sweetest version of "Here Comes the Bride." Behind me the waves of the Atlantic Ocean made their own music, and the sun set right on cue. God was painting another masterpiece. Even so, my eyes remained fixed on my bride who wore a strapless white dress flowing down her body making her look more like an angel than a human.

As she walked past our family and closest friends, about fifty people altogether, I felt my heart skipping beats. I was so happy this day was here, and Emily's smile spoke the same words as she approached me. At that moment, I completely understood why the groom waits to see his bride in her wedding gown. I knew the mental pictures I was taking would last a lifetime.

When we first started discussing the wedding, Emily wanted Ayden to be the ring bearer. As plans moved forward, she and Mom came up with another idea. Ayden was the perfect person to walk her down the aisle, and the grin on his face ensured us that Emily made the right decision.

When he joined her hand to mine, tears invaded Emily's eyes as she knelt down to hug and kiss her baby boy. The moment she let go, he latched onto my leg, and I bent down for an unforgettable hug. I wasn't sure when I began crying, but I let the tears flow even though my friends were in the audience.

As our pastor spoke, my eyes locked on Emily's, and I felt more comfortable and confident than ever. The words "I do" came as naturally as "I love you" had the day when we trekked along the dusty road.

During our rehearsal yesterday when Ayden walked Emily across the sand dunes, he said, "Mommy, this walkway to the beach from Luke's house is like our own little dusty road."

"Tomorrow, it will be your house too," she reminded him.

He grinned from ear to ear. "I'm so excited about living on the beach." He already helped us set up his new room.

When the pastor announced us as husband and wife—Mr. and Mrs. Luke Bridges, we walked along the dusty road that led to our new life together. Emily and I stepped into the house and snuck off to our bedroom where I wanted to undress my bride and make love to her for the first time. However, guests waited outside for the reception, so we held off a little longer although we shared one of the most passionate kisses we ever had.

The rest of the night felt somewhat like a blur. We danced, sang, fed each other cake, and celebrated with our friends and family. Ben gave the perfect Best Man's speech, and Colleen followed it with a tearjerker of a toast. Emily selected her as her Matron of Honor.

I was so grateful for how Emily became part of my family. Everyone loved her, and she loved them back. They felt the same way about Ayden. He already asked if he could call my mom Grandma, and he was excited about staying with Grandma while Emily and I honeymooned in the Outer Banks of North Carolina.

We spent the first night as a married couple in our house. The moment when we were finally alone, we stepped into the bedroom. I anticipated ripping Emily's clothes off her beautiful body. I played it out in my head over and over during the times that brought us to the moment we both saved for one another. But, it happened differently than I expected.

Slowly and gracefully, Emily and I removed each other's clothes. One article fell to the floor at a time, yet our eyes never lost the connection that led to our souls. We touched and kissed tenderly and passionately, and once completely naked, we guided each other onto the bed. Beneath the sheets in a candlelit room, we made love to the steady rhythm of soft music and the most sensual shared breathing I could have ever imagined. I felt more connection and chemistry than I knew could exist, and when the moment ended, more magic followed. We snuggled in our bed with our arms wrapped around one another for what seemed like hours. We embraced every ounce of energy we shared, and as we continued to caress each other's bodies, we talked and kissed and envisioned our entire lives before us.

We took a shower together and, later that night, walked along the dusty road to our beach, where we spread out a blanket near the sand dunes. The Carolina moon shined brightly and the nighttime sky twinkled with millions of stars. As Emily and I took in the beauty surrounding us, we removed each other's clothes once again. We made love as the wind brushed our naked bodies, and the waves crashing onto the shore provided the symphony.

35

Our honeymoon was more than I could have expected. It felt like we were two kids playing on the playground of life as adults. We spent more time in the house we rented than anywhere else. We made love often. Upon waking. In the middle of the day. At night. In the wee hours of the morning. It was magical. The chemistry we shared was unreal.

Just like on that first night, the deeper connection was the best part—lying in one another's arms afterward, sometimes talking for hours and other times simply embracing the quiet of each other's presence.

We wandered around the house naked. That was fun. Emily's body was spectacular, and I couldn't take my eyes off her, clothed or not. We walked on the beach. Rode bicycles. Discovered new restaurants. Ate ice cream. Kayaked. Visited lighthouses. Rode horses. Played board games. Sat on the porch. Watched the sunrise. Watched the sunset. From the moment we woke to the moment we fell asleep naked in each other's arms, we lived life to the fullest.

Not much changed when our honeymoon ended and we returned to the real world. We kept having fun together. Ayden fit into the puzzle perfectly. He loved living by the ocean. We went out to the beach almost every day. We played in the sand. Surfed. Walked. Ran. Gathered seashells. Played volleyball. Swam. Flew kites. We did all these things over and over and found new adventures as well. We even saw a nest of sea turtles hatch and then flop their way to the ocean where they fought against the waves but eventually swam into their habitat.

We ate at all the restaurants we liked. We walked along the dusty road, the one at our house and the Fort Macon State Park trail. We visited the downtown shops on the waterfront and watched the sailboats pass. We played putt-putt golf. We rode bicycles.

We became a family. Our life was surreal.

Then tragedy struck.

36

Emily and I celebrated our first anniversary with a trip back to the Outer Banks. We made love just as much as on our honeymoon. We joked and laughed and played the entire week. We did a lot of the same things we did a year ago along with some new activities.

Then, on the night we came home, Emily dropped me off at the house before heading to pick up Ayden from his dad's. I came down with a stomach virus on the ferry ride back. Even so, I tried to talk her into letting me pick him up because she complained about a headache, and I was afraid it might become a migraine. However, she assured me that my condition was worse than hers.

I crawled into bed and fell asleep within minutes.

Less than an hour later, a call woke me. I only reached for my phone because I expected it to be Emily. However, it wasn't and I didn't recognize the number or the voice. When a police detective introduced himself on the other end, my weary body trembled with fear.

"Mr. Bridges, I regret to inform you that your wife has been in an automobile accident. We need you at the hospital. Should we send a car for you?"

Adrenaline kicked in, and I somehow drove myself to the hospital. Dr. Bobbett sat me down and said Ayden escaped the wreck with minor injuries. Emily didn't. She didn't make it.

I fell to my knees. My mind flashed back to being in this same hospital with my dad where I lost him almost two years ago.

I asked Dr. Bobbett what happened, but he said he didn't know all the details and that I needed to talk to the police. Something about his mannerisms and the look in his eyes told me there was news he didn't want to reveal.

Eventually, I talked to the detective who investigated the accident and called me earlier. It shocked me when he explained that Ayden's dad also died in the accident.

What?

I suddenly had even more questions than before. Some the detective knew the answers to, some he didn't. He explained that he was still trying to assemble all the pieces himself. He admitted that things didn't add up.

According to Ayden, who was beyond shaken up, his Mom showed up at his dad's house to pick him up, but they weren't there. They were at a party, and his dad was drunk and who knows what else. His dad offered to bring him home, but Emily said no. She rushed over there to get Ayden, and upon seeing his dad stumble to his own vehicle, she offered him a ride. He accepted. Then, en route to his house, something happened, and the car ran off the road striking a light pole. No other vehicles were involved. Speed wasn't a factor. The impact shouldn't have killed her, the detective determined.

How did two people die in an accident that shouldn't have killed anyone? Foul play?

Half of my first question was answered when I found out Ayden's father hadn't been wearing his seatbelt even though both Emily and Ayden begged him to put it on. I guess the attorney we met with was right, at least in this case—a careless lifestyle caught up with Emily's ex. The choice not to buckle up cost him his life. He flew into the windshield.

Emily had been wearing a seatbelt, the detective confirmed. He considered out loud that she could have suffered a heart attack, a stroke, or any number of random tragic things. He thought whatever happened to Emily caused the accident rather than the accident causing her death.

Epilogue

The view of the world outside my salt-stained bedroom window is absolutely breathtaking. I realize this for what seems like the millionth time as I watch the sea oats dance to a breeze that appears to be blowing the Atlantic Ocean towards me one wave at a time. The seagulls, pelicans, and sandpipers patrol the air and the ground, and the sounds of the beach whisper through the screens.

However, I am finding it hard to think positively and appreciate the wonders all around even those who love me. In a world where there are more than eight billion humans, I am lonely. The sun doesn't seem to shine through the clouds as brightly as it did a short time ago, and the songs the birds sing sound more like clamor than inspiration.

I am way too young to have gone through what I've been through in the past couple years of my life. That's what those who know me say. I agree. Right now, I am not even sure who I am. My name is Luke Bridges; I know that. But that doesn't really tell me *who* I am. To me, it's just another name. It means nothing at all. It should be important; however, because it is *my* name . . . *my* heritage . . . and one day it will be *my* legacy.

I have lived most of my twenty-eight years in this small town on the coast of North Carolina. Atlantic Beach is the place I call home and always will. Some would say living in one community nearly your entire life is a waste. They're entitled to their opinion. Just as I am entitled to the one I hold. I've learned that some people travel this world chasing dreams and others running from reality. Ultimately, it's every person's choice where he or she parks his or her boat. As for me, my boat is here amongst the sandy shores, the spidery live oaks, and a small-town ambiance that soaks into the soul and, like the oil stain on my driveway, never washes out.

My father taught me to introduce myself well. "You never get a second chance at a first impression," I vividly recall him saying. If someone new met me now, however, they probably wouldn't be all that impressed. A grown man in tattered gym shorts and a t-shirt he's owned since his freshman year in college leaves something to be desired. Since you know what I've been through, your outlook might differ.

At least the hour I spent this morning hunched over on the bathtub floor beneath a steady stream of water extinguished the odor of another restless night. At some point the hot water beating on my aching bones turned cold, but I failed to notice. Honestly, I wasn't sure when the chills became a result of the temperature rather than a reaction to the thoughts constantly occupying my mind.

It took longer than I expected to figure out what happened on the road that night, but when the autopsy results surfaced, everything suddenly added up. While driving, Emily suffered a brain aneurysm. The forensics report, filled with medical jargon I didn't fully understand, included a more detailed explanation and determined she died instantly; the crash hadn't been the cause of death just like the detective expected.

This issue probably caused Emily's migraines all along but went undetected. I instantly wished I asked Emily more questions about her headaches. I'm not a neurologist, but I should have noticed the irregularities and pushed her to discuss them in greater detail with her doctor. Testing could have led to treatment. Instead, I've lost two of the most important people in my life who might have survived with proactive medical care.

It seemed like I walked through the grieving process just yesterday after losing my dad. In dealing with the loss of Emily, I felt like I crawled through the stages of grief. Even though I knew my dad far longer and was biologically related to him, there is a unique bond within a marital relationship. Two becoming one isn't just a metaphor; it's a reality.

After losing Emily, I needed to be strong for Ayden. However, I let him see me cry, and we cried together often. This time, I admitted that even though I was a counselor, I needed therapy right away. My initial sessions with Larry proved very helpful, and I was pleasantly surprised by his unique guidance. Yet, I knew healing from this tragedy would take a long time.

Nighttime is the hardest part. Without Larry, I would have only had the pointers given by friends and family on how to sleep better: open the windows and listen to the ocean, turn on a fan, read a book, flip on the television, take a pill, drink a beer, listen to music. None of them seem to work very well. The only one I haven't tried is the pill. Not that I haven't thought about it while watching the morning hours roll in on the clock sitting atop my nightstand. Tears fill my blue eyes with each flip of the hour. The truth is I learned the hard way that shattered dreams bring about uninvited nightmares. The only difference between my nightmares and the ones any regular Joe might have is that mine are real. When I wake up in the wee hours of the morning drenched in a hot sweat and realize the dream is over, the nightmare continues. Reality sets in, and there is no fast-forward button.

My life moves like the slow-motion setting on the television I rarely watch anymore. One second at a time is how I live these days, and the clock ticking on the wall to my left won't let me forget that. Time, I fear, is the only remedy to this disease, and right now time is not on my side.

I'm alone this morning unless you count a room full of flowers and cards that won't quit staring at me. The refrigerator is filled with food we probably won't ever eat. Thankfully, I'm not alone all the time. The only reason I slept any last night was the small warm body lying next to me. In Ayden's arms is where I woke up this morning. Three squeezes later, he woke up in mine.

We hardly talk over breakfast these days, but we managed to share a few words as we ate. If it hadn't been for the 'shausage' biscuits, Ayden probably wouldn't have cracked a smile. Sometimes I wonder when he first wakes up if he forgets what happened to us.

When it came time to walk him to the bus stop, he hadn't yet finished his 'shausage' biscuit, but that didn't surprise me. Neither of us finished a whole meal since Emily passed.

Ayden had no surviving relatives, so in my eyes it only made sense that he stayed with me. In fact in Emily's will, she requested that I be granted custody of Ayden if anything should happen to her. When she wrote this, his father was alive, and I knew the request was more than a longshot. At the time it made her feel better, so I went along with it for hope's sake.

Like always, this morning I waved until the yellow North Carolina school bus became a blur in the distance. The sun stole its color and broke into my house through the sliding glass door as I wiped off the table and tossed what amounted to a whole biscuit into the trash.

Six hours passed since that trashcan lid flapped shut, and I haven't worked up much of an appetite since. Probably because I've been sitting around staring at pictures and out of windows at a path that leads to a beach I'm afraid to walk on alone. I'm not sure the muscles in my legs and arms, once able to spike a volleyball like a beast on my opponent, could even muster the energy. I haven't even made it to the mailbox since the accident. Thankfully, my family has been bringing in the cards—some I've read, some I haven't. *When was the last time I checked the mail?* I find myself wondering. Not that it matters. What in that mailbox could be more important than . . . nothing, which is what I've done all day.

So who am I?

Right now I'm not very much, but on days when I used to like wearing shoes, I tied them just like the next man, and when I walked beside him, I did not look down on or up at him. That how my parents taught me to treat people.

On days like today it's hard to live up to the standards of my upbringing. I don't want to see anyone or talk to anyone. I just want to be alone. I think.

I'm not alone and I know that. Otherwise I wouldn't have been able to make it through the pain and the heartache that has burrowed its way into my bones and won't seem to loosen its grip. At times like this, I fall where I've fallen. Literally.

On my knees next to my bed, I clutch the worn Bible my father gave me in one hand, and with the other, I wipe away tears that seem as limitless as the air I gasp. I know God doesn't ordain death, but I often wonder why He allows it. I know the answer to that thought, but it doesn't stop me from yelling out loud.

"Why, God? Why? Why me? Why us? Why now?"

Today isn't the first time I've rattled the walls of this house with such questions until it hurts my throat to even speak. I'm sure it won't be the last time my neighbors hear screams that on one occasion brought three uniformed police officers to my front door.

Again I look at that old clock. Since I found this position, the hand has made it halfway around the circle. I know it's almost for Ayden to come home and for that reason, and that reason only, I allow my mind to force my hands to pick my body up off the sand floor. I look at the pictures surrounding me, constantly reminding me of what life is all about. This makes me wonder why some people's priorities are so out of balance these days. Do they realize life isn't about who can drive the nicest car, answer all no questions on Jeopardy, or pay their way out of any dilemma they can get into. Not a good life, anyway.

Life is about love, about giving love and receiving love. If there one thing I can say honestly with the book in my hand that our country's president swears on before taking office, it is that I have given love. More love than I knew my heart could pour out in an entire lifetime. More love than I thought existed in this world. And on days like today I wonder if I was able to give so much because I have received so much.

The photograph in my other hand is one of the few things I would take with me if the house beneath my body ever caught on fire and I could only carry out one load before watching the rest of my possessions burn to ashes. It was taken at my house on a whim and seemed awkward then. It was Emily's and Ayden's first visit to my house, and I was wearing clothes almost as ratty as the ones I'm wearing today. The people that I love most are all there: Emily, Ayden, Dad, Mom, Ben, and Colleen. When I stare at the picture long enough I can still hear the voices of the person on my left and right—Emily and my dad—and sometimes I think I smell them too. I always find it interesting how we each have a uniqu scent. Looking back, that was one of the best days of my life.

Since my world turned upside down, everyone in that p has been here for me in one way or another. It would following two pages to list the names of all the friends wh cards and flowers that seem to be swallowing me brought food and stopped by to spend time with bore you with names you probably won't rememb

❧

Several hundred people attended Emily's funeral, a true celebration of a well-lived life cut way too short. I cried on her casket for what seemed like hours, and I realized what my mom must have felt like at my dad's funeral. My family and friends carried me, literally and emotionally, through that day and many others that now feel like a blur in many ways.

To my surprise, Kate Johnson showed up to pay her respects and to lend her support. When I told her the story about Ayden, she offered to handle the legal process which ended up being a gift from God. She said it turned out to be a good thing that Emily included her wishes for Ayden in the will. It may have saved us some red tape in the adoption process because it explicitly stated his mother's desires. There was no guessing who she would want to raise Ayden, such as a long-lost relative, friend, or foster parent.

My heart felt a peace that surpassed understanding the day I became Ayden's legal guardian. One day after Emily's accident, I happened to be thinking about my past and all the mistakes I made. I was doing something I shouldn't have done, trying to find ways to blame myself for my wife's death as if God punishes us. He reminded me of one truth that day—we only punish ourselves when we make mistakes and even more so when we hold onto the shame and guilt we associate with them. He also showed me a miracle. My biological child, who was never given a chance to live on this earth outside its mother's womb, would have been born the same month as Ayden.

Through Emily's death, God brought Ayden and me closer together. In the following months, we built a stronger connection than I ever imagined possible. As we pulled up our bootstrings, we began to live life again. We played baseball, volleyball, surfed, skimboarded, fished, walked the beach, collected shells, drove Matchbox cars, frequented the playground, and ate more 'shausage' biscuits than needed. We finally started finishing them.

He grew up a lot that summer. We both did. We learned how to live life without Emily—my wife, his mother. We figured out who we were, both individually and collectively. He made new friends, met with a child therapist regularly, joined a youth volleyball team, and bonded deeply with my family. He began to call my sister-in-law Aunt Colleen and my brother Uncle Ben. The latter caused me to laugh every time I heard him say it because it made me think of the rice. He already titled my mom as his Grandma, and that continued.

When I needed time by myself to heal or work or spend a day with friends, our family was there for us. Ayden played video games with Uncle Ben and cards with Aunt Colleen, and Grandma taught him how to cook. He even began making a meal at home at least once a week pretty much on his own. It's amazing what children are capable of when we allow them to try new things, guide them along the way, and don't overprotect them. They fight off their fears on their own.

Ayden became best friends with Colton who lived next door. They ran back and forth between each other's houses and played in the yards and on the beach. Russ, Mary, and I took turns watching the boys and playing with them, and sometimes we all sat outside together and enjoyed the view and conversation. I learned firsthand that playing with children is one of the best ways to enjoy life and overcome tragedy. Playing in general helps, and I had to work hard to find the kid inside of me again and let my guard down around adults.

Russ's and Mary's marriage was blossoming. Counseling really paid off, and we cut back the number of sessions. The conflict of interest with them being my next door neighbors always concerned me professionally, so the bond the boys formed created the perfect opportunity for a new season. I referred the couple to Larry whom they began meeting with regularly to build their relationship. Jackie Jones made progress too. One week she showed up in my office without her sweater, and a couple weeks later she sat in a different spot.

My practice grew to the point where I had to cap it off to spend adequate time with Ayden and my family and, most importantly, take time for myself to be my best for them.

One of the biggest surprises came the day Dr. Nesbitt walked up to my door wearing a helpless look. I felt sure he was about to whine about Ayden and Colton making too much noise in the backyard although he hadn't complained about Ayden once since Emily passed. However, he shared with me that he'd been watching from afar how I dealt with Emily's loss and also noticed the positive changes in Russ's and Mary's life. He asked me if I would be his therapist. He said that the years of seeing patients die and having to break the news to their families was ripping him apart. He bottled it all up until he felt he had no more room left. That day, I cried with a man who'd been one of the biggest thorns in my side since I moved into the neighborhood, and in that one conversation we both healed more than I think either of us realized. I imagined I would refer him to Larry much sooner than I had my other neighbors but for the time being I was honored that he trusted me.

I continued to play on the coed volleyball team, but it wasn't the same without Emily by my side. I still missed her dearly, on and off the sand. I thought about her constantly, but now instead of suffering through the thoughts, I somehow began to celebrate the fond memories we made.

A new player eventually took Emily's place on the team although no one officially worded it that way. At first I kind of resented the woman, but the more I got to know her, the more the feeling dissolved. She was kind to Ayden and would play with him during our breaks. Ayden and I continued to race from one court to the next, and he was getting faster and faster, so I had to try harder to beat him. I still let him win enough to keep him wanting to run.

One day I randomly received a phone call from the teacher who would have Ayden in her classroom for the upcoming school year. I was shocked to see Mindy Lane's number pop up on my phone and hear her voice, but it warmed my heart to learn she moved to fourth grade and would be able to help guide Ayden in the classroom. The unexpected conversation allowed me to thank Mindy again for showing up at the hospital when my dad suffered a heart attack. She shared her condolences about Emily and told me she would be there if I ever needed a friend. I still owed her a favor and figured I'd have plenty of opportunities to repay her kindness by helping with the needs of Ayden's class.

I finally started spending time on the beach again. In the evenings as the sun set, I walked along the dusty road to the wide open field of sand, and there at the edge of the Atlantic Ocean, I met with Emily. I talked to her the same as I always had and felt her presence most days.

Every day, I thank her and God for our time together. She came into my life, forever changing it. Emily Beckett Bridges is and always will be my wife. These words, the ones you have read, are our story.

THE END

Photo Credit: Amy Smith

A Note from the Author

Thank you for reading ALONG THE DUSTY ROAD! I am grateful that you chose to invest your time in this book. If you haven't read my other novels, A BRIDGE APART, LOSING LONDON, A FIELD OF FIREFLIES, THE DATE NIGHT JAR, WHEN THE RIVERS RISE, and WHERE THE RAINBOW FALLS, I hope you will very soon. If you enjoyed the story you just experienced, please consider helping spread the novel to others in the following ways:

- REVIEW the novel online at Amazon.com, goodreads.com, bn.com, bamm.com, etc.
- RECOMMEND this book to friends (social groups, workplace, book club, church, school, etc.).
- VISIT my website: www.Joey-Jones.com

- SUBSCRIBE to my Email Newsletter for insider information on upcoming novels, behind-the-scenes looks, promotions, charities, and other exciting news.
- CONNECT with me on Social Media, and feel free to post a comment about the novel: "Like" Facebook.com/JoeyJonesWriter and "Follow" me at Instagram.com/JoeyJonesWriter and Twitter.com/JoeyJonesWriter (#AlongTheDustyRoad). "Pin" on Pinterest. Write a blog post about the book.
- GIVE a copy of the novel to someone you know who would enjoy the story. Books make great presents (Birthday, Christmas, Teacher's Gifts, etc.).

Sincerely,
Joey Jones

About the Author

The writing style of Joey Jones has been described as a mixture of Nicholas Sparks, Richard Paul Evans, and James Patterson. The ratings and reviews of his novels A BRIDGE APART (2015), LOSING LONDON (2016), A FIELD OF FIREFLIES (2018), THE DATE NIGHT JAR (2019), WHEN THE RIVERS RISE (2020), and WHERE THE RAINBOW FALLS (2022) reflect the comparison to *New York Times* bestselling authors. Prior to becoming a full-time novelist, Joey worked in the marketing field. He holds a Bachelor of Arts in Business Communications from the University of Maryland University College, where he earned a 3.8 GPA.

Jones lives in North Carolina with his family. Fun facts: He likes to kayak, ride his bicycle, and play disc golf. While writing part of this novel, he lived in Atlantic Beach and explored the Crystal Coast area extensively.

Joey Jones is currently writing his eighth novel and working on various projects pertaining to his published works.

Book Club/Group Discussion Questions

1. Were you immediately engaged in the novel?

2. What emotions did you experience as you read the book?

3. Which character is your favorite? Why?

4. What do you like most about the story as a whole?

5. What is your favorite part/scene in the novel?

6. Do any particular passages from the book stand out to you?

7. As you read, what are some things you thought might happen but didn't?

8. Would you have liked to see anything turn out differently?

9. Is the ending satisfying? If so, why? If not, why not, and how would you change it?

10. Why might the author have chosen to tell the story the way he did?

11. If you could ask the author a question, what would you ask?

12. Have you ever read or heard a story anything like this one?

13. Have you ever experienced professional counseling, and was it helpful?

14. In what ways does this novel relate to your own life?

15. Would you reread this novel?

Also by Joey Jones

A BRIDGE APART

A Bridge Apart, the debut novel by Joey Jones, is a remarkable love story that tests the limits of trust and forgiveness . . .

In the quaint river town of New Bern, North Carolina, at 28 years of age, the pieces of Andrew Callaway's life are all falling into place. His real estate firm is flourishing, and he's engaged to be married in less than two weeks to a beautiful banker named Meredith Hastings. But, when Meredith heads to Tampa, Florida—the wedding location—with her mother, fate, or maybe some human intervention, has it that Andrew happens upon Cooper McKay, the only other woman he's ever loved.

A string of shocking emails lead Andrew to question whether he can trust his fiancée, and in the midst of trying to unravel the mystery, he finds himself spending time with Cooper. When Meredith catches wind of what's going on back at home, she's forced to consider calling off the wedding, which ultimately draws Andrew closer to Cooper. Andrew soon discovers he's making choices he might not be able, or even want, to untangle. As the story unfolds, the decisions made will drastically change the lives of everyone involved and bind them closer together than they could have ever imagined.

Also by Joey Jones

LOSING LONDON

Losing London is an epic love story filled with nail-biting suspense, forbidden passion, and unexpected heartbreak.

When cancer took the life of Mitch Quinn's soulmate, London Adams, he never imagined that one year later her sister, Harper, whom he had never met before, would show up in Emerald Isle, NC. Until this point, his only reason to live, a five-year-old cancer survivor named Hannah, was his closest tie to London.

Harper, recently divorced, never imagined that work—a research project on recent shark attacks—and an unexpected package from London would take her back to the island town where her family had vacationed in her youth. Upon her arrival, she meets and is instantly swept off her feet by a local with a hidden connection that eventually causes her to question the boundaries of love.

As Mitch's and Harper's lives intertwine, they discover secrets that should have never happened. If either had known that losing London would have connected their lives in the way it did, they might have chosen different paths.

A FIELD OF FIREFLIES

Growing up, Nolan Lynch's family was unconventional by society's standards, but it was filled with love, and his parents taught him everything he needed to know about life, equality, and family. A baseball player with a bright future, Nolan is on his way to the major leagues when tragedy occurs. Six years later, he's starting over as the newest instructor at the community college in Washington, North Carolina, where he meets Emma Pate, who seems to be everything he's ever dreamed of—beautiful, assertive, and a baseball fan to boot.

Emma Pate's dreams are put on hold after her father dies, leaving her struggling to keep her family's farm. When a chance encounter with a cute new guy in town turns into an impromptu date, Emma finds herself falling for him. But, she soon realizes Nolan Lynch isn't who she thinks he is.

Drawn together by a visceral connection that defies their common sense, Emma's and Nolan's blossoming love is as romantic as it is forbidden, until secrets—both past and present—threaten to tear them apart. Now, Nolan must confront his past and make peace with his demons or risk losing everything he loves . . . again.

Emotionally complex and charged with suspense, *A Field of Fireflies* is the unforgettable story of family, love, loss, and an old baseball field where magic occurs, including the grace of forgiveness and second chances.

Also by Joey Jones

THE DATE NIGHT JAR

An unlikely friendship. An unforgettable love story.

When workaholic physician Ansley Stone writes a letter to the estranged son of a patient asking him to send the family's heirloom date night jar, she only intended to bring a little happiness to a lonely old man during his final days. Before long, she finds herself increasingly drawn to Cleve Fields' bedside, eager to hear the stories of his courtship with his beloved late wife, Violet, that were inspired by the yellowed slivers of paper in the old jar. When Cleve asks her to return the jar to his son, Ansley spontaneously decides to deliver it in person, if only to find out why no one, including his own son, visits the patient she's grown inexplicably fond of.

Mason Fields is happily single, content to spend his days running the family strawberry farm and his evenings in the company of his best friend, a seventeen-year-old collie named Callie. Then Ansley shows up at his door with the date night jar and nowhere to stay. Suddenly, she's turning his carefully ordered world upside down, upsetting his routine, and forcing him to remember things best left in the past. When she suggests *they* pull a slip of paper from the jar, their own love story begins to develop. But before long, their newfound love will be tested in ways they never imagined, as the startling truth about Mason's past is revealed...and Ansley's future is threatened.

Also by Joey Jones

WHEN THE RIVERS RISE

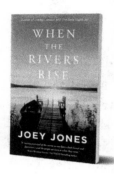

Three hearts, pushed to the limit. Can they weather another storm?

High school sweethearts Niles and Eden shared a once-in-a-lifetime kind of love until an accident—and Eden's subsequent addiction to pain medication—tore them apart. Now divorced, their son Riley is Niles's whole world, and he'll do anything to keep him safe.

In constant pain, chronically tired, and resentful of Riley's relationship with his dad, Eden is a shadow of the woman she once was. When she meets Kirk, a charismatic drummer who makes her feel alive again, she's torn between evacuating with Riley before a hurricane hits and the exciting new life that beckons.

Reese has never quite gotten over the death of her father, a cop who was shot in the line of duty. Now a detective herself and the only special operations officer on the East Ridge, Tennessee, police force without children, she volunteers to go help as a potential category five hurricane spins straight toward the North Carolina coast.

As Hurricane Florence closes in, their lives begin to intersect in ways they never imagined as each is forced to confront issues from the past that will decide the future...their own, each other's, and Riley's.

Emotions swell like the rivers in the approaching storm in this poignant story of guilt, second chances, and the lengths we'll go to protect the ones we love.

Also by Joey Jones

WHERE THE RAINBOW FALLS

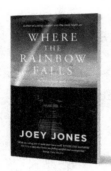

In the face of a storm, a father's love is the most powerful force.

With Hurricane Florence rapidly approaching the North Carolina coastline, all Niles North can think about is his five-year-old son Riley and how he wished he bent the law when he had the chance to evacuate him. Now, instead of being safe in Hickory with his dad, Riley is with Niles's ex-wife Eden, who's decided to ride out the storm at home with her drummer friend. Desperate to get back to his son as the storm waters rise, Niles begs Reese, an attractive police detective and rescue worker, to drive him back to New Bern.

Refusing to help Niles seems nearly impossible for Reese who quickly realizes she's in deeper than she should be—both professionally and emotionally—especially since she's drawn to almost everything about him. As the two undertake a perilous journey into the eye of the storm, Niles's worst fears come true, setting in motion a series of events that will change both of their lives forever.

Printed in the USA
CPSIA information can be obtained
at www.ICGtesting.com
LVHW040750290923
759074LV00008B/12